COMBAT FOR CUSTODY

COMBAT
FOR
CUSTODY
A PARKER & PRICE NOVEL

PAULA WINCHESTER RANK

NEW YORK

LONDON • NASHVILLE • MELBOURNE • VANCOUVER

COMBAT FOR CUSTODY
A PARKER & PRICE NOVEL

Published in New York, New York, by Morgan James Publishing. Morgan James is a trademark of Morgan James, LLC. www.MorganJamesPublishing.com

Publisher's Note: This novel is a work of fiction. Names, characters, places, and incidents are either products of the author's imagination or used fictitiously. All characters are fictional, and any similarity to people living or dead is purely coincidental.

ISBN 978-1-63195-417-7 paperback
ISBN 978-1-63195-418-4 eBook
Library of Congress Control Number: 2020922911

Cover Design by:
Rachel Lopez
www.r2cdesign.com

Morgan James is a proud partner of Habitat for Humanity Peninsula and Greater Williamsburg. Partners in building since 2006.

Get involved today! Visit
www.MorganJamesBuilds.com

To my all-time favorite partner-in-crime, Valerie. You are one of the most amazing and fascinating women I have had the privilege of knowing.

CONTENTS

ACKNOWLEDGMENTS

A special thank you goes to all those who inspired me and pushed me to fulfill my dream of writing a novel. A particular thank you goes to my husband, Joe, who supported me and allowed me the opportunity to write by transporting me all around the world and who pushed me to finish the project. Thanks to my son, Isaac, for helping me act out and stage the fight scenes, and to my son, Jared, for creating the artwork. Thanks to my focus group of readers in Amman, Jordan, who provided me so much encouragement and valuable feedback. Thank you to my publisher, Morgan James Publishing, to my fantastic editor, Cortney Donelson, and to Ethan Burroughs for introducing me to them. I also acknowledge my kickboxing instructor, Carl, who taught me how to be fierce and tenacious—beyond what I believed to be my physical limits.

CHAPTER ONE

The overhead lights flickered on in the cabin of the Egypt Air jumbo jet. Slumbering passengers stirred, murmuring to one another. Emma Parker removed the pillow covering her head and squinted at the screen on the seatback in front of her. The airplane icon on the colored map tracking their progress indicated they were just off the east coast of the United States, approaching John F. Kennedy Airport. Emma wrinkled her nose; the twelve-hour flight on the fully loaded plane had placed a strain on the effectiveness of the chemical toilets on board. The air was filled with the smells of human waste, urinal deodorizer cake, and cheap cologne. While it had seemed a good idea when booking to sit in the last row of the section because no one would be sitting behind them, the proximity to the bathrooms was a definite detraction Emma hadn't considered.

Emma gently lifted the small, curly blonde head resting on her lap. "Amber, honey, wake up. We're almost to New York." The five-year-old sat up and rubbed her big coffee-colored eyes.

"What time is it?" she asked.

"The middle of the night," Emma responded. "Almost two o'clock in the morning."

"Really?" mumbled Amber, as she slumped against the window of the airplane, closing her eyes again. Emma reached over and tickled the chubby swatch of tummy poking out below Amber's shirt. Wake up, honey." Emma helped Amber put on her shoes, placed the carry-on bags under the seats in front of them, and folded the blankets and pillows.

Emma looked across the aisle. Her friend and work associate, Morgan Price, was busy re-applying her make-up with the assistance of her lighted purse compact. Next to Morgan, eleven-year-old Lindsay brushed her long blonde hair, and then worked it into a neat French braid. Morgan and Lindsay were definitely two of a kind.

The plane began its steep descent into J.F.K. airport. Emma clutched the armrests of her seat and concentrated on breathing in slowly through her nose and out through her mouth.

"How come you get scared when we land?" asked Amber.

"I'm not scared, just nauseous," Emma replied.

"What's noxious?" asked Amber.

"It means I'm going to puke all over your lap if this plane doesn't land soon," puffed Emma between breaths.

"Yuck," muttered Amber. At that instant, the plane connected with the runway, bouncing twice before settling into the deceleration. The other passengers, most of them Arabs based on their appearance, let out a cheer and applauded.

"Why do they always do that?" Morgan asked, a little too loudly, from across the aisle. "It's like they're *surprised* we didn't crash."

Emma leaned forward and glared at Morgan. "Maybe they're just thankful that God brought them here safely," replied Emma.

"Don't you mean Allah?" asked Morgan.

"I think they're probably the same," Emma answered. "But that's a longer conversation for a different time and place."

"Whatever," retorted Morgan.

Emma and her three companions trudged along with the herd of fellow passengers, down the deserted hallway toward the immigration processing area. Amber was fully awake now and chattering incessantly. "Where is everyone else?

How come there's nobody here except the people from our plane? How long will this line be? When is our next plane? Where are our suitcases? When are we going to be home?" The child didn't seem concerned, or even aware, that no one attempted to answer her questions.

The passengers eventually reached the processing area. Rows of tollbooth-style cubicles awaited them. There were different areas for "U.S. Citizens," "Resident Aliens," and "Non-U.S. Residents." Fortunately for Emma and Morgan, the vast majority of the other passengers flying Egypt Air were in either the "Non-U.S. Citizens" or "Resident Aliens" lines. The line for "U.S. Citizens" was relatively short.

While the women and girls stood in line, Lindsay played a hand-held video game, and Amber took out her battered lunchbox full of plastic animals.

"I desperately need a cigarette," said Morgan. "If I don't get one *really* soon, I'm going to hurt somebody."

"You've waited over fourteen hours already, you can make it a little bit longer," replied Emma.

"Please don't remind me how incredibly long it's been," answered Morgan.

"Now would be a very bad time to lose your cool," said Emma. "You need to be smooth and charming to get us through this checkpoint."

"I could do that much better with a cigarette in my hand."

"This is the United States; here they mean it when they say 'No Smoking,'" replied Emma.

"Next," called out the agent from the booth in front of them. Morgan rolled back her shoulders, pulling her frame to its full fee feet, eleven inches. Tossing her golden hair over her right shoulder, she hoisted her carry-on bag to her left shoulder and sashayed up to the booth. She flashed the attendant a big smile, "Hello, how are you?"

"Fine, thank you," the red-haired gentleman replied. "How many of you are traveling together?"

Morgan leaned forward and placed her elbows on the counter, giving the young man a daring view of her full, creamy white cleavage. "My goodness, what a torturous flight!" breathed Morgan. "I thought we were never going to get here."

"Did you just come in off the flight from Cairo?" the agent asked, unabashedly staring down Morgan's blouse.

"We sure did," answered Morgan. "And, boy, am I happy to be back in the U.S.A."

"I'm happy you're here, too," the agent gushed, his neck and ears turning red.

"There's nothing like a friendly welcome," Morgan purred back. A man wearing a rumpled business suit in line behind Morgan and Emma coughed loudly. The redheaded agent started and pulled himself erect. "Ma'am, how many in your party?" he repeated.

"Just me, my sister, and her two girls," replied Morgan, smiling sweetly.

"May I see your passports," asked the agent.

"Certainly," said Morgan. She collected the passports from Emma and slowly handed them to the young man, leaning back over the counter. As the agent took the passports, Morgan let her hand linger so that the agent's fingers rested against hers. The agent grew perceptively more crimson as he looked into Morgan's eyes. While continuing to look at Morgan, he cursorily flipped through the first three passports, stamping them.

Emma slowly let out a sigh. She hadn't realized she'd been holding her breath. The agent lazily opened the last passport. He suddenly sat upright, straightening away from Morgan. The man turned to his computer terminal and scrolled down the text on the lower part of the screen.

"Are you Emma Parker?" he asked, looking at Emma.

"Yes, sir," Emma slowly answered. The agent looked at the computer screen again. He appeared to have completely forgotten Morgan and her charm. The young man leaned forward, reaching for something under the counter. He looked at Lindsay.

"Young lady, is this your mother?" he asked her, pointing to Emma.

Lindsay's eyes darted to Emma, then to Amber, who was happily marching a plastic hippo up Emma's leg." "Uh, yes, sir, she is," Lindsay quietly responded.

"Are you sure about that?" pressed the agent.

"I think I know who my own mother is," Lindsay replied, more confidently, looking the agent in the eye.

The agent opened the other three passports again and looked at the information pages. He looked at Emma. "If these are your children, Ms. Parker, why is their last name Giovanni?"

"I married after my career was established and chose to keep my maiden name. The children have their father's surname," Emma calmly replied.

"Oh, yeah?" the agent responded, "then why does your sister here have yet a different last name?"

"Because she's been married . . . repeatedly," answered Emma.

"But I'm currently single," piped Morgan.

The agent barely glanced in her direction.

"We're very tired and need to get through customs in time to catch our connecting flight," stated Emma. "Are we almost finished here?"

"We're almost done; just one more minute," replied the agent, glancing yet again at the computer terminal.

"Is there some sort of problem?" asked Emma, as calmly as she could.

"Thank you for your patience," responded the agent.

"That's not an answer," said Emma. "I asked you if there was a problem."

"I just need to check on something," the agent answered. The rumpled businessman coughed loudly again and shuffled his feet. The agent's eyes darted from Emma to the exit door from the immigration area and back again.

"It should be just another moment."

"Can we move this along?" called out the impatient businessman.

Just then, three men in dark suits with earpieces came through the exit door. Within seconds, they were behind Emma, Morgan, and the girls.

"Ms. Parker, Ms. Price," said the tallest of the three, who sported shortly cropped gray hair, "You're going to have to come with us."

"Why?" asked Emma. "Is there some sort of problem?"

"You need to come with us, and we'll discuss it." Emma looked at the man at her elbow. There was a large bulge at his side, under his suit jacket. She looked over at the shorter, slightly younger, but pudgy and balding man standing closely behind Morgan. He had the same menacing waistband lump. Emma looked beyond him. The athletic-looking third man, the youngest of the trio, stood a few paces away, between the women and the door, with his feet planted shoulder-width apart and his hands behind his back. His open suit coat revealed a handgun and holster strapped to his side.

Emma took a deep breath. "We're not going anywhere with you until you tell me what this is about."

The gray-haired man stepped closer and firmly grabbed her elbow.

"You are really not in a position to make demands," he quietly spoke in her ear. "We can do this the easy way, or we can do this the hard way. Either way, you're coming with us. Pick up your bag . . . now." The grip on Emma's elbow tightened to the point of producing a searing pain. Emma quickly scanned the room. There wasn't a single window. There were two doors—the one through which they had come, which she was sure locked upon closing to prevent people from going backward and avoid passing through immigration. Two armed men stood between her and the second door, and the third man was practically breaking her arm.

Emma slowly picked up her carry-on bag and nodded at Morgan.

"Amber, honey, pick up your animals and come with me," Emma said, resignedly. As Amber picked up her belongings, Lindsay bent to help her.

"Can I have our passports, please?" asked Emma.

"I wouldn't worry about that right now, if I were you," the pudgy man at her side replied. He placed his hand on the small of Morgan's back.

"Listen, slime-ball. Do not touch me," hissed Morgan. The man quickly removed his hand. Lindsay stepped between Amber and the men and clasped her younger sister's hand reassuringly. As the group proceeded past the lines of travelers, every eye was focused on them, and Emma realized the large room, previously buzzing with conversation, had turned completely silent.

As they passed the final line of people before the door, an unshaven man wearing a Redskins ball cap looked directly at Morgan and produced a slow smile. Morgan lunged toward the creepy man and swung her carry-on bag at his head.

"Dubrowski, you rat!" she shrieked. "What did you do?"

The passenger easily sidestepped the blow and addressed the balding man who, by now, had caught up with Morgan and twisted her arm behind her back.

"Old girlfriend. She's apparently still bitter about the break-up."

"You'll get yours," shouted Morgan.

Emma interjected, "Morgan, shut up. Now." Morgan fell silent but continued to squirm under the short man's grip and glared at the man still in line.

Emma looked at the children. They were pale and wide-eyed. "It's going to be OK, babes," she said quietly. "We just all need to cooperate with these gentlemen, and everything will get straightened out."

The three armed men escorted the group through the back corridors of the airport, until finally arriving at a door. The older man, who was clearly in charge, placed his ID badge into a reader on the wall, and the door lock clicked open. The room was bare, except for a square table, three plastic chairs, and a padlocked metal cabinet in the corner. On the wall to the right there was another door and a large rectangular Plexiglas window looking into another identical room. The room's stale air lingered with the faint odor of old coffee and cigarette-smoke-laden woolen garments.

"Sit down," the suit-in-charge commanded. Emma sat in the furthest plastic chair. Morgan kicked the second chair. It came to rest in the corner between the cabinet and the wall. The pudgy man raised his hand, as if he might slap her across the face. Morgan held her ground and glared down at him.

"Enough," the leader quietly said. "Let the suspect stand all day. It's not like she can escape." Emma's eyes went to the closed door. The young, athletic-looking goon stood in front of the door with his arms crossed.

"Girls, come here," said Emma, stretching out her arms to them.

"That won't be necessary," interrupted the leader. "The children are going to wait next door." He walked to the door on the right and unlocked it with his ID badge. "Come on, girls," he said, almost kindly. The children remained frozen. "It's OK, no one's going to hurt you," the man coaxed.

"You can't interrogate them," Emma stated. "They are juveniles, and you can't ask them anything without a parent or an attorney present."

"I'm fully aware of my responsibilities, ma'am," the man retorted. "Girls, come." Amber sat on the floor and started to cry. Lindsay looked at all three men, then at Emma. Emma nodded reassuringly. Lindsay took Amber's hand, pulled her to her feet, then picked up their belongings, and led her to the door.

Emma watched through the window as the leader settled the girls in the room next door. He brought them paper, pencils, and snacks from a vending machine. From what she could see, he didn't appear to be attempting to carry on any extended conversation. She relaxed a tiny bit and leaned forward, placing her elbows on the table and resting her chin in her hands. The fat, bald man sat in the other chair across the table. Morgan turned her back on him and perched herself on the edge of the table facing the door, keeping her back rigid and her arms crossed.

The four of them sat in silence. Emma kept an eye on the girls, who were now alone in the adjoining room. They seemed to be calm and entertained themselves. Amber had her plastic animals spread out on the table, and Lindsay was drawing or writing on the paper the man had provided.

Approximately five minutes later, there was a knock on the door to the hallway. The young man guarding the door opened it a crack, then opened it to readmit the grey-haired leader who had escorted the children to the room next door. He strode into the room and gave the short, bald man an intense look. He jumped out of the chair, yielding it to his boss. The leader sat down and pulled it close to the table. Emma sat upright in her chair, putting some distance between them, without actually giving any ground. Morgan continued to sit on the table facing the door, her back to the two men near the table.

The leader cleared his throat. "So, Ms. Parker, why don't you tell me how it is you ended up in a foreign country with someone else's minor children without the proper authority?"

"What makes you think I don't have the 'proper authority," replied Emma.

"Well, first of all, these children were reported kidnapped five days ago. Secondly, they do not have Egyptian visas, nor were any ever applied for on their behalf," stated the man.

"I obviously have their passports. Don't you think that's a little unusual for a kidnapping situation?" retorted Emma.

"That just indicates you're more clever than the average kidnapper," stated the leader. "You and your colleague here," he glanced in Morgan's direction, "have outstanding warrants against you for kidnapping and obstruction of justice. A lot of people have been looking for you and for these children. What I want to know is . . . for what purpose have you taken these girls?" he asked.

Emma paused for a moment, glanced through the window at Lindsay and Amber, exchanged a look with Morgan, and then returned her gaze to the head honcho. "If I was inclined to tell you anything, I wouldn't be allowed to do so. The information is protected by the attorney-client privilege."

"What?" exclaimed the leader, somewhat scornfully. "You're telling me that *you* are an attorney?"

"Yes," answered Emma. "And so is Ms. Price." Emma gestured toward Morgan.

"Hah! That's a good one," the pudgy man burst out, breaking his long silence. "And I'm a rocket scientist!"

Morgan slowly turned to face the numb-nut. "Hardly," she quipped.

Emma interjected, "We're working on a case. Everything surrounding these children and our travels are related to that case, so we are not free to discuss any of it. We'd be happy to show you our bar cards. They are in our purses."

The leader looked unimpressed. "All right, but one at a time. Open your purse—very slowly—and get out your identification."

Emma, then Morgan, each produced a flimsy two-by-four-inch piece of card stock and handed it to the leader. He examined the papers, turning them over a few times, as if to discern hidden information. "You're really both members of the Virginia State Bar?" he asked.

"Absolutely," responded Emma.

"Can you believe it?" said Morgan. "We're sexy *and* smart."

"We're going to go check these out," announced the leader. "Just sit tight." He rose, taking the bar cards, and gestured for the short, balding man to follow him. They exited the room, leaving the women alone, except for the ever-present door guard.

Emma looked around. "I'm going to see if I can check on the girls," she said. Morgan stood up and leaned over Emma, her lips close to Emma's ear. "You might want to have them pack up. We may be leaving soon."

"Really?" Emma whispered back. "How's that?"

"Mr. Muscles and I have been making eyes at each other for the last half hour. Just maybe, I can distract him from his duties."

"Oh, please," replied Emma. You don't really think you can get us out of this mess with flirtation, do you?"

"We'll see," responded Morgan. "Just give me a few minutes alone with our host."

Emma stood up from her chair and turned toward the young man guarding the door. "Excuse me, sir. Is there any way I can go in there and make sure the children are all right? Just for a minute?" Her head tilted toward the girls.

The door guard glanced at Morgan, who was once again perched on the table. She had her skirt hiked up to a scandalous height and appeared focused on adjusting her nylon stockings.

"Sure. No problem. I'll let you in." The young man strode to the adjoining door and passed a key card through the receptacle to the left, swinging the door open to let Emma pass. As Emma entered the doorway, she surreptitiously stuck a bent hairpin in the latch of the doorframe, preventing the door from locking completely behind her.

The girls turned to look as Emma enter. "Emma!" cried Amber.

"Mom!" exclaimed Lindsay. Amber looked sheepish.

"Oops. I mean Mom." Both girls stood to embrace Emma.

"What's happening?" Lindsay asked. "Are we in trouble?"

"I'm not sure yet what's going on," stated Emma. "But no matter what, you guys are back here in the United States, and you'll be safe."

"What about you and Morgan?" replied Lindsay. "Will you be all right, too?"

"Somehow we always manage to end up OK," stated Emma. "Sometimes things get difficult, but we always figure it out. After all the four of us have been through in the last few days, you should know that."

Lindsay laughed a small laugh. "That's for sure. So many times I thought we were done for, and you guys came up with some trick or plan to get us out of trouble."

Amber laughed, too. "I like it when you and Morgan make the bad guys look stupid. That's the funniest!"

"Yes, that is the most fun," replied Emma. "But this time the bad guys think they're the good guys, which makes it a little more difficult. No matter—we'll figure it out. Are you girls doing OK? Did you get enough to eat? Did they let you use the bathroom?"

"We're fine," Lindsay said.

"Did they ask you any questions?" probed Emma.

"No. Except the man with the Army hair asked us who our parents were," answered Lindsay. "I told him he wasn't allowed to ask us questions, just like you said, and he didn't ask anything else."

"Good girl," commended Emma. "Pack up all your things, please, just in case we need to leave very soon." The girls obeyed.

The three of them sat back down at the table. "So tell me about your drawings here," Emma asked Lindsay. Lindsay proceeded to describe to Emma her cartoons and the stories and characters behind them.

Five minutes later, there was a loud rap on the window between the two rooms. Emma looked up and realized, for the first time, that from the girls' side of the window, it appeared to be only a mirror.

Emma ran to the connecting door and pushed it open. Morgan was standing just inside, holding a service revolver. Emma looked around the room. The young man was slouched in the plastic chair between the cabinet and the wall. He appeared to be unconscious. "Oh, dear, what have you done now, Morgan?" muttered Emma.

"Just saved the day again." Morgan held up the young man's key card. "Time to go."

Emma looked over her shoulder. "Girls, time to run."

The foursome ran to the door leading to the hallway. Morgan slid the key card through the receptacle, and the door opened. She stuck her head out slowly. "All clear. Let's go."

The party ran down the deserted, white-walled hallway. Metal doors lined both sides. Emma wondered how many other unfortunately detained passengers were behind those doors, waiting to learn their fates. At the end of the hallway, there was a door marked "stairs." Morgan waved the key card, and they burst through the door. The stairwell only led up so that's the direction the four ran. At the end of the first flight, they stopped in front of another metal door.

"Hold on," said Emma. "Let's see what's out there before we go rushing through." She slowly cracked the door. A wave of noise flowed in, the sound of a talkative crowd.

"Come on," Emma beckoned them.

The group emerged into a busy concourse. Passengers hurriedly moved to and from their gates. Shops, bars, and restaurants interspersed the gates. Emma looked up at the directional signs. Large, yellow letters highlighted the way to "Baggage Claim" and "Ground Transportation." In every airport in the world, those words also meant an exit out of the terminal.

"This way," she said to the rest. "Amber, it's hurry time. Come on." Emma bent forward and reached her arms behind her. Amber took a running leap onto Emma's back. She wedged her lunchbox of animals between her chest and Emma's back, wrapping her arms around Emma's neck. Morgan grabbed Lindsay's hand, and they all jogged in the direction of the arrows.

"Excuse me, coming through," Emma called out, "We're late for our flight." The other travelers looked back and cooperatively moved aside for the thundering females. The group ran past three, then four, then five gates. There was a slight jog in the concourse and they veered to the left. As they came around the turn, they passed an airport security guard holding a radio. He watched the group run by, looked again, and then shouted into his radio.

"Oh, shizzle," muttered Morgan. "Gotta run faster, now." They picked up the pace. Amber, bouncing up and down on Emma's back, started chanting in time with the bumping: "Run, run, run, run." Shouts arose behind them. Morgan glanced back. "Here come the Heat," she panted.

Morgan spotted a smoker's lounge ahead on the right. "In here," called Morgan, as she ran toward the entry. The four burst through the door and pushed their way to the back of the crowd, where they sat down in the last row of chairs, facing the back wall. It was a small glass room so saturated with smoke that she could barely make out the faces of the occupants. The blue haze stung Emma's nose and made her eyes water. It was quite full with travelers desperate to feed their nicotine need. Nearly all of the individuals were, inexplicably, standing, although chairs were provided.

"Hey," a lady in her mid-fifties scratched out, her voice raspy from years of smoking, "this is no place for children."

"Oh, mind your own business, granny," retorted Morgan, "They love second-hand smoke."

""No, we don't," piped up Amber. "It's as dangerous to your health as smoking. Maybe worse. And I can't breathe."

"I know, baby," whispered Emma in her ear, "but the bad men won't see us in here."

"Oooh . . ." responded Amber. "Good idea. I'm OK." She suppressed a small cough.

Emma peered through the smokers. No sign of the security guards. Morgan took out a cigarette and lit it. Emma looked at her pointedly.

"Hey," said Morgan, "I haven't had a smoke in nearly sixteen hours and have no intention of passing up this one opportunity." The four sat there, not talking and watching Morgan smoke, for what seemed like forever. They saw no sign of anyone resembling security or law enforcement.

After Morgan finished her second cigarette, Emma stood up and said, "Alright, let's go." They picked up their things and moved to the door. Emerging back onto the concourse was like being hit in the face with a blast of fresh air. Everyone but Morgan took a deep breath.

"Boy, that was stinky," announced Amber. They all laughed. Amber climbed back on Emma's back, and the group continued their jog toward the baggage claim area.

After passing four or five more gates, Emma braved the thought that they were in the clear. Just then, a voice called out, "Hey! Stop!"

Emma looked back to see a lone security guard pointing at them.

"Run faster," she shouted. Fresh from their rest in the smoking lounge, they doubled the pace. They came up on an intersection with another concourse. Three more airport security guards emerged from the connecting concourse and moved to intercept them.

"In here," yelled Emma and pointed to a small bar on the left. It was crowded with travelers seated at tightly spaced high tables and bar stools. Luggage was strewed everywhere at travelers' feet. The women threaded their way to the middle of the bar to an empty table. It was waiting to be cleared and held empty beer bottles, glasses, and used dishes. The aura of less-than-fresh cooking grease hung in the air. The patrons' conversation was continuously interjected with flight announcements over the loudspeaker. Emma pulled out two stools and pushed the two girls underneath the table. "Stay here and don't come out until I say so," she commanded, as she pushed the stools back in front of them, forming a barrier.

Morgan held out her hand, "Give me your purse." Emma handed it over. Morgan gave her purse and Emma's purse to Lindsay. "If you don't mind," she requested. She straightened up and met Emma's eye. "Ready?"

"Ready," Emma affirmed. "It's on." Just then, three security guards ran into the bar. As soon as the guards spied Emma and Morgan, they started working their way toward them.

"Pardon me, sir, I need to borrow this for a bit," stated Emma and grabbed a large, wheeled suitcase with an extended handle parked beside a business-looking man at the next table.

"I don't think so," stated the man, who stood up from his stool.

"Thank you so kindly for giving up your seat," quipped Morgan, "You're a true gentleman." She grabbed his vacated bar stool by one of its legs and held it above her head.

As the security guards rushed up, Emma rapidly pushed the bottom of the wheeled suitcase into the first guard's shins, causing him to cry out and stagger backward. Morgan swung the bar stool and cracked the second guard on the side of his head. The bar patrons inhaled a collective gasp. A pre-teen boy exclaimed, "Cool!"

The third guard thought better of the frontal assault and swung around to the left, attempting to approach Emma and Morgan from the back. Just as he got within arm's reach, Morgan grabbed a beer bottle from the table, spun around, and brought it up under his chin with a *crack*. With her other hand, Morgan stabbed the guard in his right bicep with a fork. The beer remaining in the bottle sent a yeasty smelling spray over the man and Morgan. The other patrons stampeded toward the door.

The manager of the bar stood up on top of the bar and yelled, "Hey, you people have to pay your tabs before you leave!" Not one person paused.

Emma and Morgan stood back-to-back and kept the guards at bay with stools and tableware. Morgan grabbed a plate and threw it like a Frisbee, splitting open one guard's forehead, causing him to stagger backward and sit down on the floor. Sweet-smelling, sticky ketchup from the plate ran down his face. She then grabbed another bar stool and cracked him over the top of the head, rendering him unconscious. "One down," she announced.

The guard with the fork in his right arm advanced, attempting to punch with his left. Emma grabbed a hiking backpack from the floor and slung the straps around the guard's neck. Keeping the backpack between the guard and herself, Emma then used the backpack to push the guard off balance and cause him to trip over another pile of luggage behind him. Emma then tipped the nearby table, with its entire contents, onto the guard, burying him in dishes, cutlery, and food remains.

The third guard advanced on Morgan. He was short and slight of build. Morgan cocked back her long leg, adorned in its four-inch pump, and side-kicked him squarely between the eyes with the stiletto heel. The guard let out a guttural sound, covered his face with his hands, and fell to his knees. Guard number two was still trying to extract himself from the table rubble.

"Time to run," announced Morgan, pulling the two children out from their protective cage under the table. The four hurdled over the chaos and exploded back onto the concourse. Emma still had the man's large wheeled suitcase in tow.

"What are you going to do with that?" asked Morgan.

"I don't know yet, but it has come in handy so far," replied Emma.

"It'll just slow us down," responded Morgan.

"No it won't," said Emma. "Amber, get on." Amber straddled the suitcase and wrapped her arms around the telescoping handle. "Let's roll out!" she shouted, and the group was running toward the exit once again. The brawl in the restaurant had tired them, and they moved slower than before. They came to a crossroads of hallways and veered to the right, following the signs to "Ground Transportation."

Shortly after they rounded the corner, Amber, astride the suitcase, looked back and announced, "The police guys are coming again."

"Oh for the love of Pete," panted Morgan, "How do these idiots figure out where we are? They're dumb as dirt but uncannily lucky."

The group picked up speed and ducked into a women's restroom. A few women were at the sinks and several of the stalls appeared occupied. One of the women at the sinks gave the group a questioning glance, but the others at least pretended not to pay them any mind.

"In here," directed Morgan, yanking open the door to the large handicapped stall. All four squeezed into the space. Emma pulled the door shut and locked it.

"Up here, girls," Morgan ordered, pointing to the tank of the toilet. Lindsay and Amber perched on the tank. Emma leaned the rolling suitcase against the door of the stall and sat atop it, pulling her knees to her chest. Morgan turned around and sat down on the toilet. Emma placed her finger on her lips in a warning to stay quiet.

The four sat silent, almost afraid to breathe, listening for signs they had been followed. Other passengers continued to come and go from the restroom. After a few minutes, Morgan sighed impatiently and stood up from the toilet. She retrieved a bottle of water from her carry-on bag, removed the top, and turned to face the toilet. She winked at the girls and began making loud retching noise. After three such emissions of the disgusting sound, Morgan poured a large splash of water from her water bottle into the toilet bowl. Several of the fellow occupants of the restroom groaned audibly. Lindsay and Amber covered their mouths and shook with silent laughter.

Morgan repeated the charade, this time increasing the volume and adding panting and groans. The fellow restroom users hastily went about their business and in less than two minutes, the bathroom was vacant except for Emma, Morgan, and the two children. Two or three other travelers entered the restroom but quickly departed upon hearing Morgan's graphic performance.

Emma passed a bottle of cranberry juice around the group. "Everybody take a drink. We'll need the energy to keep running," she said. "You doing OK, Amber?"

"I'm good," Amber replied.

"We ready to go again?" Everyone nodded.

"Alright, let's do it," Emma announced. Amber climbed aboard the rolling suitcase, Morgan grabbed Lindsay's hand, and they picked up their carry-on bags.

Morgan bent over to peer under the stall's walls. Not a single pair of feet. "All clear!" she announced and the group slowly exited the cramped space. At the restroom exit, Morgan ducked low and stuck her head out into the corridor. No sign of airport security.

Morgan looked to the left and less than fifty feet away, she could see the exit door to the outdoors under a large sign marked, "Ground Transportation." "The door is right there," she told the group excitedly, "Let's make a dash for it."

"Amber, honey," said Emma, "Time to ditch the ride." She lifted Amber off the suitcase and settled her on Emma's hip. "Let's go," she said.

Morgan grabbed Lindsay's hand and the group sprinted out of the restroom and for the outside door. They made it to the door unhindered and emerged onto the street. A line of taxis stood in the queue. Miraculously, no other passengers were in the taxi line. Emma, with Amber glued to her side, ran to the first cab, yanked open the back door, and stuffed the girl inside. Next, she hurried in Lindsay, followed by Morgan. Emma shut the back door and climbed into the front seat of the cab.

The cab driver, a Caucasian, looked to be in his mid-thirties, was clean-shaven, and, most oddly, wore a suit. The car smelled like cleaning chemicals—new, even. Emma immediately realized that something was not right. At that moment, she noticed the pistol holstered on the cabbie's hip.

"Oh, no!" she exclaimed, "I forgot one of my suitcases at the baggage carousel. We have to go back! Get out of the car, everyone!" As she reached for the door handle, the door locks simultaneously clicked. The doors refused to open. Morgan started to pound on the window of the back door.

"What are you doing? Let us out!" she yelled.

The driver calmly sat with his hands on the steering wheel. "Ms. Parker, Ms. Price, welcome to New York," he stated in near monotone. "A lot of people have been spending a lot of time and a lot of resources looking for you and your little friends. It's time to stop running."

CHAPTER TWO

Seven months earlier

E mma Parker reclined in her office. She wore a pink and tan suit with a
short skirt. Her light brown sling-back pumps were kicked off under her
desk. Emma was leaning back in her executive office chair with her bare
feet propped up on her desk. She hated stockings, so her legs were uncovered.

Emma was pressing forty-caliber rounds into the magazine of her Glock. She
hummed and bobbed with the hip-hop music streaming from her computer. A
light knock sounded on the closed door. Without waiting for a response, Emma's
legal assistant, Kat, strode into Emma's office. A few steps in from the door, Kat
stopped and threw up her hands. "Well, aren't you just the picture of femininity?"
she stated. "I don't know which part of this picture is the most charming—your
lady-like posture, your thug music, or your semi-automatic weapon."

Emma continued pressing the ammunition into the container. "I think it's
the whole combination thereof."

"You will never find a man this way," stated Kat.

"I'm alone, in my office, with the door closed. And besides, who's looking
for a man?" Emma replied.

"Jeffrey's been gone for over three years now. You need to do more than just have male friends you hang out with. Don't you want a relationship?"

Emma looked up and thought for a second. "I don't know. Maybe," she answered.

"Well, then, practice being a little less . . . crass," suggested Kat.

"I'm not crass. Just unpretentious and . . . maybe, a little . . . aggressive," Emma responded. "Besides, men secretly want a woman who will give them a run for their money. You know, the thrill of conquest."

"Oh, good heavens," exclaimed Kat. "The last thing I wish to discuss is your romantic inclinations. Anyway, the reason I came in here was to remind you that you have to be in Motions in less than thirty minutes. Do you need any copies or orders or anything?'

Emma sat up and placed the ammunition magazine on the desk. She looked at her calendar and the list of matters on the docket for that morning. "No, I'm all set," she answered. "By the way, did you call to see what judge I have today?"

Kat nodded slowly. "That's the other good news of the day: You have Judge Steinberg," she said with a wide grin.

"Oh, that's just great," said Emma. "I've managed to avoid that particular judge for almost six months now. Apparently, my planets are misaligned today."

"Come on, Emma," Kat replied, "this whole jinxed thing is in your head and nothing more. You just have to tell yourself that nothing bad is going to happen, and you'll be fine."

"I know, I know," said Emma. "But every time I'm in front of him, I am so afraid I'm going to perform some new act of slapstick comedy that I make myself nervous and end up doing something clumsy. He looks at me through those swirly-eyed thick glasses—I know you know what I'm talking about—and I get dizzy or something. It's so humiliating!"

"Hah!" Kat burst out. "He's afraid of you, too. Remember at Logan's Christmas party last year? When you walked up to Judge Steinberg, and he held out his glass of red wine as far away from himself as possible, like he thought you'd spill it all over him?" Kat's shoulders shook with laughter.

"Shut up," Emma grumbled. "It's not funny."

"Yes, it is," stated Kat. "Anyway, why don't you send Morgan?"

"I wish I could," replied Emma, "but one of these Motions is complicated and Steinberg would confuse Morgan. Plus, I'm sending her to Juvenile Court. I just have to brave up and will myself not to do something stupid."

"Good idea," said Kat. "Hurry up, now, so you don't have to run and get all hot and flustered on the way there."

Emma loaded up her briefcase, put on her shoes, and hurried out of the office. Fortunately, the courthouse was just across the street. When Emma and Morgan had opened up their practice five years earlier, one of the criteria for office space was a location within walking distance of the courthouse.

There was a line of people waiting to get through the security checkpoints at the courthouse door. Emma skirted up the side of the line and rushed through the metal detector, without putting her briefcase or purse on the conveyor belt for the x-ray machine. Several people glared at her or stood there watching, mouths agape. The private security guard, a handsome young Nigerian, glanced up but didn't move from his metal folding chair behind the x-ray machine.

"Ms. Parker," he called out, "if you're going to go around security, you need to display your credentials."

"Eddie," Emma called back, "you've seen my I.D. card a million times. It looks the same today as yesterday and the day before that."

"It's standard procedure," Eddie shouted. "We all have to follow the procedure."

"I keep hoping you'll get suspicious and give me the special search, Eddie," Emma retorted.

"Maybe next week, counselor, if the line isn't so long," said Eddie.

"I'll dress accordingly," Emma called over her shoulder as she walked off toward the bank of elevators.

The doors of the center elevator were starting to close as Emma approached. "Rugger," she called, spying an attorney she knew, "hold the elevator for me!" The man pushed the "door open" button and the doors reversed their squeeze. Emma rushed to get aboard. Her overstuffed briefcase caught on the edge of the door. Emma yanked to pull it free. Suddenly, the bag disengaged from the door and sprung forward to smack a grumpy-looking man in the stomach.

"Oomph!" the man grunted. "Watch it, lady."

"Oh, I am so sorry, sir," stated Emma. "Are you alright?"

"Fine," the man replied.

Emma realized she really should have taken her rolling litigation case. She was such a bad judge of spatial relations.

Emma got off the elevator at her floor and made her way to Judge Steinberg's courtroom. The judge was not yet on the bench. The courtroom was crowded with attorneys and their clients. Emma stopped a few feet inside the door and scanned the room for two of her clients, whom she expected to be there that morning. Before she could locate either of them, the judge entered the courtroom from the door behind the bench, preceded by the deputy sheriff.

"Ladies and gentlemen," the deputy announced, "the Circuit Court of Exeter County is now in session. Please be seated and come to order." Emma thought that would be a fine suggestion, if there were enough seats for everyone.

Judge Steinberg took his seat behind the bench and began to call the docket. As he called each case, the counsel for the parties stood up and stated the time estimate for the arguing of the motion. A few minutes into the docket call, Emma noticed, from the corner of her eye, that Cindy Linton, an attorney who stood approximately four-feet-ten, entered the courtroom. Cindy had only been practicing about a year and was already known by everyone in the domestic relations bar as the attorney who had broken down and cried in the middle of a divorce trial. She had been unable to continue and had called a partner in her firm to finish the case. Needless to say, Cindy had promptly been fired from her position at the firm and lost the respect of every one of her colleagues. Cindy was trying to establish her practice but was rumored to have very few clients.

Emma returned her attention to the docket call, while at the same time, continued looking for her clients. Her back started to ache from the weight of the overloaded briefcase. Emma shifted the briefcase further back on her hip, letting it rest her left side. Judge Steinberg droned on with the calling of the cases. It was then that Emma spotted one of her clients, Rosemary Wood. She was seated in the benches. With just a few people between Rosemary and Emma, Emma tried to tap Rosemary on the shoulder to gain her attention. As Emma leaned to her right, reaching toward Rosemary, the giant briefcase slid off her back and it swung heavily off her left shoulder. Emma reached her hand back to catch the shoulder strap but not before the briefcase lurched forward, catching Cindy Linton solidly between the shoulder blades and slamming her face-first to the floor. The file folder Cindy had been clutching flew into the air and the papers contained inside fanned out around Cindy's outstretched arms.

Judge Steinberg stopped his litany of cases mid-sentence and looked up from his computer printout of the docket. His Coke-bottle-bottom glasses glittered, as he looked first from Cindy splayed on the ground to Emma clutching her briefcase to her chest, her mouth wide open in horror.

"Ms. Parker," Judge Steinberg slowly asked, "Do you perhaps know what has led to Ms. Linton's unfortunate accident?"

"Uh," stammered Emma, "Your Honor, I am so sorry, I didn't mean to hit her, I mean, my briefcase, um, got away, and, um, I really don't know how—"

"Ms. Parker," interrupted Judge Steinberg.

"Yes, Your Honor?" Emma responded.

"Perhaps you would like to help Ms. Linton up off the floor and assist her in retrieving her documents?" the judge suggested. The courtroom erupted in laughter.

"Quiet in the courtroom," cautioned the deputy.

Emma set down her briefcase and hurried to assist Cindy.

"Now," continued the judge, "let's finish calling the docket."

After the docket was called, the judge worked his way through the cases, calling them with the shortest time estimate first and working his way toward the longer estimates. Emma located her clients and motioned for them to meet her in the hallway. She got them seated on the sofas in the corridor and excused herself to go to the ladies' room.

Emma entered the restroom and looked at her image in the mirror. Her cheeks were two bright red spots. Her forehead had tiny sweat beads, and little curly strands of hair had sprung free from her bun.

Emma attempted to collect herself. She wet a paper towel and wiped her forehead. She combed and re-fastened her hair, took a deep breath, and returned to her clients. They seemed a little apprehensive at first, but Emma soon disarmed them with her comfortable manner and reassuring presence. After making sure the clients were set, they all returned to the courtroom and took their places in the gallery.

Emma's first case was called. She grabbed the file from her case and approached the podium. She argued flawlessly. She was calm, her arguments were concise, and her speech flowed like honey. The opposing counsel stammered with "ums," spoke in circles, and, in general, stunk. Judge Steinberg smiled and announced that Emma's motion was granted. "Thank you, Your Honor," she replied and returned to her seat. Emma sighed deeply and dared to think the curse with Judge Steinberg was broken.

Other attorneys argued three more cases. Then, "Wood v Wood," called Judge Steinberg. Emma nodded to Rosemary, and the two made their way to the counsel table. Mr. Wood was a no-show, and no attorney appeared on his behalf.

"Ms. Parker," asked the judge, "did you properly serve Mr. Wood with notice of today's Motion?"

"Yes, Your Honor," replied Emma.

"I don't see an Affidavit of Service in the file," stated the judge, "Do you have a copy of the Affidavit?"

"Yes, of course, Your Honor," Emma responded and pulled the file-stamped copy from the folder.

"Please approach the bench, Ms. Parker," the judge requested. Emma started toward the bench, but there was not enough room between the podium and the counsel table for her to pass.

Emma inwardly cursed her curvaceous hips. She grabbed the corners of the podium and attempted to push the podium. Looking down, she realized this particular podium did not have handy castors. Emma pushed harder. The podium clung to the carpeted floor. Emma started to rock the podium back and forth to free it from the carpeting, in hopes that she could then "walk" the podium forward enough to squeeze past it. Suddenly, the podium tipped away from Emma. She reached to grab it back, but caught her right foot behind the forward leg of counsel table. In what seemed like a slow motion movie reel, the tall wooden podium fell to the ground, like a tree in the forest. The courtroom was silent until the podium landed with a thundering crash. The attached microphone issued a feedback scream.

Emma's client, Rosemary Wood, her supposed ally, laughed first. Judge Steinberg glared at her, and Rosemary covered her mouth with her hand. The entire courtroom reverberated with suppressed laughter. Emma stood frozen in horror, wishing she were anywhere but in that courtroom at that moment in time.

"So," asked Kat as Emma dragged herself and her evil briefcase back into the office an hour later, "How'd it go?"

"I don't want to talk about it," Emma muttered as she walked into her office, slamming the door behind her.

Emma plopped into her chair and leaned back. She closed her eyes and breathed deeply and evenly, trying to calm herself down. Slowly, she felt the stress back off and her pulse and blood pressure return to normal.

There was a knock on the door and Emma's law partner, Morgan Price, strode in. As usual, she was stunning. Morgan wore a lemon-colored, silk suit with a low cut camisole revealing her impressive cleavage. Emma had hired Morgan as her associate just after opening her law practice ten years earlier. Morgan proved to be a natural litigator and when Emma later invited Morgan to buy into the firm as a partner, Morgan happily accepted. The two women shared a passion for justice and a fierce tenacity.

Morgan settled herself into the client chair across from Emma's desk and crossed her long legs.

Emma opened her eyes. "So, how did things go in Juvenile Court?" Emma asked.

"Amazingly well," announced Morgan. "Judge Larson was in a benevolent mood and gave me everything I asked for."

"Wow!" Emma replied. "Good for you. Was the client happy?"

"Ecstatic," Morgan answered. "How did Motions go?"

"Less than amazingly well," Emma replied. "I won my motion, but I really need for this day to be over."

"It's only one o'clock," Morgan pointed out. "Maybe lunch will help."

"Alright," Emma said, "but we have to be quick because I have a new client coming in at two o'clock. And I'll only go if we can have Mexican."

"We eat Mexican practically every day," protested Morgan.

"That's why we're so spicy!" laughed Emma.

———

Emma was seated at her desk when Kat led the new client into her office. He was a handsome, olive-skinned man with luxurious curly black hair. He wore a designer suit without a tie and had the top two buttons of his dress shirt unbuttoned, revealing a silver necklace nested in dark hair.

Emma stood up and extended her hand. "Mr. Giovanni, I'm Emma Parker. This is my partner, Morgan Price." Morgan smiled engagingly. The man shook Emma's hand. She was surprised by the rough calluses, which were incongruous to his attire.

"Have a seat, Mr. Giovanni," Emma motioned.

"Please, call me Alexander," the man offered.

"Alright, Alexander," said Emma, "why don't we start with you telling us a little bit about what brings you here today."

Alexander sat uneasily on the front of his chair. He rested his elbows on his knees and clasped and unclasped his hands. "It's my wife. I'm very worried about her and our two little girls. I just don't know what she is up to.

Contessa is three years older than I am. I'm thirty-five; she's thirty-eight. We've been married for thirteen years and have two daughters—Lindsay, who's eleven, and Amber, who's five. When I met Tessa, I knew she had a past, but she never really wanted to talk about it. She was married before, when she was very young, to an Arab guy. All she really told me was that he took her to Saudi Arabia to live and that she hated it there. They were only married for four years and never had any kids. She and I met about a year after her divorce and got married after dating for a year. I was attracted to Tessa because she was just so full of energy and life. Early on in our relationship, she sometimes partied a little too hard and would stay out late and come home drunk. But after she got pregnant with Lindsay, she settled down a lot. She seemed to enjoy motherhood and said she was content taking care of the girls and the house. She was a good mother.

My only complaint was regarding Tessa's spending. I make a good living, but Tessa always wanted to live as if we were rich. After our youngest, Amber, was born, Tessa insisted on getting a tummy tuck and breast implants. She said the two pregnancies had destroyed her body, and she was unhappy with the way she looked. She goes to the hairdresser and the nail salon all the time. She shops like crazy and has tons of clothes and shoes and jewelry. Most of the time, she puts all this stuff on credit cards, which I struggle to pay. If I try to talk to her about her spending, she says I am mean, controlling, and selfish. I want her to have nice things, but I don't want to be saddled with debt. My father always told me to never buy anything on credit that didn't appreciate. I have tried to abide by that philosophy, but Tessa refuses.

Kat entered the room with a tray bearing coffee and shortbread cookies. She served everyone and quietly slipped back out again.

"Please go on, Mr. Giovanni," Emma prompted, once they were all settled again.

"That was about a year ago. Since then, it seems she's lost interest in the girls. Around three years ago, I was working on a project in New York and living up there during the week. I had an affair with the project manager. It was a huge mistake and completely my fault. I felt terrible about it, broke off the affair, and confessed to my wife. She was devastated. However, she took me back and we went to marriage counseling. Things seemed to be going better in our marriage. She became pregnant again, and she was thrilled. I tried working less, and we were happy. Then, she lost the baby. After that, she went into a deep funk, and things got out of control. She started drinking a lot, to the point now it's most of the day when she's at home. She goes out three or four nights a week and comes home really late, past two o'clock. Sometimes, not at all. In the past two months or so, she has disappeared for two or three days at a time, without warning or explanation. If I ask her where she's been, she just screams at me.

"That must be really hard for you," Morgan inserted.

"I'm sad about our relationship, but I am more concerned about our girls. I'm a general contractor, and I work long hours, often at job sites two or three hours away. Amber only goes to school half days, and I am afraid Tessa is either leaving her home alone or is drunk when she's supposed to be taking care of Amber. The other disturbing thing is the sort of role model she is being. Lindsay, my eleven-year-old, drew this picture of her mother."

Alexander pulled a piece of notebook paper from the file folder in his lap. He handed the picture to Emma. The picture was drawn in pencil and depicted a woman in very high heels and short skirt, with teased hair and exaggerated eye makeup, dripping in jewels, and holding up an oversized martini glass, as if making a toast. A speech bubble above her head read, "I am Contessa, and I am far more fabulous than you'll ever be."

Emma examined the picture and passed it to Morgan. "I can see why you are concerned."

"It's not just that. There have been several specific instances when I've felt the children have been in danger or at least seen things they shouldn't," Alexander said.

"Could you give us some examples?" asked Morgan.

"Well, one evening I came home from work. As I opened the front door, I smelled smoke. I followed the smell to the kitchen. The toaster oven was flaming inside and smoke was pouring out of the edges of the door. The cord was sparking. I called out for Tessa and the girls, but they didn't answer. I put the fire out and went to find them. Tessa was passed out on the sofa, a mostly-empty vodka bottle next to her. I searched the whole house, calling the girls' names. Amber finally came out of her bedroom closet. I eventually learned Lindsay was at a friend's house. I tried to talk to Tessa about it the next day, but she insisted it was no big deal."

"Another time," he went on, "Lindsay called me on my cell phone at work. She was hysterical. She said Tessa was drunk and in the upstairs bathroom, threatening to jump out of the window and kill herself. I left the job site and kept Lindsay on the phone the whole time. Fortunately, I was able to calm Tess down when I got there, but both the children were very, very upset. Tessa is drunk more and more frequently when I get home from work, and I am almost afraid to leave her alone with the children. She and Lindsay bicker all the time. On a few occasions, Lindsay has told me Tessa has slapped or hit her. I don't want to leave them there with her, but my work is so demanding. This is our busiest time, and I can't just take off work without threatening our financial stability."

Emma said, "This is definitely a tough situation for you. However, your children are more important than your job."

"The children will be more harmed if I can't make a living and am unable to put a roof over their heads and food on the table," Alexander protested.

"I doubt it would come to that," said Emma. Alexander didn't respond to the comment.

"There's one other thing," Alexander continued. "Strange people are calling the house and Tessa's cell phone all hours of the day and night, looking for Tessa. On several occasions, I have noticed men I don't know sitting in their cars out in front of my house. Tessa claims she hasn't noticed anything odd and says I'm paranoid. I just don't know what to do. I am starting to think maybe she is having an affair."

Emma paused in thought for a minute. "Have you ever known your wife to use illegal drugs, Mr. Giovanni?"

"What?" Alexander exclaimed. "No. Not that I know of. But I have never used drugs, nor been close to anyone who has, so I wouldn't necessarily know the signs. Why do you ask?"

"Unexplained disappearances for days on end are frequently due to drug use," said Morgan. "Also, what you may think are the effects of alcohol may be something more."

"No," Alexander stated. "I refuse to believe Tessa would be that irresponsible."

"Right," Morgan interjected. "Because she hasn't done anything else irresponsible?"

"I see your point," Alexander responded. "I guess almost anything's possible with her at this point"

Emma put down her pen and leaned back in her chair. "Well, Alexander, the very first thing we need to do is make sure these girls are safe. Is there anyone who can help you out with them?"

"I suppose I could get my mother to come down from New Jersey to stay for awhile. She doesn't work and loves to spend time with the girls. Tessa won't be very happy because they don't necessarily get along, but . . . she caused this problem, so she'll just have to deal with it," answered Alexander.

"Good," Emma replied. "Plus, she can keep an eye on Tessa and tell you what else she does during the day. In the meantime, Morgan and I will try to find out where your wife goes at night and whom she associates with. Do you have her on your cell phone account?"

"Yes," said Alexander.

"Great," replied Emma. "Get me copies of the detailed bills for the last six months, showing all the calls coming and going. I also need a list of the names and addresses of all her friends and a list of places you know she hangs out."

"No problem," stated Alexander. "I'll get you all the information first thing tomorrow."

"As soon as we know the extent of the facts, we can talk about what legal action would be effective in protecting you and your children," explained Emma.

"But no judge would ever take custody of two little girls away from their mother," said Alexander. "Tessa has been a stay-at-home-mom since they were born. We agreed I would be the breadwinner and she would take care of the kids. She can't change the plan now. I never wanted to be the primary parent."

"In the eyes of the law, Mr. Giovanni, the determining factor is what is in the best interest of the children," Emma explained. "If their mother is doing things that would endanger them, or even just exposing them to inappropriate things, it may very well be in their best interest to be with you, their father."

"I don't want custody of the kids. I just want my wife to get her act together and go back to being a mother," Alexander complained.

"Mr. Giovanni," said Emma, "that would be the best scenario. But you can't make other people change unless they want to. If your wife continues on her current path, and your girls are in danger of being harmed physically or emotionally, you need to prepare yourself to step up to the plate and be a father to your children. I know you can do it."

"I guess you're right," said Alexander. "But let's first try to see if we can get Tessa to turn herself around."

An hour later, Alexander had filled out the necessary paperwork to officially hire Emma and Morgan as his counsel and laid down a hefty retainer fee. After Alexander departed, Morgan and Emma sat alone in Emma's office.

"Oh, yeah," Morgan announced, "I'm putting my money on drugs *and* a boyfriend. Although, if I had a guy like Alexander at home, and someone with money, to boot, I wouldn't be out running around."

"You'd think not," answered Emma, "but the grass is always greener on the other side of the fence. It's human nature; we want something other than what we have. Apparently, the stability she thought she'd get from Alexander has become boring for Tessa. Or maybe she simply has a substance-abuse problem that she managed to control for a time but has now gotten out of control. Whatever it is, it's probably not going to end well for any of them: Tessa, Alexander, or their two little girls."

"As soon as we get the details from Alexander tomorrow, I'll start the legwork," said Morgan. "In the meantime, feel like kicking some rubber butt?"

Emma looked at the clock on her bookshelf: 4:15 p.m. "OK. Let me wrap up a few things, and we should be able to make the five o'clock class."

CHAPTER THREE

Later that afternoon, Morgan and Emma, dressed in gym shorts and sports crop-tops, crossed the parking lot in the strip mall to the High Kicks Tae Kwon Do studio. It was an open storefront, with one big room covered floor to ceiling in red and blue mats. The dojo always emitted the unique odor combination of stale sweat and grease from the fast-food restaurant next door. Several years earlier, when Emma's two boys were in elementary school, they had started taking tae kwon do. The owner and karate master convinced Emma to take an evening kickboxing class as a means of staying in shape. She had instantly fallen in love with the sport and convinced Morgan to join her. Except for one awesome Korean lady in her late fifties, Emma and Morgan were the oldest students. Most of the other women were high school and college athletes, looking for a challenging workout to keep them in condition for their various sports.

"Tonight's goal," announced Emma, "is the same as every other night—to not throw up. I can feel it; tonight's the night."

"Just face it," Morgan responded, "you are the type of person who throws up a lot. It's part of your unique charm."

"I do not," said Emma.

"Yes, you do," said Morgan. "You throw up when you exercise too much, when you drink too much, when you eat too much, when you have too much stress, and in every type of vehicle or vessel. That, my darling, is a lot."

"Fine," said Emma. "But I am *not* throwing up in class today."

Both women bowed as they entered the studio and took off their shoes. The other students were filtering in and preparing for class.

"So," Emma asked, as she and Morgan pulled their boxing gloves out of their gym bags and selected spots at the back of the room, "how's it going with your boyfriend *de jour*?"

"I don't know," Morgan responded. "When we're together, he seems to be all about me—attentive and affectionate. But then he doesn't call me or return my calls for three or four days. He always has some odd, lame excuse as to why he was unresponsive. It makes me crazy. But then, when I see him again, he's so nice to me that I forget how annoyed I was."

"Haven't you dated his type before?" asked Emma.

"You mean the male type?" answered Morgan. "They're all jerks in their own special ways."

The instructor entered the class and signaled for quiet. He towered above others, well built and completely bald. He had done wonders for teaching Emma's unruly boys discipline, respect for authority, and general tae kwon do. Although he had always been perfectly courteous and friendly, Emma was a little afraid of him. His classroom manner was quite intimidating.

The class started with stamina training exercises. The master barked out commands: "Jumping jacks! Push-ups! Squat-thrusts! Push-ups!" The students obeyed and kept count in loud unison. Emma and Morgan kept up with the class until they got to the push-ups. Morgan started on her knees, while Emma balanced on her toes with the other students. At fourteen push-ups, Morgan flopped down on the mat. Emma struggled on to twenty-eight, then collapsed.

The master yelled out, "Ladies, I see you slacking in the back! There will be extra laps for you later!" Emma and Morgan pretended not to hear. A few of the younger women snickered.

After calisthenics, the students paired off and practiced kicks and punches. Emma held the padded board while Morgan kicked. The master yelled out the types of kicks as he had the aerobic exercises: "Roundhouse! Snap! Sidekick!"

"Going back to what we were talking about earlier, I see the disappearing man trick," grunted Emma between Morgan's kicks, "as a way of men showing us they are in charge. Everything is going to be on their terms. They'll see us when they want to see us. They'll talk to us when they want to talk to us. If they answer when we call, they perceive that as us calling the shots."

"I can see that," huffed Morgan, "but how do we keep them from disappearing?"

The women switched roles, and Emma kicked, while Morgan held the target. Every time Emma landed a kick, Morgan stumbled back a few steps. Although Morgan was three or four inches taller, Emma was stockier, more muscular, and outweighed Morgan by at least twenty pounds.

"Not that I'm any expert—" replied Emma, "remember, I was married at twenty-one and stayed with the same man for over fifteen years—but I think we, as women, need to turn the tables. We need to make them chase us. Don't call, don't e-mail, just wait. And then when they do call, don't answer right away. Make them wait a little. Keep them guessing."

The class moved on to punching the targets held by their partners.

"You mean, play their own game against them," said Morgan.

"Exactly," Emma said.

"Worth a thought," said Morgan. "But I'm not sure I have the self-control to do it."

"Yay!" exclaimed Emma, looking to the front of the room. "Time to beat up Bob!" The master directed several students to push three big, rubber practice mannequins into the center of the studio. They resembled a peach-colored man from the waist up but without arms. The base was weighted and wrapped in mats. When struck, the mannequin would bend and give slightly but not tip over.

"It's a little scary how much I enjoy attacking this guy," said Emma. "I don't know if it's that he's just so passive, or if it's the way his gummy flesh sinks in when you strike him. Whatever it is, it just feels so good!"

The students formed three lines to take turns kicking and punching the mannequins. As Morgan's turn approached, Emma asked, "Who's Bob today?"

"The coffee store barista who got my order wrong and then tried to tell me I ordered something else," Morgan answered. Morgan ran forward and pummeled the rubber man with a series of kicks and punches.

Emma clapped and cheered, "Yeah! Get him! That's *skim* milk, not *soy!*"

Morgan ran back and gave Emma a high-five. "For me, today Bob is the pompous arse, Maxwell, who laughed his stupid bow-tie off when I tipped over the podium in court today!" Emma ran to the mannequin with a warrior yell. "Hah! Hah! Who's smiling now, jerk!" She attacked the rubber man with a vengeance, kicking, then punching, circling the mannequin, raining blows on his sticky body.

The other students clapped and chanted, "Go Emma, Go Emma, Go Emma." By the time the master indicated it was time to switch to the next student in line, Emma's face was dark red, and sweat ran down her temples. She ran to join Morgan at the back of the line.

"That was intense," noted Morgan. "Maybe a little creepy."

"I'm just channeling my aggression in an acceptable manner," retorted Emma. She bent forward, resting her hands on her knees, breathing heavily. "And now, I'm going to go channel my stomach contents into the gutter." Emma ran out the front of the studio and vomited in the parking lot. A couple exiting the fast food restaurant veered around her in disgust.

"Sorry," called Emma. "The karate place doesn't have a bathroom."

When Emma returned to the class, the master was pairing up the students according to size and ability for sparring. He called out Emma's name and she stepped forward. Her partner stepped forward at the same time. She was enormous. Audrey Walynski was at least four inches taller and forty pounds heavier than Emma. She had muscles like a man. Emma and Audrey stood looking each other up and down.

As soon as the master finished pairing all the students, Emma trotted up to him. "Sir, I can't spar with her! She's twice my size!"

"I'm sorry, honey, but you're the next heaviest person in the class," the master answered.

"That's not true! And I'm not fat. I'm just thick," Emma retorted.

"Take a look around. Tell me who else weighs more than you do," the master challenged. Emma frantically scanned the class. Sadly, it was true. Other than Audrey the Giant, Emma was the largest woman in the class.

"Fine." Emma admitted. "But I'm still going to get killed."

"Not if you practice good defense," said the teacher.

Emma trudged back to her position. The students all donned padded helmets, chest guards, shin guards, and padded foot covers, along with their boxing gloves. They inserted mouth guards to protect their teeth. Emma thought they all looked a bit like hockey goalies.

The master called for the sparring to begin. Audrey lunged toward Emma. Emma retreated. Audrey took another step forward. Step by step, Emma retreated until her back was against the wall and Audrey loomed over her. Emma ducked under Audrey's left arm and ran back to the middle of the room. Audrey followed. Emma squared her stance and held her fists at chin level, waiting for Audrey to catch up.

Audrey approached and began to circle Emma. *Pop!* Audrey landed a right jab in the middle of Emma's padded forehead. Emma took a step back. *Bam! Bam!* Audrey hit Emma again in the forehead with a right/left combination. Emma reeled. *Crack!* Audrey landed a right hook on Emma's left temple.

"Stop that!" yelled Emma.

"Hands up, Emma!" called out the master. Emma lifted her cocked hands higher. *Whack!* Emma attempted to land a roundhouse kick to Audrey's ribs but ended up striking the outside of Audrey's left thigh. Audrey looked confused. Emma quickly aimed a kick at Audrey's belly. *Pop!* It connected and Audrey took a step back.

"How do you like that?" taunted Emma. Audrey's eyes narrowed, and she advanced on Emma. One! Two! Three! Audrey nailed Emma in the forehead again. Emma staggered back four or five steps. Audrey chuckled.

"Emma!" directed the master, "You *gotta* keep your hands up!"

"OK. Now I'm mad," said Emma, catching her breath and advancing on Audrey. Emma held her fists up high in front of her face and circled Audrey quickly. Audrey struggled to keep pace. Emma circled again and caught Audrey in the ribs with a right roundhouse, followed by a snap kick to the jaw. Emma danced up and down, waiting for Audrey's counter-attack. Suddenly, Audrey brought up her right foot and—*BAM!*—kicked Emma in the stomach.

"Ow!" grunted Emma, but she held her ground. Emma came back and landed a spinning right and left roundhouse combination to Audrey's mid-section. Audrey dropped her hands. Emma jumped up and hit Audrey in the forehead with a right/left jab combination.

"Time!" called the master. Emma and Audrey bowed to one another and retreated to opposite walls. Emma slid her back down the wall until she rested her rear end on the floor. She turned to Morgan, who was seated against the wall next to her.

"Now *that* was fun," Emma exhaled.

"You're so weird," Morgan responded.

———

As Emma walked in the front door of her house, Sadie, the family's chocolate lab greeted her. "Hi, baby," Emma said and petted the dog's head. Loud, metal rock music issued from the family room. Emma walked into the room and waved her arms. Her seventeen-year-old son, Jason, looked up from the computer where he was working on an animation, waved back, and touched the computer keyboard. The music volume decreased.

"Hi, Mom," Jason said. "You're home." He got up from his seat and walked to Emma. As he leaned down to hug her, Jason's shoulder-length strawberry blonde hair tickled Emma's cheek.

Justin, Emma's dark-haired fifteen-year-old son, glanced up from the video game he was playing. "Hey, M," he greeted her. "What's up?"

"Not much," said Emma. "I just kicked butt at kickboxing class."

"Uh-huh," said Jason. "That's why you have a giant red welt in the middle of your forehead."

"You should see the other girl," responded Emma.

Justin paused his game and walked over to his mother. He leaned in toward her and sniffed. "Did you throw up today?"

"Only once," retorted Emma, "and not until almost sparring time."

Claudia, the family housekeeper, entered the family room from the door to the laundry room. She smelled vaguely of bleach and spray starch. "Hola, Claudia," said Emma. "How was your day?"

"Fine, missus," Claudia answered.

"Did you make dinner tonight?" asked Emma.

"No, I am sorry. I didn't have the time. I was very busy."

"Oh, yeah," Jason spoke up, "'Court TV' was particularly gripping today."

"Hey," responded Claudia, "I was folding the laundry."

"For, like, two hours," said Justin. Emma's middle child was the studious one, always looking for a debate.

Jasmine, the boys' thirteen-year-old blonde sister, came down the stairs. "Justin's just annoyed because Claudia was using the TV, and he couldn't play video games," she said.

"There are two other televisions in this house," said Emma.

"But, Mom," replied Jason, "they're not high definition."

"I see," said Emma. "So, what should I make for dinner?"

"Chicken curry!" suggested Justin.

"Kusherie!" said Jason. "You haven't made Egyptian food in a long time."

"It must have been at least ten days," Emma replied. "What's your vote, Jasmine?"

"I already ate," Jasmine said.

"Really? What did you eat?" asked Emma.

"I drank a Slim Fast shake," Jasmine said.

"That's not dinner. That's a snack," said Emma.

"Nuh-uh. It's called a meal replacement," Jasmine said.

"Some little drink couldn't replace one of my meals," said Emma.

"Obviously," said Jasmine, looking pointedly at Emma's mid-section.

"Hey," Emma laughed, "I'm not fat. I'm thick."

"Shut up, Jasmine," said Jason. "Mom looks fine."

"I think you're beautiful, M," Justin joined in.

"Thanks, boys," said Emma. "Chicken curry, it is. Jasmine, you will at least sit at the table with us."

"Maybe I'll have a little," Jasmine replied.

"I'll make the rice," Claudia said.

"Jason and I will set the table," Justin offered.

"I'll feed the pets," Jasmine said. Everyone set about their tasks.

"Hey, guys," said Emma, "after dinner, want to play Scrabble?"

"Sure!" the boys responded.

"Claudia, do you want to play?" Emma looked at her housekeeper.

"Can I use the Spanish words?"

"Sure."

"Can I use French?" said Jason.

"All Romance languages allowed," Emma decreed. "But bring your dictionaries so we can double-check you."

CHAPTER FOUR

Emma was sitting at her desk, perusing Mr. Giovanni's cell phone bills, which she had received that morning. Morgan strode in, carrying an enormous cup of coffee. Emma glanced up. "I thought you were going to cut back on caffeine," she commented, eying Morgan's nearly quart-sized drink.

"That was last week. It didn't work out so well." She plopped herself down in one of Emma's client chairs.

"So, what are we doing today?" asked Morgan.

Emma put down her highlighter and looked up from the cell phone bills. "Well, first of all, I'd like you to finish the Austin uncontested divorce package. Then, please do a first draft of the proposed Property Settlement Agreement for the O'Leary case. I e-mailed you a bullet-point list of the items I want included," Emma instructed.

"OK," agreed Morgan. "What are you going to do?"

"I'm going to start researching what Mrs. Giovanni has been up to. I've got her cell phone bill details here. I also got her bank statements from the past three months from Alexander that show her debit card transactions, " Emma said. "In addition, I have some orders to draft from a few cases I argued last week."

Morgan yawned. "How very exciting. Paperwork drudgery."

"Whoever said the practice of law was exciting?" smiled Emma.

"Fine," said Morgan, rising from her chair. "Might as well get started." She left Emma alone.

After going through three months of cell phone details, Emma had compiled a list of six telephone numbers that Contessa Giovanni had called frequently, including many at odd times of the day and night. She took out her cell phone and dialed. The first three numbers she tried resulted in voice mails.

"Hi! I got your number from a friend of mine. My name is Emily. Call me back, please—at the number I called from. Thanks!" said Emma to each machine. No one answered the fourth number, and no voice mail activated. Emma dialed the fifth number. After three rings, a woman with a Southern drawl answered.

"Hello," Emma said. "My name is Emily. I'm a friend of Contessa Giovanni's. I haven't heard from her in a few days, and I'm a little worried. Do you happen to know where she is?"

"Who is this?" the woman asked.

"My name is Emily. I'm a friend of Contessa Giovanni's."

"Really," the woman replied. "Then why don't you know nobody calls her Contessa?"

"I met her at tennis lessons, " Emma improvised. "I guess she wanted to show me her fancy side."

"Ha!" the woman guffawed. "That is so like her, trying to be someone she ain't! I can just see her playing that tennis. That'd be hilarious!"

"So," Emma prompted, "have you seen her lately?"

"Hmm . . ." the woman thought. "Two nights ago I saw her at karaoke night at our usual spot."

"Really? And where's that?" asked Emma.

"At Digger Dan's," the woman said.

"And that is where?"

"Why, in Scanton, where we all live," the woman said, seeming perplexed. "Don't you live here, too?"

"Oh, no," Emma manufactured. "I live a couple towns over. How often does she show up at Digger Dan's?"

"Oh, I reckon she and her boyfriend are there four or five nights a week," the woman replied.

"Yeah, what was his name again?" asked Emma.

"Marvin," the woman helpfully stated. "He's such a great guy, but she treats him something terrible—like he's a dog or something. I know she's glitzy and all, but he deserves to be treated better.

"Oh, I'm sorry. I know she's your friend, but he's just such a sweet old guy. Anyway, I gotta go pick up my kid from the kindergarten bus, so I gotta hang up. Hope you find your friend."

Emma disconnected the call. She was not at all shocked to hear Mrs. Giovanni had a boyfriend. Emma read the last number on her short list and dialed it. A man picked up and answered in a language Emma could not understand.

"Sorry," Emma stammered, "wrong number." Emma thought the man could possibly have been speaking some dialect of Arabic she didn't know, but it seemed more like Farsi or maybe Urdu. Emma wondered why an Italian girl from New Jersey frequently called this guy? Then, she remembered Alexander had said his wife had previously been married to an Arab and had lived in Saudi Arabia. Maybe that was the connection.

Having called all the telephone numbers she had deemed interesting, Emma switched her attention to Contessa's debit card transactions. She was just getting started when Kat buzzed her intercom. "Ms. Parker," she stated, "there is a gentleman here to see you."

"Who is it?" Emma asked.

"He does not wish to give his name," Kat replied.

Emma thought Kat sounded odd. She rarely called her "Ms. Parker" and her voice was more tremulous and less energetic than usual.

"Ask him to wait," Emma said. "I'll be up in a minute."

Emma walked to the waiting room. As soon as she entered the area, Kat jumped up from the reception desk and quickly exited to the rear of the office. Emma looked at the only person remaining in the waiting room. He was wearing wrinkled black jeans, a black T-shirt advertising some metal band, and work boots. His heavily tattooed arms protruded from his T-shirt. His long, unwashed, wavy black hair was pulled back in a ponytail. He stood up as Emma approached him.

"Did you call me?" the man asked. His breath smelled of marijuana.

"I don't know," Emma answered. "What's your name?"

"You don't need to know that," the man snapped.

"Well, I can't really say whether I called you unless you tell me your name."

"Sharky," the man replied.

Emma's eyes widened slightly. "I'm pretty sure I didn't call you. I would remember calling someone named Sharky."

Sharky looked around the waiting room, then out the window, then back to Emma. "Can we talk alone somewhere?"

Emma glanced around the waiting room. Kat was long gone, and no one else was in sight. "We *are* alone," she pointed out.

"I mean in private," Sharky said.

"No. I think I'm fine right here," Emma stated. "What's this about?"

"You want something?" Sharky asked.

"No," said Emma. "You came to me."

"Because you called me," Sharky replied, obviously irritated. "Look, I don't need you to be wasting my time. Do you want to buy something or not?"

"What, precisely, is it that you are selling?"

"Whatever you are looking for," Sharky said.

"Look," said Emma, now annoyed herself, "I don't have time to play guessing games with you. Just tell me why you are here."

Sharky stepped forward until he was within inches of Emma's face. "Look, sugar, someone obviously gave you my number. It's not like it's listed in the yellow pages. You called me. I don't know what game *you* are playing, but it's not cool." Emma could smell stale cigarettes and last night's bourbon mixed with the weed on Sharky's breath. His teeth were clenched tight. Emma's mind raced to make the connection.

"Do you, perhaps, know Contessa Giovanni?" asked Emma.

"Tess gave you my number?" exclaimed Sharky, raising an eyebrow

"Uh, yes," said Emma. "I didn't know your name, obviously, but, yes, I got the number from her."

"That chick is crazy," Sharky said. "She'll run her mouth to anyone, anytime. What's a business-looking woman like you doin' running around with that piece of trash?"

"It's a long story," Emma said. She desperately wanted to step back away from Sharky but didn't want to agitate him. "Actually, I was just trying to find her. I haven't seen her in a few days, and I'm a little worried."

"Shoot," snarled Sharky, "she's probably off on a bender. Unless somebody up and killed her, which wouldn't surprise me."

"Why?" Emma exclaimed. "Who would want to kill Tess?"

"She's your friend, right?" asked Sharky.

"Yes, kind of," Emma said.

"Well, I heard from some people that Tess and her boyfriend stepped on some people's toes. Those West Virginia boys ain't used to newcomers in the business, and they're gettin' pretty annoyed with your little friend." Sharky ran his eyes from Emma's face to her toes and back up again. "Tess may dress nice and pretend she's fancy, but she ain't nothin' but trash underneath. But you, honey, you're the real deal. You don't want to be messin' with that girl or that business. You're likely to get yourself hurt," Sharky warned.

"Believe me," Emma said, "I have no intention of getting involved in her 'business.' But I would like to find her. Any idea where she might be?"

Sharky shook his head. "Don't know why you think she's worth the trouble. But I hear she stays somewhere near Scanton. She must also have some sort of D.C. or P.G. County connection, but she's been operating mainly in West Virginia. That's why the boys are so irritated with her. Other than that, I don't know. If I see her, I'll tell her that you're looking for her. What's your name again?"

"Emily," said Emma. "Her friend from tennis."

"Alright," Sharky said, as he turned and headed for the door. He stopped and looked back. "Oh, and Emily," he said, "forget my number."

"Yes, sir," said Emma. "But what number was that, exactly?"

Sharky laughed. "It ends in seven, eight."

"Gotcha," said Emma and gave him a thumbs-up.

With that, Sharky breezed out the door, closing it firmly behind him.

Emma sunk down on the waiting room sofa and took a deep breath. Obviously, Sharky was one of the numbers from the cell phone bills she had called that morning. But she hadn't left her real name and had deliberately used her cell phone so her office number couldn't be traced to her. She wondered how Sharky had known where to come? How had he come so quickly? Mrs. Giovanni was certainly an interesting girl.

So, thought Emma, even though Contessa's husband and children live in Northern Virginia, she was, apparently, spending most of her time in West Virginia. And, as Emma had originally suspected, Tess was having an affair with someone named Marvin and was using drugs. Furthermore, she was also apparently involved in some sort of illegal business. Not a good combination for the mother of two young girls. No wonder her husband was concerned. If only he knew the half of it. In any event, those children had to be kept away from their unstable mother and her unhealthy lifestyle. To do that, Emma had to gather the evidence to show to a court.

Emma got up from the sofa and headed to her office. On the way, she stuck her head into Morgan's office door. "What do you have on your agenda this afternoon," she queried.

"I have to go to Bethesda to depose the doctor in the Mitchell case, remember?" said Morgan.

"That's right," replied Emma. "I remember now. I have to go do some investigation."

"Why don't you hire investigators, like normal attorneys do?" said Morgan.

"You know why," replied Emma. "I need to know the information is accurate. I'm a control freak." Emma smiled.

"No kidding," replied Morgan. "Have fun. Be careful."

"Always," said Emma. "I'll most likely be out of the office tomorrow, too. Can you handle my temporary support motion in Juvenile Court?"

"No problem," agreed Morgan. "Just bring me the file before you go, and I'll take care of it."

CHAPTER FIVE

Emma returned to her office and picked up the phone. If she was going to go poke around in West Virginia, she knew just the person she wanted to take along. Emma and Stan had been friends since they were young attorneys, fresh out of law school. Stan and his wife, Amy, had previously spent a lot of time with Emma and her husband, Jeffrey, when Jeffrey wasn't traveling overseas. When Jeffrey had been traveling, and even more so since Jeffrey died, Amy was great about taking Emma's kids for the evening or even overnight so she could get some time to herself without feeling guilty about leaving them home with the housekeeper. Emma's boys loved spending time with Stan and Amy's two boys, even though the latter were a few years younger.

"Hey, Stan," said Emma, once Stan's receptionist put her through. "What are you doing this afternoon and tomorrow?"

"As it turns out, I just convinced the prosecutor to *nol pros* the charges in my case that was supposed to go to trial tomorrow. So . . . nothing. Why?"

"How do you feel about a road trip to Scanton, West Virginia? I need to do some investigating and don't feel comfortable going by myself," Emma explained.

"Oh, please," said Stan. "You have been to Paris, Cairo, Rome, and who knows where else alone, but you're afraid to go to West Virginia?"

"Rome didn't turn out so great. Remember the night club incident?" Emma said.

"Oh, yeah," replied Stan. "Who knew it wasn't smart for a blonde, American girl to go alone to a night club full of frisky Italians?"

"I'm not blonde; my hair is light brown," pointed out Emma, "and I thought all Italians were civilized, like the rest of Europe. Apparently, I was mistaken. Nonetheless, I am even more afraid of rednecks."

"Right," said Stan. "Anyway, you know I'm always up for slumming. Can Chuck go, too?"

Emma sighed. "I guess. Is he going to be nice?"

"Of course not," said Stan. "That wouldn't be any fun. Let me call him and also make sure Amy doesn't have any conflict, so she can cover the kids. Assuming everything is cool, I'll meet you at your office at 1:30."

"Sounds good. See you then."

Emma called Claudia to let her know she'd be out of town overnight and asked her to stay with the children. She then spent the next half hour returning phone calls and e-mails to keep her other cases from blowing up in the next twenty-four hours.

At 1:22, Emma realized someone was in the parking lot, honking a car horn. Emma looked out the window. Chuck was at the wheel of his beat-up, old, two-door Saab. Stan was in the passenger seat. Chuck continued to tap the horn. Emma quickly gathered up her things, went to the parking lot, and approached the driver's window.

"Is it necessary to disturb the whole office complex?" Emma demanded.

"If you would have been ready, we wouldn't have had to honk," quipped Chuck.

"Stan said you would be here at 1:30," said Emma. "It's just now 1:25."

"Whatever," replied Chuck, unabashedly. "Get in." He pointed his thumb over his left shoulder.

"Hi, Stan," said Emma, looking past Chuck. "Don't you want to take my car? It's bigger and more comfortable than this old thing."

"No way," objected Chuck. "Number one: I get to drive, and I'm sure you wouldn't let me drive your car. Number two: I wouldn't be caught dead in a mini-van. Shut up and get in before we hit rush hour and can't get in the HOV lane."

"HOV restrictions don't start until 3:00," Emma retorted. "It's only 1:30."

"Come on, Emma," interjected Stan. "Just let Chuck drive. Let's go." Stan exited the car and flipped the seat forward to allow Emma to get in. Emma walked around the car, shuffling her feet on the way. She reached into the back seat to stow her briefcase and immediately stood back up.

"There's no room back there for me," Emma complained. "Can't we put the cooler in the trunk?"

"No!" Chuck and Stan exclaimed in unison.

"It's not like you're going to drink the beer on the way," said Emma. "It's illegal, remember?"

"No, it's not," said Stan. "Just give me your briefcase, and I'll put it in the trunk."

"It is too illegal," said Emma. "You know that; you're a criminal defense attorney, for Pete's sake."

"Emma, just give me the briefcase. You don't want to go to visit the Bubbas alone, do you?" said Stan.

Emma sullenly handed Stan her bag and crawled into the tiny backseat. The driver's side of the backseat held two nylon gym bags. On the floor, covering the entire driver's side and more than half of the passenger's side, sat a huge cooler, lid up, full of beer on ice. Emma had to lean her knees into the door and wedge her feet under the cooler in order to fit into the compact space. She glared at Stan as he returned the seatback of the front passenger seat to its original position.

Emma pouted in silence for more than forty-five minutes. By the time the group reached the outer suburbs, Stan and Chuck had already managed to down two beers each. Emma hoped she would avoid a fatal traffic accident on the way to conduct her investigation.

Chuck and Stan, on the other hand, seemed to be having a great time. They were both singing along to the Nora Jones CD—a music selection that greatly amused and surprised Emma.

"So, guys," Emma said, finally speaking up, "you want to know what we're looking for?"

Chuck turned down the music. "Oh. I almost forgot *you* were here," he said. "Shoot."

Emma filled them in on Mr. Giovanni's problems with his wife. She also mentioned the foreign-language voice mail she had reached when calling one of Tess's frequently called numbers.

"So, Stan," Emma queried, "you represent a lot of shady people. Have you ever heard of a guy named 'Sharky?'"

"I've heard of a lot of people, Emma," Stan replied, speaking slowly. "But the attorney-client privilege prevents me from disclosing anything I do, or do not know, to you or anyone else. All I will say is that you should probably exercise caution."

"What does that mean?" Emma asked. "I haven't given him any reason to want to hurt me," Emma said.

"That you know of," said Chuck. "These people sometimes just sort of manufacture reasons."

"I don't have time to worry about that," responded Emma. "He can just stand in line with all the other people who hate my guts for imagined wrongs I have allegedly committed against them. Can you tell me *anything* about Sharky? Like what kind of 'business' he is in?"

"Nope," Stan said. "Sorry. I would imagine there are a number of individuals called 'Sharky.'"

By the time the trio left the interstate and entered the two-lane state highway in Harrisonburg, Virginia, Emma had relaxed and decided to drink a beer herself. Soon, she was singing along with the guys. Cheryl Crow, now.

Two or three more beers later, the group crossed the West Virginia border, and the alcohol had run right through Emma. "Hey, Chuck," Emma shouted over the music, "I need to go to the bathroom."

Chuck waved his hand in front of the windshield. In case you haven't noticed," he said, "we are in the middle of nowhere."

"Well, just keep an eye out for a bathroom, please," said Emma. "Soon."

Approximately fifteen minutes later, Emma spotted a sign that read: "Covered Bridge Park 2 miles." She pointed it out. "A park is sure to have a bathroom," she said.

Chuck and Stan looked at each other. Chuck shrugged. "Sure, why not?" said Stan.

Chuck turned off the paved highway onto a well-groomed gravel road. At the end of the half-mile drive, the road widened to reveal a small gravel parking lot situated in front of an idyllic pond with a small dam at one end. Crossing the dam and the narrow end of the pond, to the left of the parking lot, was a picturesque covered bridge. It appeared the bridge was only open for foot traffic. Chuck pulled into a space, and the trio tumbled out of the car. Actually, Stan and Chuck tumbled; Emma, more accurately, hauled herself out of the backseat of the Saab. Both of her feet felt numb, and her lower back was reluctant to let her unbend to an upright position. As soon as she could walk again, Emma hurried toward the building that housed the bathrooms. Fortunately, the ladies' room turned out to be modern and clean.

When Emma emerged from the bathroom, Stan and Chuck were out of sight. Two or three groups, which appeared to be families, were gathered around separate picnic tables under the trees rimming the pond. It seemed to be a big crowd for a Wednesday afternoon. Perhaps the locals were not as overly ambitious as the inhabitants of Northern Virginia. Emma frequently thought the Washington D.C. culture of relentless striving to get ahead of the other guy left a lot to be desired in the way of quality of life.

Emma looked toward the covered bridge and wondered if Stan and Chuck might have gone to check it out. As she approached the bridge, she heard the echoes of their voices. As Emma entered the opening, she saw Chuck at the other end, attempting to run up the curved side. Stan sat cross-legged on the floor directly opposite. On each try, Chuck got a little bit farther up the wall before pushing off and dropping to a crouch.

Emma walked up and sat beside Stan. "What's he doing?" she asked.

"I'm trying to do a Jackie Chan backflip off the wall," Chuck answered. "It isn't very often you find a curved wall with traction this good," he panted. Chuck took another run at the wall. This time, his feet made it as high as his original chest-level. "Almost got it!" he stated. "But I need a little breather."

Chuck strolled to the side of the bridge on which Emma and Stan were seated and perused the graffiti on the walls. After a moment, he chortled. "I like this one," he said. "It says: 'I banged Becky Sue here on July 18, 2000.' That's beautiful. I can just see it. Good ole' Skeeter, or Scout, or whatever his name was, brings little Becky Sue here to show her the beauty of the antique bridge. He starts showing her the graffiti—little does she know she'll soon be mentioned, too. He backs her up against the wall and starts kissing her. She can smell the warm sap in the natural wood, along with the faint scent of urine from pranksters past. Skeeter caresses little Becky Sue with his magic hands. Before she knows it, Skeeter escorts her into the wonders of womanhood! Yahoo! And just so they won't ever forget it, Skeeter writes Becky Sue this heartfelt tribute!"

Chuck stepped back and dramatically waved his arm toward Becky Sue's memorial graffiti. Emma and Stan applauded. Chuck turned, sprinted toward the other wall of the bridge, ran up the wall, and executed a perfect backflip, landing firmly on his feet in the middle of the bridge. He pivoted, bowed to Stan and Emma, and ran out of the other end of the bridge.

Laughing, Stan and Emma got up and followed. When they emerged into the sunlight on the other end, they found Chuck standing, hands on hips, looking up a very steep embankment to the left. "What do you think is up there?" Chuck mused.

Stan and Emma looked up the embankment. "Most likely a train track," Stan speculated.

"You really think so?" said Chuck. "Cool! I'm going to climb up there!"

Emma looked at him. "Why?" she asked.

"Because train tracks up high are really cool, and I've never been on one like that," Chuck said. "You guys coming with me?"

Emma looked down at her attire. "No thanks. I'm not exactly dressed for mountain climbing today."

"Guess not," said Chuck, looking Emma up and down. Emma was wearing navy blue pumps with three-inch heels, navy-and-white-checked gabardine dress pants, a white eyelet camisole, and a navy silk blazer. "How about you, Stan?"

"Nah, I'll hang here with Emma," Stan answered.

"Alright. Watch for me at the top!" Chuck took off at a run toward the embankment. As he started up the bank, a scramble of small stones and dust rolled down behind his feet.

Stan and Emma strolled down toward the pond and sat on a wooden bench along the shore. A small group of hopeful ducks paddled over to the pair, looking expectant. "Think they've maybe been fed before?" Emma chuckled.

"So, girl, how have you been?" Stan asked. "I haven't seen you in over a month."

"I've been good, " Emma responded. "I've been really busy at work, and the kids always keep me running. You know, the usual."

"Yes, but how are *you*?" Stan asked more pointedly. "Are you taking care of you?

"Oh, yeah," Emma assured him. I've been getting the right amount of sleep, exercising regularly, and only occasionally eating things that are terrible for me but taste really good."

"Well, I'm glad to hear that, " said Stan, "but that's not really what I meant, either. Are you dating?"

"What, you think a woman can't possibly be happy unless she has a man?" objected Emma.

"I think for some women it's possible, but I think you would be happier if you at least had someone to give you companionship, if not love," Stan said. "So . . .?"

"Yes, I've been dating. I even occasionally find someone I actually want to go on a second or even a third date with. The problem is I always end up comparing that guy with Jeffrey, and he never measures up. So, I break it off." Emma looked away and appeared to study the ducks.

"Emma," Stan said gently. "Jeffrey's been dead over three years now. Do you think it's possible that your memory of him, the one to which you are comparing these other guys, is better than he actually was? Don't get me wrong; I loved Jeffrey. I thought he was really cool and a great guy. But he was not perfect. None of us are perfect. Maybe you're just afraid to get involved."

"Maybe," Emma admitted. "But maybe all the decent guys are already taken. If a guy is single in his forties, he's either so weird that he hasn't been able to convince any woman to marry him, *or* he's a jerk and failed in at least one marriage. Either way, I don't necessarily want to be part of it."

Stan laughed, then sobered. "Maybe you're right. In any event, at least promise me you'll keep looking. You never know when the right guy might come along."

Emma chuckled. "Don't worry, Stan, I like men and their company too much to lock myself in a convent just yet. For now, I promise I'll have fun, not worry about true love, and just see what happens. How about you? You OK?"

"I'm great," Stan answered. "Living the life of suburban Dad—coaching football, basketball, and baseball, going to Boy Scout meetings, and keeping my lawn expertly manicured."

"Uh-huh," said Emma. "And if I know you, playing poker, hustling pool, making your own wine and staying up until three o'clock in the morning, playing online video games where you kill people."

"Well, of course," said Stan. "I'm not dead yet."

"HELLOOOOOOOOOOOO!" rang out from across the pond, echoing off the rock formations on either side. Stan, Emma, and everyone else at the Covered Bridge Park looked toward the source of the sound. At the far end, a railroad trestle crossed above the pond. Chuck stood in the center of the span. "Anybody have a bungee chord?" he called out. Several people laughed. Emma looked worried.

"What if the train comes?" she asked Stan.

"I guess he'll run really fast," Stan said.

Chuck started walking toward the right end of the trestle. After a few steps, he did a handspring. You could almost hear the picnickers collectively catch their breath. Chuck waived to his impromptu audience. He then did two more handsprings in a row. After landing, he waved again.

A middle-aged man at the other end of the picnic area, near Chuck, cupped his hands and shouted to Chuck, "Hey, Buddy. Don't be crazy. Knock off the stunts and come on down."

Chuck waved again and set off on a run of handsprings. One, two, three, four . . . he started to drift to the left . . . five, six, seven . . . he was near the end of the trestle when, suddenly, Chuck disappeared from sight! The picnickers fell silent. Several of them rose to their feet. Stan took off at a dead run toward the other end of the pond beneath the trestle. Emma stood up on the bench and strained to see where Chuck might have gone. Before Stan had traversed half the length of the pond, and just as a few people started to climb the embankment under the trestle, Chuck jumped out from behind one of the trestle supports.

"I'm OK!" he shouted to the watching park-goers. Some people laughed; others muttered profanities. Stan ran to meet Chuck at the bottom of the embankment and promptly slapped him upside the head.

Stan and Chuck returned to join Emma on the bench. "You know you're crazy, don't you?" Emma said to Chuck.

"Clearly," said Chuck. "But you can't say I'm not fun."

"True," said Emma. "It's also clear why you're not married."

"Baby, I'm too fabulous to be enjoyed by only one woman," boasted Chuck.

"I'm sure," said Emma.

"Enough of this dilly-dallying," Chuck said. "Time's a ticking. We need to get going."

"Sorry to hold you up," Stan replied sarcastically. "We need to get to Scanton and find this Digger Dan's bar."

"Perhaps I should have mentioned this before," Chuck said, looking intently at Emma, "but we can't go slumming with her dressed like that. Do you have any other clothes in the car?" he asked Emma.

"No, " Emma replied. "When I dressed for work today, I didn't know I was going to West Virginia. What's wrong with my outfit?"

"You look like a big-city lawyer. You can't go into a redneck bar looking like that," Stan said. Stan wore running shoes, athletic socks, khaki shorts, and an un-tucked golf shirt. Chuck was dressed in a Hooters T-shirt, Levi jeans, and red high-top Chuck Taylor canvas basketball shoes. Emma knew from experience that Stan and Chuck always kept two or three suits at the office and wore them only when they had to, such as to go to court. Otherwise, they dressed similarly to the way they appeared that day.

"I can work with this," said Stan, standing up and approaching Emma. "First, take off the blazer." Emma complied, exposing her white eyelet camisole.

"I like this better already!" said Chuck. Emma shot him a dirty look.

"Now, the pants still scream 'old lady,'" said Stan. He stuck the four fingers of his left hand in the front of Emma's pants and pulled the waistband out. His thumb rubbed up and down on the wide, high waistband. Emma looked at Chuck. He raised his eyebrows. Stan unbuttoned Emma's pants and folded the waistband over toward him. He examined the inside of the waistband.

"I'm getting a little uncomfortable here," said Emma.

"Me too," said Chuck. "I'm not sure I ever needed to know that you have a belly button ring."

"Shut up," said Emma.

"Did it hurt?" asked Chuck.

"What do you think? Emma responded.

"When did you get it?"

"About seven years ago."

"What? You were married then. What's the point? Nobody would see it."

"My husband liked it," Emma said.

Emma was distracted by her exchange with Chuck and didn't realize Stan had taken out his pocket knife, and after plucking at a few stitches at the end of the band, gave one hard, quick jerk of the waistband, and the entire waistband tore free from Emma's pants. Her pants now sat low on her hips, a good three-and-a-half inches below the bottom of her camisole.

Emma shrieked. "Stan! Those were expensive pants!"

Stan handed her the waistband. "I didn't hurt them. Your dry cleaner can put it back together later."

"But I'm naked!" protested Emma. "My disgusting stomach is hanging out!"

"I wouldn't say disgusting," Chuck opined. "I wouldn't say hot, but not heinous, either. It's basically flat. The stretch marks are mostly faded and won't show up in the muted lighting of a bar. I like the sexy curve of your hips, too. Also, most people will be staring at your breasts, anyway, and won't pay any mind to your stomach."

"We are done discussing this topic," pronounced Emma. "Stan, I was not aware you had fashion designer skills."

"Amy makes me watch all those fashion-design reality shows with her," Stan explained. "Apparently, I've learned a few things."

"Yet another reason why I refuse to get married," Chuck said. "Now that we're all properly costumed, let's roll."

CHAPTER SIX

I t was a little before 6:00 p.m. when the trio of lawyers crossed the overpass approaching Scanton. Several factories and warehouses sat scattered in the area below the overpass. Tall smokestacks from the factories spewed black smoke into the clear blue sky. One of the smokestacks also flared a bright orange flame. A smoky, acrid stench permeated the car. Emma wrinkled her nose. "Eww! What an awful smell! Didn't Congress enact the Clean Air Act to put a stop to air pollution like this? It looks like Chernobyl!"

"Oh, please, Emma," Chuck scoffed, "this is nothing compared to the pollution in the third world. And, by the way, dummy, nuclear energy is the cleanest energy there is *and* if there is an accident, like Chernobyl, nuclear waste is mainly invisible to the eye . . . and odorless."

"Thank you so much, 'Mr. Answer Man,'" retorted Emma. "If you recall, I have spent my fair share of time in the developing world. My point was that this is *not* the third world, and we're supposed to have our pollution under control here in the U.S."

"I think most of the Clean Air legislation has delayed enforcement dates. It's more of an aspiration than actuality, I'm afraid," said Stan. "What's silly is that Congress can make legislation to take effect five or ten years later, but by the time that date rolls around, there is a whole different Congress in place and probably a new Administration, and they can just change the legislation the past lawmakers made. So, in reality, very little progress actually happens."

"Well, that stinks," said Emma. "Literally."

"OK, ladies and gentlemen," said Stan, "now to find Digger Dan's fine drinking establishment."

"How hard can it be? There's probably no more than two main streets in this town," said Chuck.

As they drove through what appeared to be the newer part of town, there were fast-food restaurants, several gas stations, two newer-looking chain grocery stores, and a Super Wal-Mart. Emma scanned the signs above the two or three strip malls, looking for Digger Dan's. No such luck.

"Look," Stan said, pointing at a sign, "that way to the 'historical district.' I bet that's the original downtown." Chuck turned at the intersection to follow the sign's indicator.

The old downtown lay quiet at 6:00 p.m. The hardware store, seed store, real estate office, and accountant's office all appeared closed. Only a few cars were parked outside the tiny Piggly Wiggly food store. The businesses were located around a town square. The courthouse, with the requisite tower clock, sat on one corner. Adjacent to the courthouse were a few attorney's offices, a bail bondsman, and one establishment that advertised: "Court Reporting, Private Process Service, Notary Public, Fax, and Photocopying Services."

"Wow," Chuck commented, "all your legal support services in one-stop shopping."

In the middle of the square sat a fountain surrounded by benches, trees, and flower gardens. "Don't you just want to bring your lunch and have a picnic by the fountain?" Emma said.

"Nothing like Spam and American cheese on Wonder Bread to perk you up after a long morning at the seed store," said Chuck.

"So, where is Digger Dan's?" wondered Emma.

"I have an idea," said Stan. "Park here, Chuck." He indicated a nose-in diagonal parking space in front of a paint store. "This store is still open."

Stan, Emma, and Chuck entered the paint store. The front of the store was quiet and devoid of customers. Four employees were sitting on the counter, their feet swinging, and talking loudly among themselves. They stopped their chitchat and looked up only after the three strangers stood in front of them for a few seconds.

The oldest of the employees, sporting a nametag on his red vest that read "Bill," turned to face the lawyers. "Well, good evening. Is there anything I can do for ya'll?" He looked the three over, his eyes pausing a little too long on Emma's exposed cleavage. Emma folded her arms.

Stan stepped forward. "We were just passing through and were wondering if you could suggest a good place to chill out and have a few drinks, maybe shoot a little pool?"

"Well," said Bill, "what sort of place you have in mind?"

"A regular people place," Chuck said. "The kind of place the locals go after work, to unwind."

Bill looked at the other workers. "There's the bar at the Holiday Inn," suggested a young man named Steve, according to his nametag. He had a goatee and a tattoo of a snake on his neck.

"No," said Stan, "precisely *not* the type of place we have in mind."

"There's John's Place," suggested Mac, the employee with red hair and a full beard to match. "But . . . no, tonight's Ladies' Night, and for some reason, only women show up."

"What about Digger Dan's?" suggested Ted, the fourth employee. "It's kind of small but pretty laid back. And tonight's dollar beers until 7:30."

"Sounds perfect," said Stan. "How do we get there?"

———

Digger Dan's was, indeed, small. The one-story, white cinderblock building sat in the middle of a gravel parking lot on the corner of a residential part of town. The windows were covered. Two neon signs, one advertising, "Pabst Blue Ribbon" and the other "Miller High Life," flashed erratically.

"Now, that," said Chuck, pointing at the beer signs, "tells you so much already about this joint."

The trio entered the building. It was dimly lit, and it took a minute for their eyes to adjust. A bar ran along the left side of the room. Ten or so patrons sat perched on the red vinyl stools and chatted with one another. To the right of the door sat two pool tables, and a jukebox. Four small tables sat under the windows, immediately to the right of the door. Along the far right wall was a row of stools and a narrow rail on which to set drinks. Two men, dressed as if they had just come from work in one of the factories, played pool. Two other men sat hovering on the stools along the walls, watching the game and heckling the players.

Stan, Chuck, and Emma selected three stools in the middle of the bar. Stan, who had always had the ability to start up a conversation with anyone, began to chat up the bartender. The bartender, a long-legged, muscular woman in her early forties, had a pleasant face, free of make-up, and blonde hair, which was pulled back in a ponytail. She seemed wary at first but warmed up to Stan quickly. Stan explained they were in the area to visit friends but had been struck by an urgent need for alcohol. The bartender, who introduced herself as Sally, laughed. "Well, baby, then you've come to the right place. We've got plenty of liquor here, and I think you'll find the price is right. In fact, tonight we have dollar draft beers until 7:30."

"Perfect," said Chuck. "I'll take two Bud Lights."

Emma looked around. A string of multi-colored NASCAR flags hung above the bar counter. An open cooler beneath the taps held bottles of beer on ice. Behind Sally, there was an old porcelain sink, the two-foot deep type that hasn't been manufactured anywhere since 1965. To the right of the sink sat an ancient refrigerator, with rounded corners and a big steel handle that actually lifted up on the bottom edge to release the latch. Emma ordered a Screwdriver. Sally opened the refrigerator and took out a plastic pitcher of orange juice and gave it a shake. Emma gathered the juice must be from frozen concentrate. She hoped the water used to mix it was safe and not contaminated by any industrial waste that was spewing into the skies from the local factories.

Stan and Chuck discussed the upcoming NASCAR race with Sally. Emma wondered how it was that Stan and Chuck seemed to know something about everything. What Emma knew about NASCAR could fit in a thimble. She sat quietly, sipping her drink. Then Sally turned to Emma. "I think that Jeff Gordon is just so sexy. Who do you like, honey?"

Emma's mind frantically searched for the name of any NASCAR driver, handsome or not. "Well, I must admit I am fond of Dale Earnhardt, Jr.," she stammered.

"Junior?" said Sally. "He's alright, I guess, but a little too full of himself. Who's your all-time favorite?" asked Sally.

Emma was desperate. She couldn't think of any other NASCAR drivers. "Hmm . . . let me see. You know, I've always thought that Richard Petty was pretty hot."

Stan, Chuck, and Sally all stopped and looked at Emma in surprise. "Really?" Sally exclaimed. The two guys chuckled.

"Well, yes," Emma covered, "in a rugged, manly sort of way."

"OK," conceded Sally. "I maybe can see that. I definitely think his money's sexy."

"That's for sure," piped up the woman sitting next to Emma. "I'd date the ugliest man on earth if he was filthy rich. My name's Peggy, by the way." Peggy extended her hand to Emma.

"Emma. These are my friends, Chuck and Stan."

"Pleased to meet you," said Peggy. Sally floated off to the other end of the bar to wait on customers. "So, what brings you to town?" Peggy asked Emma.

"Oh, we just decided to look up a friend of mine," Emma replied. The two ladies began chatting about kids, cooking, and gardening. Sally refilled their drinks. As the alcohol took effect, the conversation flowed easier and faster between Emma and Peggy. Before long, they were giggling and bemoaning the shortcomings of men, in general. Stan picked up his beer and wandered off toward the pool table. Chuck was debating global warming with the old farmer in overalls to the right of him who had a long, unkempt, white beard.

Emma kept looking at a glass gallon jar on the bar—what looked like hard-boiled eggs floated in a brownish-red liquid. "What is that?" Emma asked Peggy.

"Pickled eggs," Peggy said. "Haven't you ever had them?"

"No," said Emma. "Can't say that I have. What's in them?"

"Oh, there are a bunch of different ways to make them," Peggy answered, "but it's always hard-boiled eggs, of course, vinegar, and then either beet juice, Tabasco sauce, or brown sugar and cinnamon. Looks like these have beet juice."

"Yummy," replied Emma.

"Want to try one?" Peggy asked.

"Not today, thanks. I'm watching my cholesterol," said Emma.

"So," asked Peggy, "who's your friend? Maybe I know her. It's a small town, you know."

"Tessa Giovanni," said Emma.

"She's your friend?" asked Peggy, wrinkling her nose ever so slightly.

"Well, yes," Emma replied. "I'm worried about her . . . that she may have gotten herself into some trouble."

"Hmmm," said Peggy. "I don't know, personally, but from what I hear, you might be right."

"Oh, dear," said Emma. "Her husband and kids are so worried."

"What?" exclaimed Peggy. "She's *married*?"

"Yes, of course," said Emma. "Why? Didn't you know?"

"No, I didn't know. And I doubt if her boyfriend, Marvin, knows, either," said Peggy. "She told us she was a stewardess and traveled for work a lot, and that's why she was gone for days at a time. Is she not a stewardess?"

"Not a stewardess," said Emma. "So what do you hear she's involved in?"

"I'm not sure, exactly, but I have an idea," said Peggy. "She hangs out with a lot of people who you wouldn't think she'd be friends with. Young guys, mostly, in their twenties, some a little older. They're all unemployed. Most of them worked in the coal mines or in the factories and got hurt. They seem to do nothing but lie around and drink, and who knows what else. It's really sad, and their families are heartbroken. Their mamas don't know what to do with them. They can't throw them out on the street, them being hurt and all, but a lot of them have been stealing from their families. One guy, Butch Ayers, killed his daddy over trying to steal his daddy's guns to sell. He went to prison. A bunch of these guys are always at Marvin's house, just hanging out. Also, Tess will be in here and one of these guys will come in and talk to her. She'll go out in the parking lot with him, and then she'll come in alone. The guy never stays, not for even one drink. It's very odd."

"Do you think Tess uses drugs?" asked Emma.

"Oh, definitely," Peggy replied. "She's always high on something, and I think it's something other than alcohol. Every time she's been in here lately, she's totally out of it. It's embarrassing, really. Marvin has a hard time keeping her from making a fool of herself or even from just falling on her face. I feel sorry for him, really."

"Wow," Emma said. "Do you think her drug use might make it difficult for her to take care of her little girls?"

"Absolutely," Peggy said. "I wouldn't leave my dog alone with her. She's a mess."

"Well, Tess's husband is trying to get custody of their little girls so Tess doesn't go off with them and let something bad happen to them. Do you think there's any way you would come to Virginia and testify for him?" Emma gently asked.

"I don't know," Peggy said. "I don't want to get involved in other people's business."

"I understand," said Emma, "but these little girls really need your help. Besides, from what you've said, Tess doesn't have a lot of fans around here. Even if they found out, who would really be upset with you?"

"Nobody, I guess," admitted Peggy. "Except maybe her young buddies."

"Exactly," said Emma. "Look, here's her husband's attorney's card. Her name is Morgan. Give her a call. She'll let you know how you can help."

"OK," Peggy said. "But don't mention it to anyone else, OK?"

"No problem. I don't know anybody, anyway," promised Emma. "Where else does Tess hang out?"

"I don't know for sure," said Peggy. "I mostly only come here. But a pretty, man-crazy girl like her might like to go to the Elk Horn Inn. It's on the highway, a few miles south of town. I've never actually been there, but I hear it's a wild but high-class kind of place.

"You know what I think?" Peggy continued, raising her voice a few notches louder. "I think it's time for shots!"

"Yeah, shots!" agreed several customers up and down the bar.

"Sally," called out Peggy, "bring us some shots!"

"Sure thing, honey," said Sally. "What you want?"

"How about SoCo and lime?" asked Peggy.

"Yes!" called out a huge man from the very end of the bar. "SoCo and lime!"

"How many?" asked Sally. Several people up and down the bar, including Peggy, Chuck, and Chuck's new friend with the ZZ Top beard, raised their hands. Sally quickly counted. "Eight," she announced. Peggy looked at Emma.

"Nine," said Peggy.

"Oh, no, not me," Emma protested. "I don't drink shots. Besides, I've had several drinks today already."

"Oh, come on," said Peggy. "You can't be a sissy here in West Virginia!"

"Yeah, Emma," Chuck interjected. "You can't be a sissy here like you are back home."

"I'm not a sissy," said Emma. "I'm just trying to pace myself."

"Who's driving?" asked Peggy.

"Not her," said Chuck.

"Well, then," said Peggy, "you have no excuse. We're friends now, and I'm buying you a shot. It would be rude to not drink it. Make it nine, Sally."

Sally nodded and lined up nine shot glasses in a row. She poured a large amount of Southern Comfort, a small amount of lime juice, and a few ice cubes in a voluminous shaker. After giving it several vigorous shakes, Sally smoothly poured the concoction up and down the row of glasses, amazingly making them all equal and pouring the last drops in the last glass. She then slid the shot glasses down the polished bar, much like a bartender in the Western movies that Emma's father loved to watch.

Peggy raised her shot glass and winked at Emma. "To Richard Petty!" she shouted.

"To Richard Petty!" yelled the bar patrons, as they raised their glasses before throwing back the shots. Emma couldn't help but laugh.

"To Richard Petty!" Emma responded and gulped her drink. Chuck laughed aloud.

"Another round—on me!" shouted Chuck, and everybody cheered.

Several more people entered the bar in ones and twos. Everybody seemed to know each other by name and called out greetings as they arrived. Someone started up the jukebox, and the customers had to raise their voices to be heard over the country music tunes blaring from the back wall.

A woman in her fifties entered the bar and came over to Peggy and Emma.

"Maisy!" cried Peggy, who jumped off her stool to hug the woman. Maisy smiled widely and pulled Peggy toward her, practically smothering Peggy in her ample bosom.

"How the heck are you?" Peggy asked.

"Oh, another day above ground is a good day," Maisy replied.

Peggy laughed. "Emma," said Peggy, "this is my good friend, Maisy. She used to go with Marvin."

"Until he ran off with that Italian tramp, that is," Maisy added.

"Sit down, Maisy," Peggy said, offering Maisy her barstool. "Have we got some interesting news for you." Peggy quickly filled Maisy in on Tessa's marital status and the impending custody suit.

"Well, well," said Maisy. "Can't say I'm very surprised. From day one, I knew something wasn't right with that girl. And I'm not sayin' that just 'cause she stole my guy. She come rollin' into town, acting like she's all that and like her poo don't stink. But her stories don't add up. She said she was an airline stewardess but never said what airline. She'd go away for days and when she come back, we'd ask where she'd been and it was a different place every time. I had a cousin once who was an airline stewardess, and she always went to the same city, every time, for years. Then she switched, but it was the same place for years again."

Peggy reached out and placed her hand on Maisy's arm. Maisy covered Peggy's hand with her own opposite hand.

"I also don't get what a woman in her thirties wants with Marvin. He's fifty-three and not rich or anything. And I think he's handsome enough but no catch for a young woman. At the same time, she's running around with a bunch of young stoner boys. If you ask me, that Tess is up to no good."

"Do you think Tess is involved in some sort of illegal activity?" asked Emma.

"I was just getting to that," Maisy stated. "My friend, Louise, caught her oldest boy with illegal drugs in the house. She had a lot of trouble with him in the past for stealing people's pain medicines. Louise took the drugs she found to her nephew in Rockford County—he's a deputy sheriff. He said it looked like heroin. Louise was shocked. Her nephew said if she would let him destroy the drugs right off he wouldn't tell anybody, but that she better get her boy straightened up, or he would go to jail sooner or later—if he didn't kill himself first. Louise sent her boy off to a rehab place in Mississippi, and now he's living with some of their kin down there."

"Did Louise's son say where he got the heroin?" asked Emma.

"No, he wouldn't say, but Marvin had mentioned to me how he was annoyed that the boy kept showing up uninvited at his house when that Tessa was staying with him. Marvin said the boy would show up, stay for twenty, thirty minutes, drink a beer, and then Tess would walk him to his car. Marvin took it that the boy had a crush on Tessa and just dropped by to see her."

"Why would Marvin put up with such behavior?" wondered Emma.

Both Peggy and Maisy laughed. "That's Marvin," said Maisy. "He's just such a nice guy that he lets people walk all over him. He doesn't have a mean bone in his body. Even when he broke up with me to be with that hussy, I couldn't stay mad at him. He came to me and explained so nicely how he couldn't help but be in love with her—she's so beautiful and young and full of life . . . and so classy. What man could resist? I was mad at first, but I had to admit I couldn't compete with her. Marvin and I stayed friends. I figure she'll eventually get sick of him and move on. Maybe then he'll realize what a good deal he had with me and will beg me to take him back. And you know what? I probably will. I know it's pathetic, but I love him."

"Oh, I don't think you're pathetic," said Emma. "If I've learned anything over time, it's that the relationships between men and women are complicated and that pride often gets in the way of love."

"Wow," said Maisy to Peggy, "your new friend's a smart one."

"She is, isn't she?" agreed Peggy.

Before long, Maisy had agreed to testify for Mr. Giovanni and promised to get her friend Louise, to do so, as well. The conversation turned to lighter topics, such as favorite reality television shows and how to best defeat tomato bugs.

Emma excused herself and went to find the bathroom. Peggy had indicated it was located on the right side of the bar, behind the pool table. On her way there, Emma stopped to talk to Stan. Stan was leaning against a stool next to the pool table and near the front door. His pool opponent, a hairy man who looked like some sort of mechanic, judging by the grease on his work pants and shirt, was walking round and round the pool table. He bent down to table level, eyed the balls, then straightened up and moved to another location to do the same.

Stan smiled at Emma. "What's up, lady? Learn anything?"

"Oh, yeah," Emma answered, keeping her voice very low, "I'm making friends and getting a lot of information."

"Good," Stan said. "I'm getting ready to relieve this gentleman of his paycheck."

"I'm shocked," Emma replied, giving Stan a wink.

Just then, the largest man Emma had ever seen, other than on television, strode through the front door. Emma and Stan couldn't help but stare. The man's height and girth seemed to overwhelm the small building. His head nearly touched the ceiling and his hands brushed against the furniture and patrons as he passed by. He continued to the bar and called Sally over. The bartender immediately went to him, a draft beer in her hand. She placed the glass in front of him. The man picked up the glass and drained it without lowering it once. He then set the glass on the bar and wiped his mouth with the back of his hand.

"Wow," Emma commented. "He must have been really thirsty."

"Apparently," said Stan. "Or he was on the drinking team in college."

"Something tells me he didn't go to college," Emma said.

Sally gestured toward Stan and Emma. The huge man turned around and scowled at them. He headed straight for the pair.

"Yikes!" Emma said under her breath.

The giant lumbered up and stopped uncomfortably close, in front of Stan. "I'm Tiny Johnson," he announced.

Stan appeared unflustered. He ran his eyes up to the big man's face and then back down his torso. Stan's gaze stopped and focused on the fly of the man's jeans. "Of course you are," Stan said in a flat tone.

Emma looked pointedly at Stan, eyes wide in disbelief. Fortunately, Tiny Johnson didn't seem to note the insult.

"Are you folks friends with Tessa Giovanni?" Tiny growled.

"Well," Stan replied, "we know her if that's what you mean."

Tiny pointed at Emma. "I heard you were telling people you're a friend of hers," he accused.

"I may have said that," Emma admitted. "I was trying to figure out where she was and what she's been doing."

"Is that right?" said Tiny. "What she's doing is butting in where she don't belong. What she's doing is trying to get herself in trouble. What she's doing is ticking people off. "

"What people?" asked Emma, in the most innocent voice she could muster. Stan rolled his eyes.

"Just people, that's all," Tiny grumbled. He took a step toward Emma. Emma noticeably swallowed but did not retreat, nor even lean away.

"This is my place," Tiny said menacingly.

"I thought it was Digger Dan's" Stan inserted.

"Don't try to be cute, boy," Tiny snarled at Stan. "We don't need any more outsiders coming here and cutting in on us."

"We have no plans to cut in on anybody," said Emma, placating the giant. "We are just here for the day and dropped in to have a few drinks, relax a little. We have no plans to stay. I am sorry if you got the wrong impression." Emma gave Tiny a winning smile. "Can I buy you a drink to apologize?"

Tiny's shoulders relaxed. "Shoot, I never pay for my drinks here anyway, but I'd like to buy you a drink, sweetheart." He extended his hand and Emma shook it.

"Sure," Emma replied. "Why not?"

Stan looked at Emma and gave her a tiny, almost imperceptible wink.

Stan's pool opponent, who by now had finally finished taking his shot—and missed—interrupted: "Are we going to play, buddy, or not?"

"Sure," said Stan. "Let's do it."

Emma looked up at Tiny. "What about you? You care to hit a few balls?" She indicated the second, now empty, pool table.

"If you want to, darling," said Tiny, moving closer to Emma. "I'd be happy to. Why don't you set up, and I'll get us some refreshments." Tiny moved off toward the bar.

Emma set up the game, and Tiny returned with two beers and two shots of a dark amber liquid. Emma's stomach turned over. She had already gone far beyond her usual drinking limit for one night.

Tiny handed Emma one of the shots. "Try this, darling," he said. "It'll put some hair on your chest."

"Not something I ever felt I was missing," Emma muttered. She smelled the liquid. It burned the inside of her nose. "What is it?" she asked.

"Jack Daniels," said Tiny. "Go on, try it." Emma shook her head.

"I don't think so," Emma said. "I'm really not much of a hard liquor drinker."

"Oh, don't be such a city girl," said Tiny. "Give it a try."

"I'm not a city girl, " Emma protested. "I grew up in a very small town."

"Well, then, you got no excuse," Tiny replied. "Bottoms up!" He drained his shot glass instantly. Emma shrugged and took a sip. The liquid didn't want to go down, and her gag reflex nearly pushed it back up. After getting control of her nausea, Emma took a deep breath and swallowed the remainder. Her stomach felt like she'd just swallowed a charcoal briquette. She grabbed one of the beers from Tiny's left hand and quickly took a few swallows.

"So," said Emma, "want to show me how this game is played?"

"Absolutely," said Tiny. "You ever played before?"

"A couple of times," said Emma. "But I'm not very good, I'm afraid. You'll have to give me some tips."

"My pleasure," said Tiny, a big grin spreading across his face.

As Emma chattered and played the eager student, Tiny visibly relaxed. He began to loudly guffaw at Emma's jokes. He drank beer after beer and regularly fed the jukebox, telling Emma each song was for her, something she'd just love. Tiny stood close to Emma between pool shots and leaned down to her level to breathe his hot, liquor-laden breath in her face. Emma tried not to grimace.

It was Emma's turn to shoot. The cue ball had stopped squarely in the center of the table. Tiny leaned against the back wall, his head barely under the television set, which hung from the ceiling. Emma moved between Tiny and the table to take her shot. She looked back at Tiny to see if he was going to move so as not to interfere. He made no signs of doing so. Emma had to lean over as far as she could to reach the cue ball with her stick. She breathed, took the shot, and the number four ball rolled smartly into the corner pocket.

"Nice shot, girl," Tiny said. "Better yet was the view I got from here while you were bent over that table." Emma looked over at Tiny. He was positively leering. Emma felt nauseous again.

"Don't be naughty," she said, trying to keep her voice light.

"Why—will you spank me if I am?" asked Tiny.

"Probably not," Emma said. As if she could.

Tiny kept bringing beers. With every round, he became more flirtatious and sexually suggestive. Emma looked over at Stan, but he was engrossed in his game of pool. Chuck was still sitting at the bar, deep in conversation with "overalls man."

Emma realized she had never made it to the bathroom, which was where she was headed when Tiny had entered. She told Tiny where she was going and approached the door in the corner marked "Women." Emma opened the door. It was a pea-sized room with one toilet, a small pedestal sink, and a trashcan. A bare light bulb hung in the middle of the ceiling. Emma entered and closed the door. Or, at least, she tried to close the door. The door seemed too big for the frame and refused to fully latch. Emma tried slamming it. It bounced back and hit her in the nose. She tried lifting up on the door and jiggling the doorknob, both to no avail. She tried pushing down on the doorknob. Nothing. Finally, Emma shut the door as far as she could and pushed the tall metal trashcan in front of it to prevent it from swinging wide open. Feeling less than secure, Emma used the bathroom as quickly as possible. The entire time, she kept her eyes focused on the open crack, looking for signs of anyone in general, Tiny in particular. Happily, not a soul came near the door. Emma washed her hands and exited.

Tiny was perched on the edge of the pool table when she returned. "I missed you," he said.

"I highly doubt that . . . seeing that I was gone less than five minutes," Emma said lightly. "You didn't cheat while I was gone, did you?" she teased.

Emma and Tiny continued their game of pool. "So," said Emma, after a few turns, "what, sort of activity of yours is Tessa cutting in on anyway?"

"She's just taking away my business," Tiny said.

"What sort of business?" asked Emma.

"Sales, that's all," Tiny replied.

"Do you sell the same things as Tessa?" Emma asked casually while taking her pool shot.

"Not the same but similar," said Tiny. "Let's just say she took a lot of my customers. I hope you're not planning on doing more of the same. If so, we're going to have a problem."

"Oh, no, honey," laughed Emma. "I don't need any problems. I'm not in the same line of work as Tessa. In fact, the person I'm working for is very interested in finding her and convincing her she should get out of that line of work."

"Smart idea," said Tiny.

Loud voices drew Emma's attention to the second pool table. Stan and his opponent were arguing. The opponent angrily slapped a wad of bills in Stan's hand and stomped out of the bar.

As the patrons became more inebriated, the volume in Digger Dan's increased. The jukebox continued cranking out country tunes and old-school rockabilly. Tiny brought another round of Jack Daniels. Emma nearly vomited at the mere smell of it.

"Cheers," said Tiny, holding up his glass.

"Cheers," Emma weakly replied. She took a small sip. When Tiny turned to contemplate his next shot on the pool table, Emma poured the remainder of her Jack Daniels into the dusty plastic plant standing in the corner.

As Emma was leaning over the pool table to take her next shot, Tiny came behind her and pressed himself against her. Emma's heart raced and not because she was aroused. "Excuse me," she said, "I can't pull back my elbow. Would you mind moving back a little?"

Tiny didn't move back. He slid his long arms around her midsection, crossing them over and around Emma's sides again. Emma found it hard to breathe. She stretched her neck to look across at Stan. He was deep in negotiations with his next hustling victim. Chuck was across the bar with his back to her. Peggy and Maisy were gone. Sally was busy serving the customers at the bar and oblivious to all else. Emma was on her own.

"Really, sweetie," Emma cajoled, "I can't possibly make a shot now with you squeezing me."

"I thought maybe we'd play a little different game now," Tiny panted in Emma's ear. His right hand moved back to Emma's front side and slid up to cup her left breast. Emma jumped and put her hand on top of Tiny's, trying to push it down.

"Come on, baby," Tiny said. "Don't play hard to get now. You owe me; I've been buying you drinks all night."

"I didn't ask you to," said Emma. "I'm more than capable of paying my own tab." She wriggled side to side but was unable to loosen Tiny's grip at all.

"You know you want it," Tiny said. He removed his hand from Emma's breast. She breathed a sigh of relief. However, in the next instant, Tiny slid his hand lower and inserted it in the front of Emma's pared-down slacks. "What else you got pierced, you little tease?" Tiny snarled, trying to wriggle his hand even lower.

Emma strained forward, as much as she could while held tightly in Tiny's grasp. She lifted up her right foot and stomped it down as hard as she could on the top of Tiny's big foot. Tiny roared, removed his hand from Emma's pants, and released his grip. Emma took the opportunity to round the corner of the pool table and head for the door. She got no more than three steps when Tiny grabbed her right shoulder with his meaty paw and spun her around. Tiny pushed Emma's back against the pool table, on the short end of the rectangle, closest to the back wall. As soon as he was facing her, Tiny picked Emma up by the sides of her waist and set her on the edge of the pool table. With his left hand, he gave Emma a violent push to the center of her chest, forcing her to fall back on the table. With his right hand, Tiny pulled at the front of her pants. Emma instantly realized what Tiny had in mind and was terrified.

"Stan! Chuck! Help me!" Emma screamed. But it was so noisy in the bar and so much activity was going on that no one seemed to notice. Emma's right hand searched frantically behind her on the table. She located a billiard ball and threw it at Tiny. It hit him squarely in the forehead and bounced off to the floor. Tiny grunted loudly and slapped Emma across the face. Emma found another ball and threw it at Tiny. He caught it. She threw another ball, and he caught that one, too.

"Now you're going to see how it feels, you little bit—," said Tiny as he wound up to throw one of the billiard balls back at Emma. Emma's hand located the pool cue, which was leaning against the table. She suddenly remembered her weapons classes with the tae kwon do master. Emma cocked her left foot and kicked Tiny in the crotch. He hollered again and bent forward.

Emma did a backward roll on the table and came to a standing position with the pool cue balanced in both hands. She began to spin the cue, in windmill fashion, keeping her eyes on Tiny.

"Stan! Help, please!" she screamed again. Stan looked up, saw Emma standing on the pool table, and headed toward her. Stan's opponent punched Stan in the face and then tried to put him in a headlock. Tiny threw a billiard ball at Emma. She dodged it. He threw a second ball. It hit the spinning pool cue, bounced off, and rolled across the floor.

"Wow!" Emma exclaimed. "It worked!"

Tiny quickly threw another ball. It went wide to Emma's left and smashed into a beer bottle sitting on the bar rail against the wall.

Stan couldn't extricate himself from his tussle with his billiards opponent. The other patrons began yelling and cheering as if these shenanigans were things they saw every day. Emma continued spinning the pool cue. Tiny lunged toward her and the cue cracked him alongside his head. The patrons applauded. Emma landed another blow with the cue into Tiny's ribs, along his left side. The crowd cheered in appreciation.

Tiny dove onto the pool table, grabbing Emma around the ankles. She fell backward, and Tiny's hands broke free of her as she flipped over the opposite end of the table, losing her grip on the pool cue and landing on the floor. Looking up, Emma spotted the wooden triangle used to rack the balls hanging on a nail placed in the table. She scrambled under the table and came up on the side behind Tiny. Leaping up, Emma popped the triangle over Tiny's head. It barely fit. When the triangle reached Tiny's neck, Emma placed her right foot on his tailbone area and threw all her weight backward. Tiny bent backward, choking. He spun around, swatting at Emma with one hand while trying to pull the triangle off his trachea with his other hand. Emma clung on tightly, leaning back with all her weight.

Tiny spun away from the table, with Emma still on his back, as tenacious as a rodeo rider. His face had turned a scary shade of red. He turned his back toward the wall and staggered backward. Crashed into the wall, he crushed Emma. She let go of the triangle and of Tiny's shoulder and slid to the floor, landing on her rear end, with her legs in the air. Tiny, infuriated, took a step backward and pulled the triangle up and off his head. He threw it at Emma, but she dodged it. The triangle scuttled toward the bathroom door. Tiny pulled back his right leg, preparing to kick her.

Meanwhile, Chuck had torn a string of the NASCAR flags from the ceiling and just as Tiny prepared to kick Emma, Chuck flung the flags around Tiny's neck and pulled them taught. As Tiny clutched at the string around his neck, Chuck ran around Tiny with the end of the string of flags, pinning Tiny's arms to his side. Emma rolled out of Tiny's reach and stood up. She ran for the door.

Tiny spun around and lunged toward Chuck. His massive chest hit Chuck squarely in the face. Chuck's neck snapped backward, and he dropped the end of the string. Tiny took another step forward and kneed Chuck in the stomach. Little Chuck flew backward, where he hit his head on the rung of a barstool and landed dazed under the bar.

Tiny angrily pulled off the NASCAR flags and looked around for Emma. She had gotten as far as the pool table closest to the door, where she was on the back of Stan's opponent, trying to poke him in the eyes to slow down his pummeling of Stan. Tiny peeled Emma off the man's back and threw her down on the pool table. Emma couldn't help but realize she was back in the same position she had started on the other pool table.

Stan managed to duck under his attacker's blows and grabbed a barstool. He swung it horizontally, hitting his opponent squarely on his left ear. The man fell to the floor unconscious. Stan then came up behind Tiny. Stan lifted the barstool above his head and brought it down with all his force over Tiny's head.

Tiny was enraged. He bellowed and swung his fist as hard as he could at Stan. Stan ducked. Tiny staggered forward with the momentum of his punch and smashed his fist through the glass of the jukebox. Sparks flew everywhere, and the music abruptly stopped.

The other patrons decided to join in the melee and began punching each other and throwing furniture. Two men in overalls pulled the television from its brackets suspending it from the ceiling. They then smashed the television on the floor. Sally ran into the back room and slammed the door.

While Tiny was trying to pull his bloody fist out of the jukebox, Stan grabbed Emma by the wrist and pulled her off the pool table. "I think we need to go," he said. "Where's Chuck?"

"Over there, under the bar." Emma indicated the area where Chuck had landed with her finger. Chuck had managed to land at the farthest point in the bar from the front door.

"You wait outside," said Stan. "I'll get Chuck."

"I'm not going outside alone," said Emma. "We'll get Chuck together."

"Fine. Let's go," Stan said. Stan headed toward the other side of the bar. A fat, greasy guy with a belly the size of a flour sack blocked their way. Stan gave him a right hook to the jaw. The man staggered. Emma gave him a roundhouse kick to his right flank. The man sank to the floor. A second man, apparently in defense of his buddy, came forward and grabbed Emma by the arm. Emma twirled under her own arm, dropped to her knee, and flipped the man over her shoulder, where he landed on his back on the floor.

"Nice," said Stan.

"Thanks," said Emma. The pair battled their way across the room to Chuck. By then, he was sitting on a barstool, watching the action, and drinking a beer.

"Thanks for the backup, buddy," said Stan.

"Hey, I was recovering from my certain concussion," Chuck replied. The three looked toward the door. Between them and the door stood several brawling patrons and a few rednecks that eyed them angrily.

"How are we going to get out of here?" asked Emma.

"I have an idea," said Chuck. He lifted the giant jar of pickled eggs off the counter and unscrewed the top. "Ready?" he said, looking at Stan and Emma.

"I like it," said Stan, smiling. "Ready."

Chuck stood up and tossed the contents of the pickled egg jar across the bar floor. The patrons didn't notice the eggs underfoot, and pandemonium broke out as people stepped on the eggs and slipped. As they fell, they grabbed onto other patrons, bringing them down with them. They wallowed together in the purple, vinegary mix. Some of the people became angry and threw punches at their fellow victims.

Chuck, Stan, and Emma avoided the slippery egg mess by running around the far end of the pool tables. They hurdled the smashed television, dodged the strewn billiard balls, and squeezed past the still-sparking jukebox. Tiny was sitting on the floor, slouched against it, holding his bleeding hand, and looking dazed. Reaching the door, they ran through the parking lot to Chuck's car.

"I still got shotgun!" shouted Stan, and they piled in. They were safely five miles down the road before Emma started crying.

CHAPTER SEVEN

"Emma, why on earth are you crying?" said Chuck. "That was *fun!*"

Emma stared at Chuck for a long moment. "Some of us don't consider attempted rape fun," she finally replied.

"Aw, come on, Em," Stan piped in. "You love a good brawl and you know it. Gives you a chance to show off your fancy martial arts moves."

"Kickboxing is not technically a martial art, I don't think," Emma said. "But I do have to admit there is some satisfaction in defending myself against a bully."

"You're fine, I'm fine. Chuck is totally unscathed. That's all that really matters," opined Stan. "And Digger Dan's will never forget us."

"I know I won't forget Digger Dan's, either," Emma said.

"So what's our next step, 'Fearless Leader?'" Stan asked Emma. "The night is still young."

Emma took a deep breath and thought for a moment. "Peggy, the woman I talked to in the bar who knew Tessa, suggested we might look for her at a place called the Elk Horn Inn. She said it was on the highway, a few miles south of town. Want to see if we can find it?"

After stopping at a gas station to freshen-up and find some snacks, they located the highway and headed south out of Scanton. There was little traffic other than large trucks. Five minutes out of town, they spotted a large, wooden sign demarcating the Elk Horn Inn. It was a one-story building made of rough-hewn vertical boards painted a dark cocoa brown. The front of the building had one large picture window that was covered from the inside with what looked like posters or flyers. There were no lights in the parking lot or on the exterior of the building, despite the fact, there were several cars parked out front. Chuck parked the car at the end of the lot.

"Notice how I backed in and parked right in front of the driveway?" Chuck said. "It facilitates a faster get-away."

"Well, I'm glad to see you are learning from your past experiences," said Emma.

They approached the door. It was all wood, except for one small window, which was covered from the inside by a shutter or flap. A sign underneath the window said, "Private Club. Members Only."

Emma stopped. "Oh, no. We can't go in. We're not members."

Chuck and Stan stopped and looked at Emma, smiling. "Honey, I guess you don't get out to these parts much, do you?" Chuck commented. "They're not really private. They just say that so they can legally deny admission to any person, or category of person, they don't want to let in. Most of them let you become a member on the spot. Stan and I have never been denied entry to this type of private club."

"That's ridiculous," Emma said. "You're making that up. People can't get away with that kind of blatant discrimination."

"Sad, but true, my dear," said Stan. "Are we going in or not?"

"I guess we can try," Emma said. "The worst that can happen is they don't let us in."

"Actually, I think the worst that can happen almost did already happen back at Digger Dan's," said Chuck. "I hope they have a jar of pickled eggs." They all laughed.

"To improve our chances of getting in," Chuck instructed, "you have to go first, Emma. Here, pull your shirt down," he said, grabbing the bottom of Emma's camisole, exposing more cleavage. "Make sure you lean forward, giving them a good view," he said, "and don't forget to smile." Emma rolled her eyes.

"Fine," she said.

Emma approached the window, Chuck and Stan behind her. "I feel like I'm at a speak-easy," Emma said. She knocked on the door. No response. She knocked again, louder. The window shutter behind the window slid back, and a grey-haired man, who appeared to be in his late fifties, peered out.

"Yes?" said the man.

"Excuse me," Emma said in her sweetest voice, "I know this is a private club, but we're visiting from out of town and heard your place was really great. We were wondering if there was any way we could come in for a little while and have a few drinks?"

"Step back for a second, darling," the man said, "and let me see the fellows you got with you." Emma stepped back. Stan and Chuck smiled and waved. The man shut the shutter and a few seconds later opened the door. "Come on in, folks," he said. "My name's Randy."

The bar was tastefully decorated and surprisingly quiet. The establishment consisted primarily of three rooms. As they entered, they saw a dark mahogany, highly polished bar that ran along the left side. Liquor bottles and a variety of glasses gleamed on shelves in front of a mirrored wall behind the bar. Three flat-screen televisions were mounted above the shelves. Two middle-aged men sat at opposite ends of the bar. Across from the bar, there were two table-curling games, powdered with sawdust. Behind the room with the bar was a small, brightly lit room filled with video poker games. This room was full, with at least ten men and one woman, all focused on their games. The machines were muted. To the right of the room with the bar, a doorway between the table curling games led to a large room. It contained a jukebox, a raised dais at one end, and a dance floor surrounded by several small tables. Six young men sat bunched around one table, drinking and smoking. The jukebox was silent. Emma noticed that all the patrons in the Elk Horn Inn were white.

Emma, Chuck, and Stan took stools at the bar and ordered a round of drinks from the young, fit bartender. "So, what brings you folks to Scanton?" the bartender asked.

"How do you know we're not locals?" asked Chuck.

"Because I grew up here, and I know just about everybody in the county, that's how," the bartender replied. "By the way, my name's Bucky." He extended his hand. Stan, Chuck, and Emma introduced themselves.

"I wanted to look up a friend of mine who moved out this way," said Emma. "We sort of lost touch, and I was wanting to see her again. These fine gentlemen agreed to come along for the ride in the country."

"Well, that's right kind of them," said Bucky.

"That's just the sort of guys we are," Chuck said. "Always ready to help out a pal."

"So who's your friend?" asked Bucky, resting his elbows on the bar and leaning in toward Emma. "Like I said, I know just about everyone round here. Maybe I can help you out."

"That's a good idea," Emma replied. "Her name is Contessa Giovanni, but she goes by Tess or Tessa."

Bucky's smile turned to a frown. He straightened up, took a step back, and crossed his arms. "You're a friend of Tess's?" he asked. "She's not welcome in here anymore, and we don't want any more of her kind here, either." He glared at Chuck and Stan.

"Well, actually, to be perfectly honest, Bucky," Emma said sheepishly. "We're not really what you would call friends. Her husband is trying to track her down, and we are helping him out."

"She has a husband?" Bucky said. "You mean Marvin? I don't think they're married."

"No, her actual, legal husband, Mr. Giovanni," Emma replied.

"Wow. Never knew she had a husband. I guess he probably would have a lot of questions."

"If I may ask, why isn't she welcome here?" Stan interjected.

"Not once, but twice, she ran up a big bar tab and then used a stolen credit card to pay for it. Of course, the owner of the credit card disputed the charge, and we didn't get paid," said Bucky. "The first time, she gave me some crock story about how it was her mother's card, and she had permission to use it, how it was all some big misunderstanding. She paid back the tab eventually, so I gave her a break. Then, when she did it again, I had had it. She told me that a friend of hers, in the other room over there, had given her his credit card and asked her to close the tab. That also turned out to be a lie. She was just a little too rowdy for this place. As you can see, it's pretty quiet here. People come in, have a few drinks, relax a little, and go home. That's the advantage of being a private club; you can keep out the undesirables."

"What do you mean when you say 'rowdy,'" asked Chuck.

"She's really not your friend?" asked Bucky, looking at Emma.

"No, she's not," said Emma. "Sorry I lied to you. I just really need to find her."

"If I were her husband, I'd let her stay lost," said Bucky. "Anyway, to start off with, she usually hit the door already with a buzz on, or maybe high on something other than alcohol. She talks too loud and demands immediate service. *And* she seems to prey on the young guys—the ones under thirty or so—but only the ones who have problems. She would single one out, honey up to him, get him to buy her a bunch of drinks, and then leave with him. It was disgusting. Everybody knows, even the guys she hit on, that she is involved with Marvin. And everybody likes Marvin. I guess when you're young and horny, and a pretty lady like that, who seems classy and all . . . dangles it in your face, it's hard to say no. But it's just not right." Bucky stood up. "Anyway, I've said too much already. Ya'll let me know if you need another round of drinks." Bucky walked to the far end of the bar, picked up the remote control, and ran through the channels on the television set above his head.

"Wow," said Chuck. "Tessa sounds like my kind of girl." Emma and Stan just stared at him.

"Think I'll go win me some drink money," Chuck said and, picking up his beer, sidled over to the table curling area.

"Hmm," Emma said to Stan, "there appears to be a theme regarding Tess and the young deadbeat guys. What do you think is up with that?"

"I'd have to say it has something to do with sex, drugs, or both," Stan replied.

"Not rock and roll?" said Emma with a smile.

"No. Sex and drugs almost always follow rock and roll, but rock and roll do not necessarily follow sex and drugs," Stan said with a grin.

"But, seriously," said Emma, "a woman of her age and social class would not otherwise give these guys the time of day. If she's seeking them out, there has to be a reason. Since she could get sex just about anywhere, from any guy she wanted, my money is on drugs."

"Sounds reasonable to me," said Stan.

"I wonder if this has something to do with that creepy guy, Sharky, who came to my office?" asked Emma. "He said Tess was operating a business in Scanton and stepping on toes. Do you think the business has to do with illegal drugs and these boys?"

"I obviously don't know, Emma," said Stan, "but I think your logic appears sound."

"Hey, Stan," called Chuck from the curling table, "these gentlemen would like to challenge us in a doubles match. Come over here," Chuck beckoned to Stan.

"Ah, let the games begin," said Stan, as he stood to join Chuck, leaving Emma alone with her thoughts.

Emma sipped her beer and glanced up at the row of televisions above the bar. Every one of them had the sound muted. One was showing some form of auto racing. Big surprise. Another program seemed to be about fishing. The third one, directly above Emma's head, was showing a concert of the latest pre-pubescent boy pop star. Emma's daughter was a fan, as were many elderly women. Emma thought it was a very odd selection for the Elk Horn Club. The patrons did not seem to be the type to be interested in a skinny little boy soprano pinging around the stage like a Mexican jumping bean. Emma giggled to herself.

"Hey, Bucky," she called out to the bartender. He looked up and wandered down the bar to Emma. "Are you a big Justin fan?" She pointed to the television screen.

Bucky followed Emma's indicator. "Who, him?" Bucky said. "Are you kidding me? He's absolutely ridiculous. I'd like to punch him in the face."

"Wow," said Emma, "how do you really feel?" She smiled. "Then why is he on the television behind your bar?"

Bucky chuckled. "That television is stuck on that channel, that's why. We have to watch whatever comes on."

"I bet your customers love that," said Emma

"Actually, as you just found out, it's frequently a source of amusement, or at least a conversation starter."

Emma and Bucky were exchanging small talk when several young men in their mid-twenties came in. They ordered beers from Bucky and took their drinks into the large room beyond the table curling games.

"See those guys?" Bucky asked Emma. "I think some of them are dudes that left here with Tessa before. Not exactly age-appropriate for her, huh?"

Emma wrinkled her nose. "Not hardly. Very bizarre."

Chuck and Stan came over to the bar. Chuck said, "After three games (and sixty dollars), those guys said it was their turn to use the table, and we should step away. Sore losers."

"I'm starting to think you guys have a gambling problem," said Emma.

"Funny thing about that," Stan said, "people only say someone has a gambling problem when he continues to gamble when losing, thereby placing himself and his family at financial risk. I always win, thereby benefitting my family. How can that be a problem?"

"You never lose?" Emma asked, incredulously.

"Nope," said Chuck. "We never lose."

"If that's true," said Emma, "it's hard to argue with you. I apologize."

"No offense taken," said Stan.

"I think it's time for shots!" said Chuck

"Yes!" Stan agreed.

"Oh, no!" said Emma. "I have already had way, way too much to drink in the past twelve hours. I let myself get talked into shots at Digger Dan's and look how that turned out."

"It turned out great!" said Chuck. "We kicked some tail! Five lemon drops, bartender!" Bucky nodded.

A few moments later, Bucky set down five shot glasses rimmed with sugar and filled to the very top with a translucent yellow liquid.

"Hey, guys," Chuck said and gestured to the two men at the table curling game. "Come here a minute. Here's a peace offering." The two men looked at each other, shrugged, and walked over to the bar.

Stan placed a glass in front of each of the two men, Chuck, himself, and Emma. "No, thanks," said Emma, pushing her glass toward Bucky.

"Oh, honey," said Bucky. "I made it just for you. You will hurt my feelings if you don't drink it. It's basically lemonade."

"What's in it?" asked Emma.

"Fruit juice and some other stuff," said Bucky.

"What other stuff?" Emma grilled.

"*Good* stuff," said Chuck. "Like I always say, 'If you can't run with the big dogs, stay on the porch, Chihuahua.'"

Emma glared at Chuck. "I am not a Chihuahua." She picked up her glass and downed the contents in one swallow.

"Yeah!" said Bucky.

"Yeah!" shouted all the other guys, and they downed their shots, as well.

"Another round!" said Stan

This time, Emma didn't even bother protesting. The lemon drop had tasted like fruit juice and went down easy. A third round followed.

The table curling guys challenged Stan and Chuck to a rematch.

Emma stood up to go find the ladies' room. As she started across the room, she realized that perhaps she had been affected by the lemon drops. Walking in a straight line was suddenly quite difficult. She concentrated on putting one foot directly in front of the other and made her way to the ladies' room.

In the restroom, Emma walked in front of the mirror and gasped. Was that her? She had forgotten about Stan's re-adjustment of her wardrobe. Her cleavage was popping out of the top. Her midsection was exposed. Her hair was wild and scarily voluminous. And, to top it all off, her cheeks were flushed, and her eyeliner was smudged. Emma thought how thankful she was that, out here in West Virginia, she could not possibly run into anyone who knew her.

When Emma returned to her previous seat at the bar, a nicely dressed Black man with scholarly-looking glasses occupied the seat next to hers. He seemed young, in his mid-twenties like the "boys" in the large room. He was sipping a dirty martini. Emma sat down on her stool.

"Hi," Emma said to him. "I'm really surprised to see you here!"

He turned and looked her up and down, from head to toe, and back again. "I could say the same about you," he said coldly. "I come here all the time, but I've never seen you in here before."

"I'm sorry," said Emma, "Sometimes I say things and immediately think, 'Did that just come out of my mouth?' I really didn't mean that the way it sounded."

The young man smiled. "No, it's a fair question. My name's Anthony, by the way." He held out his hand, and Emma shook it.

"I know I don't exactly blend in here. Neither do you, incidentally. They decided to let me be a member, I think, because I'm not originally from around here. Also, I'm a college graduate; I teach history and coach football at the local high school. I played ball for West Virginia University. For all these reasons, the locals think I'm OK."

"I grew up in the Midwest and totally understand how the high school football coach is a local celebrity," said Emma.

"Especially when the team is having a winning year," smiled Anthony.

"Is your team having a good year?" asked Emma.

"They let me in here, didn't they?" Anthony replied. "What brings you to Scanton and the Elk Horn Inn?"

Emma told him she was looking for Tessa and asked Anthony if he knew her.

"You mean Marvin's wife?" Anthony asked.

"Um . . . yes," Emma replied, unwilling to explain, yet again, that Tessa was actually married to someone other than Marvin.

"Well, I don't know her personally, but I have heard about her from my students."

"Really?" said Emma "And what have you heard from your students?"

Anthony picked up his beer and finished the last couple of inches in one swallow. He set down his glass. "My mama always taught me, 'if you don't have something nice to say, don't say anything at all.' I don't have anything to say about her.

"But like I said," Anthony continued, "I don't know her personally. And I make it a point to not repeat gossip. All I can say, is, from what I hear, she is trouble. That's all I have to say. Now, if you will excuse me, I am heading home."

"But you just got here," complained Emma.

"I just came in to have a couple beers and relax a little before bed. I need to head home. And I don't mean any disrespect, but from the looks of things, maybe it's time for you to call it quits, as well."

"I should have called it quits about six drinks ago," said Emma.

"Do you have a ride?" asked Anthony.

"Yes," said Emma. "My friends are over there." She gestured toward Stan and Chuck, deeply engaged in a heated argument about the wager over the last table curling game.

"Oh, great," said Anthony, "the drunk driving the drunker."

"Don't worry," said Emma, "I'm sure we won't leave for hours. By then, someone should be sober enough to drive."

"Well, that's reassuring," Anthony replied. "Yet another reason for me to get safely home now. It was nice meeting you. Good luck with your search. Oh, and Emma . . . be careful. Scanton doesn't take to kindly to strangers."

"I sort of already experienced that at Digger Dan's," said Emma.

"Ohhhhh, how'd that work out for you?" asked Anthony.

"I bet you'll hear some stories around town tomorrow. They're mostly not true, I'm sure." Emma smiled. "Thanks, though. Have a good night." Anthony picked up his jacket off the back of the bar stool, gave Bucky a wave, and headed out the door.

Emma looked over to Stan and Chuck. They and their two fellow curlers were just agreeing on a "triple or nothing best of seven" series. Emma surmised they were going to be a while. She asked Bucky for a diet cola and took her drink to the video poker room.

The room was so brightly lit by the overhead fluorescent lights that Emma had to squint when she entered. The patrons were hunkered over their video consoles, robotically pressing the touchpads on the screens. The machines issued competing but quiet digital *deetle-ettle eep* noises. In a sad, cheap, worn-out way, it reminded Emma of the one time she had been to Las Vegas but without the glitzy people, the buffets, and the spectacular architecture.

Emma went to stand behind a mature man with greying hair, wearing blue work pants and a short-sleeve dress shirt, unbuttoned at the collar. "Any luck tonight?" asked Emma.

The man glanced over his shoulder at Emma. "As a matter of fact, darling," the man said, "I'm on a roll. Now that you're here, I'm sure it will hold out."

"Well, aren't you sweet," said Emma. "I'm Emily. What's your name?"

"Bob," he said.

"Go, Bob!" said Emma.

"Go, Bob!" said the man at the machine to Bob's right.

Bob won the next two hands against the computer, lost the following three, and then won two more. Emma stayed by Bob's side, alternately cheering him on and consoling him.

Emma decided to try a new tact on the Tessa investigation. "Say, Bob, I thought that while I was in town, I might look up an old classmate of my older brother's who lives around here. His name is Marvin. I can't remember his last name. I hear he has a younger, really pretty girlfriend. Do you know him?"

Bob looked up at Emma. "You're older brother? He must be a lot older; Marvin's an old guy."

Emma patted Bob on the shoulder. "You are such a flatterer! So you know him?"

"Well," Bob said, "it's more like I know his mom. She's a wonderful woman! Her name is Betty."

"That's great!" said Emma. "Any idea where I can find Betty? I'd love to meet her!"

"Betty loves visitors. Folks round here just drop by her house. She lives in town, just off the town square, next to the Piggly Wiggly. Little white house with green trim. Go hungry because she will stuff you with coffee cake, homemade doughnuts, and whatever else she is making that day."

"Sounds fabulous!" Emma commented. "Are you sure she wouldn't mind a stranger just dropping by?"

"You're not a stranger. You're Marvin's friend's sister, right?" Bob replied.

"Right," said Emma. "Thanks! I think I'll look Betty up tomorrow. That would be fun."

Bob looked at his watch. "Uh-oh. Time to go before I turn into a pumpkin. The Mrs. gives me a curfew. Nice meeting you. Thanks for being my good luck charm." Bob left the poker room, exchanging farewells with the other players.

Another man on the opposite side of the room called out to Emma, "Hey, darling, want to be my good luck charm for a while?"

Emma laughed. "Aren't you the rascal? Let me go refresh my drink, then we'll see."

Emma walked back out to the bar and got another diet cola from Bucky. "How you feeling, girl?" Bucky asked. "Sobering up a little bit?"

"Working on it," Emma said.

Chuck and Stan's prior table curling opponents had departed and two newcomers were in the process of losing their money to Emma's colleagues. Emma wandered into the big room. Several young men hunched around two small tables at one end.

"Hi, guys! What's going on?"

All eyes turned to Emma. "Not a heck of a lot," said one young man wearing jeans, cowboy boots, and a plaid western-style shirt with snaps down the front. "What's up with you, ma'am?"

"Not a darn thing," said Emma. "My friends are busy playing that stupid game over there, and I'm bored. Anybody mind if I put some music on the jukebox?"

A skinny, pale boy in faded jeans and a WVU t-shirt stood up. "Not at all. Come on. I'll help you pick out something. I think I even got a couple of dollar bills."

"Great!" Emma said. She wasn't surprised to see the jukebox contained mainly country selections. The boy, Mike, and Emma finally agreed on classic Southern rock, including Lynyrd Skynyrd and Eagles. They walked back to the table. "Who wants to dance?" she asked, looking around the table. The young men dropped their eyes to their feet or raised them to the ceiling—anywhere but at Emma.

"Fine. I'll dance by myself." Emma went out into the middle of the dance floor and started dancing, feeling quite vulnerable, but just drunk enough to not care. After a minute or so, the young man dressed in cowboy attire sauntered out onto the floor.

"I felt sorry for you," he said, as he joined Emma and began to dance.

"Gee, thanks," said Emma. "A pity dance. Did your buddies bet you money you wouldn't come dance with me?"

The young man grinned broadly. "Nah, nothing like that. I actually like to dance, but not many girls come in here."

"Yeah, why is that?" Emma asked.

"Not really sure. Most of the nice girls are married or engaged. The wild girls don't like to come here. And my buddies and I go other places to pick up wild girls. We come here to relax and drink in peace."

"Do you think I'm a wild girl, Mike?" asked Emma.

Mike grinned again. "No, ma'am," he said. "You're sort of dressed like one, but you don't act like one. And . . . you're not a girl."

"Oh, thanks! You think I'm too old to be wild?"

"One thing doesn't have anything to do with the other. I know one chick that used to come in here that was old *and* wild," Mike said.

"Oh, really?" said Emma. "Is her name Tessa?"

"How did you guess? Do you know her?" Mike replied.

"Not really. I just know of her," said Emma. "Do *you* know her?"

"All my boys know her. She's pretty cool," Mike said. He pulled Emma in close, then spun her out and back again.

"Is she cool or wild?" asked Emma.

"Both," said Mike. "And she's got connections."

"What kind of connections?" asked Emma.

"Necessary connections," Mike answered. "Do you have the kind of connections Tessa has?"

"No. I wish." Emma said.

"You should talk to my boy, Spike," said Mike. "He has worked with Tessa before."

"Maybe I will," Emma replied.

After the song ended, another young man came onto the dance floor, and Mike took his leave. Emma danced song after song with one partner after the other. Finally, on the seventh song, her new dance partner introduced himself as "Spike." After a little inquiry, Emma learned that Spike had once driven to a club in Washington, D.C. to pick up a package for Tessa. He described where the club was located, although he couldn't remember the name of the club, other than it had the word "City" in the name.

"Who did you get the package from?" asked Emma.

"From some Arab guy—I mean, not an Arab. I called him an Arab, and he got mad and said he wasn't Arab; he was from Afghanistan," Spike explained.

"Hmmm," said Emma. "Doesn't ring a bell. Guess I don't know him."

Emma and "the boys" danced for over an hour. By that time, Emma's feet were killing her, and she needed to use the bathroom again. She excused herself and headed to the front of the bar. Stan and Chuck sat on stools at the bar, drinking brown shots.

"Hey!" Emma said, indignantly. "Why are you guys still drinking? Someone needs to drive!"

"We sort of passed that window of opportunity about an hour ago," said Stan. "We're just going to have to find a hotel within walking distance."

"Are you kidding me?" Emma exclaimed. "We're in West-BeJinky. There's not going to be a hotel within one hundred miles of here! We are screwed!"

"*Au contraire*," Chuck said. "There is a motel less than one hundred yards from here. When they close this joint down, we will head right that way. Now, in the meantime, you need to be introduced to Mr. Walker."

As if on cue, Bucky set a rocks glass half full with a dark brown, pungent liquid in front of Emma.

"What the heck," Emma said and took a sip.

CHAPTER EIGHT

Shortly after the last call—around 1:30 a.m.—Emma, Stan, and Chuck, along with the other few remaining patrons, stumbled out of the Elk Horn Inn.

Emma looked down the highway to the right, then to the left. "So Chuck, just where is this hotel of which you speak?"

Chuck sloppily gestured with his right arm. "Just over the top of that hill, that way," he said. I saw it when we came in."

Emma staggered toward Chuck's car. "Give me the keys, Chuck," she slurred, "I'll drive. I'm the least drunk."

"Nobody's driving," said Stan. "We are walking. Remember, we had this conversation about an hour ago."

"I don't think I can walk," said Emma.

Stan held out his bent arm toward Emma. "You'll be fine. Come on, hold on."

Emma grabbed Stan's arm. "OK," she said, "but it better not be far." Emma and Stan started after Chuck, who was already ahead of them, weaving his way up the hill on the shoulder of the highway.

"Last one there's a rotten egg," Chuck called over his shoulder.

"Is he serious?" Emma asked Stan, speaking very deliberately, trying to lessen the slur in her words.

"Obviously not," Stan said, smiling. "You're not an egg." He patted Emma on the head.

"That's. A. Very. Good. Point," Emma said.

"I know," said Stan. "I'm just full of wisdom and insight."

"Particularly after a hundred drinks," said Emma.

"Particularly so," said Stan.

As they crested the hill, Emma spotted the motel. It was a tired-looking, one-story building consisting of six rooms strung consecutively together, with the reception lobby in the center. A neon sign advertised "OTE" and shined atop the twenty-foot pole in the parking lot. The line below read, "VACAN." Six vehicles were parked in front of the structure.

"Wow," said Stan. "There's a lot of people here."

"Didn't you know that Scanton is a vacation hot-spot?" giggled Emma.

Chuck was waiting for Stan and Emma outside the lobby.

"Everybody, try to act sober," said Stan. "Emma, I think it's best if you don't say anything at all."

"Fine by me," said Emma.

The three entered the blinding fluorescent glare of the lobby and approached the dingy counter. A skinny man wearing black jeans and a flannel shirt was tipped back in the office chair, watching a reality television show on a small, fuzzy-pictured TV. His cowboy boots were resting on the edge of the table that held the television. As the three approached the counter, the man turned his head toward them but otherwise did not alter his posture.

"Help you?" he said.

"Yes, please," said Stan. "We need three rooms for tonight."

"Only got one," said the man, turning his head back toward the television.

"Excuse me?" said Chuck. "You say you only have one room available?"

"Yep," the man replied.

"That seems pretty unlikely," said Chuck. "I find it hard to believe that this P.O.S. motel is fully booked."

Stan glared at Chuck and stepped in front of him. "What my friend meant to say, is," said Stan, "are you certain you only have one room available?"

"Not that hard to figure," said the man. "Have six rooms, five of them full. I reckon that leaves one, don't you?"

"Let's just go somewhere else," said Emma.

"We can't go anywhere else," whispered Stan. "We are all well over the legal limit of intoxication. Even if we don't get arrested, it is dark, the roads are curvy, and we don't know where we are going. We will die. We have to stay put."

"We'll take your one room, sir," Stan said. He took a credit card out of his wallet and placed it on the counter. The man slowly put his feet on the floor, stood up, and sidled over to the counter. He looked down at Stan's credit card.

"We don't take plastic," he said.

"You don't need a credit card as security against incidentals?" asked Stan.

"Ain't got no 'incidentals,'" said the man. "Cash only."

"Alright," said Chuck. "How much is it?"

"Thirty-two dollars, including tax," the man said.

"Great!" said Stan. "Here's forty. Keep the change." He handed the man two twenty-dollar bills.

"Oh, good grief," said Emma. "I hope the price is not comm-sem . . . consum . . . com-mens-urate with the quality."

Stan elbowed Emma in the ribs. "Emma," he said, "just wait for me over there, please." He gestured toward a pair of yellow vinyl chairs near the door. Emma looked at Stan. He looked intently back at her.

"Alright," Emma said and went to one of the chairs. Chuck followed and plopped himself down in the other chair.

Stan completed the necessary paperwork, and the front desk clerk handed him a large metal key with the number "1" imprinted on it.

As the three went out the door, the man called out, "You three have a real good time now!" He winked knowingly.

"As if," said Emma, under her breath.

Stan, Chuck, and Emma made their way to the end of the building, to the first room, labeled with a large, green metal "1" on the door. The door stood ajar by more than a foot.

"Maybe someone is in there," said Emma. "You guys go in first."

Stan knocked loudly on the doorframe. "Hello," he called. "Anyone in there?" There was no response from the dark room. Stan reached in and turned on the lights. Chuck walked into the room. Stan followed him. A few seconds later, Stan gestured for Emma to enter. Emma walked into the room, pulling the door closed behind her. The door hit the doorframe and bounced back open. Emma turned around and grabbed the doorknob with both hands. She pulled the door toward her a second time. The door would not fit into the frame.

"The door won't close," Emma said.

"You're such a girl," said Chuck. He grabbed the doorknob and pulled the door toward him forcefully. The door bounced off the doorframe and flew all the way open. After several tries by both Chuck and Stan, they concluded the door, in fact, would not close.

"It's freezing in here," said Emma. "What is it about this town and doors that won't shut?"

Stan took off his belt. He tied one end around the doorknob and buckled the other end around a pipe running from the ceiling to the wall radiator. "That will keep the wind out, at least," he said.

"Who's going to sleep where?" asked Chuck, eying the two queen-sized beds. "I'm not sleeping with any guy, ever," he said.

"Well, I can't sleep with Emma," said Stan, "I'm married. It would be very inappropriate, and my wife would kill me if she ever found out."

"I'm definitely not sleeping with *her*," Chuck said, pointing at Emma and scowling.

"As if I would ever sleep with *you*," Emma said, wrinkling her nose.

"How about you sleep on the floor, Mr. Picky?" Stan said to Chuck.

"Oh, heck no," said Chuck and then promptly took off his pants and shirt, leaving him in his boxer shorts and T-shirt. He then jumped into the bed farthest from the door and positioned himself diagonally across it.

"I paid for the room," said Stan. "I'm not sleeping on the floor."

Emma looked as if she might cry. "You can sleep with me, Emma," Stan said. "But NO ONE EVER hears about this! You hear me, Chuck?"

"Oh, please," said Chuck. "Like that would be the juiciest secret of yours I have ever kept. Never leaves this room." Chuck then threw his arm across his eyes. "Hurry up and shut off the light."

Stan turned off the light, leaving the room dark but for the light emanating from the bathroom. "I'm beat," he said and took off his pants and shirt and crawled into bed in his underclothes. Emma realized she hadn't brought anything with her to sleep in.

Emma looked at Chuck. He still had his arm over his eyes and seemed to be asleep. She headed toward the bathroom and on the way, picked Chuck's shirt off the floor and took it with her. In the bathroom, Emma closed the door. It was much warmer in there. She sniffed Chuck's shirt. It wasn't too malodorous. Emma was thankful she had left her purse in the car during their bar hopping. Otherwise, it would certainly have been lost in the fray. She washed her face, removed her makeup, and thought how happy she was that she always carried a toothbrush and travel-sized toothpaste in her purse. You never knew when you would need a toothbrush, such as after having onions for lunch. Emma took off her pants, folded them neatly, and placed them on the counter. She took off her shirt and bra and slipped into Chuck's shirt. Now she was ready to sleep.

When Emma re-entered the room, both Chuck and Stan were sound asleep. Chuck snored loudly. Emma placed her purse on the nightstand, climbed into bed with Stan, turned her back toward him, and moved as close to the opposite edge of the bed as possible. Within seconds, she was asleep.

Emma awoke to the rhythmic movement of the bed bouncing up and down. She sleepily opened one eye. In the darkened room, she could barely make out the outline of a figure straddling Stan and moving up and down. Emma's sleep-and-alcohol-hazed mind tried to conceptualize what was happening. What were Stan and Chuck doing? Then, from the other bed, she heard Chuck still snoring loudly. Chuck was still in the other bed? Then who was on top of Stan?

"Chuck!" Emma screamed, "Intruder!"

Emma rolled onto the floor between the two beds and crawled to the foot of the beds. Chuck sat up then jumped onto the bed with Stan and the intruder. Emma got up and turned on the desk lamp. The person sitting on Stan's chest was wearing a camouflage print ski mask and had his hands around Stan's throat. His knees were pressed down on Stan's biceps. Stan's arms flapped uselessly, attempting to hit his attacker but to no avail. Chuck was on his knees next to them. Chuck cocked back and punched the stranger in the jaw. The man's head jerked to the opposite side of the punch, but otherwise, he appeared unaffected. Emma jumped on the bed behind the attacker, straddling Stan's spasming legs. She wrapped her left arm around the attacker's neck and poked at his eyes with her right hand. The attacker elbowed Emma forcefully in her breast with his right elbow, causing Emma to fall backward off the bed. To elbow Emma, however, the attacker had to release Stan's throat with his right hand. Stan reached out with his newly freed left arm and grabbed the lamp on the bedside table. Stan smashed the lamp on the side of the attacker's head.

The intruder, dazed, rolled into the space between the two beds, taking Chuck with him on the way. The two struggled on the floor. Emma tore the bedspread off the empty bed, threw it over Chuck and the intruder, and jumped on top of the bedspread, bouncing up and down and thrashing at the bedspread with her fists. "Emma, get off!" yelled Stan. "You're crushing Chuck!"

"Oh, yeah," breathed Emma, backing out of the breach and moving to space by the front door. Stan moved to the foot of the bed. With one hand, he pulled off the bedspread, and with the other, he grabbed the intruder by the back of the shirt, pulling him off Chuck. Using the momentum and his body weight, Stan pushed the intruder face-first into the wall opposite the entry door. Chuck lay between the two beds, gasping for breath. The intruder pushed back off the wall, causing Stan to take a few steps back. The intruder spun around to his right and into the recess in front of the bathroom.

"I can't die in West Virginia!" yelled Stan. "I told my wife I was going to a seminar in Roanoke!" Stan grabbed the wooden, straight-back desk chair and rushed toward the intruder. The man ran into the bathroom. Stan slammed the bathroom door closed and wedged the desk chair between the bathroom door and the opposite wall of the niche.

"Time to check out, people!" yelled Stan, jumping into his pants and grabbing his shirt and shoes. Chuck crawled out from between the beds and likewise, grabbed his pants and shoes. "Where's my shirt?" Chuck hollered. "Hey, you're wearing my shirt!" he said, pointing at Emma. "Where are your clothes?" he shouted.

"They're in the bathroom," Emma said, unhappily, just realizing it herself. "We need to get them."

"Oh, sure," said Chuck. "Just go knock on the door and ask the nice gentlemen to please hand them out." The intruder was banging on and kicking the door and yelling.

"Emma," said Stan, "we have to go."

Emma looked dejected. "At least I have my purse. I guess we better just go. "

"Good idea," said Chuck.

Chuck, Stan, and Emma ran outside. "It's freezing!" said Emma. "And the gravel is killing my feet. Ow! Ow! Ow!"

Chuck turned his back toward Emma and bent over. "Get on!" he said. "That guy's going to get out of the bathroom before you make it out of the parking lot."

"Thanks," said Emma and jumped on Chuck's back, wrapping her arms around his neck.

"Don't choke me!" Chuck said. Emma lowered her grip.

As the trio crested the hill, they could see Chuck's car, the lone vehicle left in the Elk Horn Inn's parking lot. Something sparkled in the moonlight on the ground surrounding the car.

"Oh, you've got to be freaking kidding me!" said Chuck, straightening up, causing Emma to slide to the ground. "They busted out all the glass in my car!" Chuck took off running toward the parking lot. Stan took off after him. Emma walked to the grass alongside the road. It was much easier on her bare feet. But she began to run, too.

When Emma reached the parking lot, she stopped at the edge of the gravel, eying the broken glass surrounding Chuck's car. Chuck circled the car, mumbling and kicking the tires. Stan walked over to Emma.

"It looks like someone isn't too happy we've come to town," he said. "I'm starting to think these are not random acts of violence. It's a bit too much to think that, in what is most likely a relatively low crime area, the same people would be attacked in their motel room and have their car shot up."

"What do you mean, *shot* up?" asked Emma.

"There are bullet holes in the interior of Chuck's car and a couple in the external body. Boy, am I glad we didn't bring my car! Bullet holes would be hard to explain to my wife. We need to get out of here before our motel visitor gets out of the bathroom. Come on." He turned his back to Emma, and she jumped on. Stan deposited her in the backseat.

CHAPTER NINE

A short time later, the three pulled into the Wal-Mart parking lot. "I say let's get Emma some clothes, buy Chuck a shirt, get some chow, then head for home," said Stan.

"No!" protested Emma. "I still need to talk to Marvin's mom!"

"And I need to get the glass replaced in my car out here in the boondocks where it's cheap," said Chuck. "It will cost Emma a fortune back in Northern Virginia."

"Why do I have to pay for it?" asked Emma.

"Because I came here because of you," said Chuck. "And because you're obviously the one who ticked off half the county, making us targets."

"Won't your insurance cover it?" said Emma.

"Insurance never covers intentional acts, dummy," said Chuck.

"We'll split it three ways," said Stan. "Wal-Mart doesn't open for two hours. Let's try to get a little rest before then." Stan and Chuck reclined their seats. Emma curled up in a ball on the backseat.

———

"Wake up, Emma," Stan said, opening the back door. "We got you clothes."

Emma sat up and rubbed her eyes. She took the Wal-Mart bag Stan held out. "Thanks. Take a walk for a minute, and give a lady some privacy."

Stan and Chuck complied and scooted away from the car. Emma pulled the clothes out of the bag. Jeans and a yellow, lightweight cotton sweater: Not terrible. However, as Emma put the clothes on, she realized the jeans were skin-tight and ultra low-rise. The sweater was also tiny, and her midriff and cleavage were exposed, again. Both had seen more sunlight in the past few days than in recent years. The shoes the guys had purchased were basic slides but with three-inch heels.

When Stan and Chuck returned, Emma said, "I can't go see Marvin's mom looking like a streetwalker. You need to take these clothes back and get bigger ones that are more appropriate."

"Oh, come on, Emma," Chuck whined. "We *hate* shopping. If you send us back, we won't do any better. Besides, this way you fit in with the locals."

"He's right," said Stan. "We had a hard enough time picking out this stuff. It fits; it's just not your usual lawyer costume. Chuck's not complaining about his shirt." Emma looked at Chuck. He was wearing a plaid cowboy shirt with fake pearl buttons.

Emma sighed. "You guys are hopeless. But I'll wear these clothes if you find me some biscuits and sausage gravy for breakfast."

"That, my dear, should be an easy task in this town," said Chuck.

Bev's Diner sat on Scanton's town square, kitty-corner from the courthouse. It was a small storefront structure, with hand-lettered signs in the window boasting "Homemade Pies!" and "Daily Blue Plate Specials." As Emma opened the front door, steamy warmth enveloped her, along with the delightful smell of fresh coffee and frying bacon. "I'm in heaven!" she said.

Chrome and grey-speckled Formica tables hovered above booth benches covered with cracked red vinyl. The black-and-white-checkered floor gleaned from years of buffing. The diner was bustling with the breakfast crowd. Lawyers in suits sat alongside farmers in seed company ball caps and mechanics in blue work pants and shirts. A woman wearing a pink uniform dress and white nursing shoes came to meet them at the door. A plastic nametag, pinned to her lapel on top of a white, lace handkerchief read, "Tina."

"Can I help you?" Tina asked.

"Yes, please," said Emma. "Can we have a table for three?"

"Sorry, honey," said Tina. "No tables open right now. You want to sit at the counter?"

"But there are two tables available over there," said Chuck, pointing to a pair of empty tables in the front corner.

"Those are reserved every day for the judge and his staff," said Tina. "But you can sit at the counter," she repeated.

"The counter will be great," said Stan.

"Dibs on the mechanic," said Chuck, pushing past Emma and perching himself on the black vinyl and chrome stool next to a man in grease-stained work pants and shirt.

Emma and Stan took two stools to Chuck's left. All three accepted Tina's offer of coffee.

Emma, of course, ordered the biscuits and sausage gravy. Stan selected the "Big Breakfast," complete with three kinds of pork products. Chuck settled for two slices of homemade rhubarb pie.

As Emma finished her breakfast, she noticed her lips felt moisturized and slippery, as if she had just applied a coat of lip gloss. "People who consistently eat a high-fat diet must never get chapped lips," she said.

"And that would be their only positive physical attribute, I'm sure," laughed Stan.

In the course of conversation over breakfast with Tina and their fellow diners, Emma learned where the Piggly Wiggly was located, and Chuck found the best place to have his auto glass replaced. The three lingered in the diner until just before 10 a.m., by which time they were the only patrons left, except for two elderly men in a corner booth. Emma ordered two large cinnamon rolls to go.

"Aren't you full yet?" asked Stan.

"Very," admitted Emma. "But hopefully these are my admission ticket to Marvin's mom's house."

"Smart," said Stan.

While Chuck and Stan went to fix the car, Emma paid a visit on Marvin's mother, Betty. Fortuitously, the Piggly Wiggly was just off the town square. It stood on the corner, so there was only one house that could be described as "next to the Piggly Wiggly." Emma supposed this was Betty's house.

Emma strolled up the front walkway. The small front lawn was well kept and decorated with whimsical ceramic and cement garden ornaments, such as frogs, butterflies, and a pig playing the cello. Emma climbed the two steps of the stoop and knocked on the screen door.

"Coming!" called a muffled voice from inside the house. Emma could hear slow but deliberate steps gradually grow louder. Eventually, the storm door opened. An elderly woman wearing a clean and pressed housedress stood before her. "Can I help you?" she said.

"I'm looking for Betty," Emma said.

"That would be me," said Betty.

"You don't know me, and I apologize for showing up unannounced like this," said Emma, "but I was wondering if I could talk to you for just a few minutes. I brought treats," Emma said, holding up the cinnamon rolls wrapped in plastic wrap.

"Are those Bev's?" asked Betty, eying the cinnamon rolls.

"They certainly are," Emma replied.

"Oh, Bev's coffee rolls are my weakness," Betty admitted. "You aren't one of those Jehovah's Witnesses, are you? I don't have time to listen to that nonsense this morning."

"No, ma'am," said Emma, smiling. "I actually wanted to talk to you about your son, Marvin. And about Tessa."

Betty frowned. "You aren't a friend of hers, are you?"

"No, ma'am," Emma reassured her. "I am certainly not a friend of hers. Actually, some people asked me to try to find out what she may be up to here in Scanton."

"Up to no good, that's what," said Betty.

"Yeah, I keep hearing that," said Emma. "Could I maybe come in, just for a little bit?" Emma held the cinnamon rolls up higher.

"Pardon my manners. Of course, honey, come on in," said Betty. She opened the door and gestured for Emma to enter.

Emma and Betty settled in the kitchen, and Betty made a pot of coffee. The kitchen was warm, cozy, and sparkling clean. The ladies sat at Betty's chrome-and-Formica kitchen table, which looked to be of the same era as the furnishings in Bev's Diner. Apparently, the look was all the rage at some point in time.

"So," said Emma, as she swallowed a bite of the cinnamon roll, "tell me about your son."

"Oh, gracious," said Betty, "I am so worried about him. Marvin is such a kind, sweet, generous man. But that woman has put some sort of spell on him and is ruining everything good about him."

Betty told Emma that Marvin had never married. When Tess showed up in town and paid him some attention, Marvin lost his mind, as Betty put it. After meeting Tess, Marvin stopped going to church, neglected all his friends, and even nearly cut off all communication with his family. "He used to come over for dinner every single Sunday," said Betty. "I haven't seen him in two months."

Betty didn't know what Marvin and Tess were up to, but she figured it was nothing positive. Betty had heard around town that "unsavory people" were frequenting Marvin's house, and that Marvin was behind in his bills.

"I'll tell you one thing," said Betty. "No one in this town would be sad to see that Tess leave and never come back."

CHAPTER TEN

"**M**om! You're home!" Emma's children greeted her as she walked in the front door.

"Where did you go?" asked Jason, her eldest, giving her a hug.

"I was in West Virginia, working on a case," Emma answered.

"What in the world are you wearing?" said Jasmine, scowling.

"It's a long story," said Emma. "My clothes got lost." Jason raised his eyebrows.

"I guess they don't have malls in West Virginia," Jasmine commented.

"Not really," said Emma.

"Maybe you should have at least bought something age-appropriate," said Jasmine.

"I figured you and I both could dress like we were twenty-five and even things out," Emma retorted with a smile. "Something smells good. What's for dinner, Claudia?" she called toward the kitchen.

"Hello, missus," said Claudia, emerging from the kitchen. "I made cilantro rice with chicken. It will be ready in about thirty minutes. Welcome home."

"Mom," said Justin, the middle child, "I made a new movie. You have to watch it tonight."

"That sounds great," said Emma. "We can all watch it after dinner."

"I already watched it three times," said Jason. "I helped him with the audio."

"I don't want to watch it," Jasmine complained.

"After dinner, we will all watch it together," said Emma. "End of argument."

———

At 8:30 the next morning, Emma was back in her office listening to her plethora of voice mail messages when Morgan walked in.

"Did you have fun with the hillbillies?" Morgan asked.

"You mean Chuck and Stan?" said Emma.

"Yeah, them too," laughed Morgan, "but I was referring to the West Virginians."

"Oh, I had a real blast," said Emma. "I drank way too much, almost got sexually assaulted, started a barroom brawl, stayed in a seedy motel room that got broken into, and lost my clothes. Oh, and someone shot the crap out of Chuck's car. Other than that, it was pretty mundane. I did learn a lot about Contessa Giovanni, though. How about you; how went your investigation of dear Tessa?"

"Very well, actually," said Morgan, settling herself in one of Emma's client chairs. "I called Tessa's first husband's sister. Giovanni gave me her number. We had lunch yesterday."

"Did you learn anything useful?" asked Emma.

"Very useful, I think," said Morgan. "Ms. Ziad told me that Contessa pretended to be this sweet, innocent girl to attract Ms. Ziad's brother. Then, as soon as they were married, beginning on their honeymoon, Tessa's party-girl side came out. According to Ms. Ziad, Tessa got drunk one night on the honeymoon and flirted with other men at the bar at the resort where they were staying. Her husband got upset and went to the room, and Tessa didn't show up until the next morning. Apparently, things just went downhill from there. Tessa said she didn't want children. She shopped all the time, ran around with friends her husband didn't know, and drank heavily. After three years, her husband decided to move back to Saudi Arabia, where he figured Tessa would have to settle down. He convinced her to accompany him by telling her she would live in a big mansion with a swimming pool and a pile of servants. What he didn't tell her was that she wouldn't be allowed to leave the mansion without a male escort and only then, with his permission and dressed in an abaya. Obviously, she hated it. When they came back to the U.S. for a visit, Contessa left him and refused to return to Saudi Arabia with him. After a year of separation, they were divorced by the court here."

"Wow. I can't say I'm terribly surprised," said Emma, "given her recent behavior."

"It gets better," said Morgan. "After Tessa separated from her husband, he still had hopes of reconciliation. So he had his sister check up on Contessa. Ms. Ziad, with the help of some private investigators, learned that her sister-in-law was running around with some Afghani guys. These guys didn't come from rich families yet, inexplicably had tons of cash for fancy restaurants, illegal drugs, and expensive gifts for Tessa. Ms. Ziad believes the guys were involved in some sort of illegal activity. When she told her brother all these things about his lovely bride, he gave up and did not contest the divorce."

"Hmmm," said Emma. "Afghanis again. Yet Tessa's first husband and his sister were Saudi, is that right?"

"Correct," said Morgan. "What do you mean 'Afghanis again?'"

"Some of the folks I talked to in West Virginia talked about Contessa being involved with some Afghani guys. I wonder what's behind that connection?"

"Weird," said Morgan. "Afghanistan is a long way from West Virginia."

"Maybe things will become clearer as we continue our investigation. What do you have going on this afternoon?" Emma asked.

"Not too much," said Morgan. "Why?"

"Alex is meeting me at the house when his girls get out of school, so we can meet them. I thought you and I could go over a little early and talk to some of the neighbors," Emma explained.

"I will go if you will buy me sushi on the way," Morgan replied.

"It's a deal," said Emma.

———

The neighbor across the street from Alex Giovanni's house was working in his yard when Morgan and Emma pulled up. Emma started a conversation with the man by complimenting him on his landscaping.

Morgan further won him over by telling him his impressive physique must be due to all the manual labor he was doing in his yard. The ladies learned from "Mr. Gardener" that one Afghani man, in particular, who drove a brand new E-series Mercedes, frequented the Giovanni's residence when Alex was away from the house.

"How do you know he is Afghani?" asked Morgan.

"He told me," the neighbor said, smiling. "He kept parking in front of my driveway, so I couldn't get out. I got after him one day and said, 'You Arabs have no respect for other people.' He got very irate and said, 'I am not an Arab. I am Afghani.' Like there's a difference."

"Do you think Mrs. Giovanni is having an affair with this man?" asked Morgan.

"I really have no way of knowing that, but I doubt it," the neighbor replied. "The guy never went inside the house for more than five or ten minutes, and I never saw Tessa leave with him. They seemed to have more of a business relationship . . . if you know what I mean."

"What do you mean?" asked Emma.

"Don't quote me on this," said the neighbor, "but the guy looked like some sort of mobster. Expensive car, expensive but tacky clothes, gold jewelry, lots of hair gel, and cologne. My guess would be more along the lines of illegal sales of some sort, like drugs or stolen property, or something. But, really, I don't know anything for sure."

The woman whose house was next door to the Giovanni's was happy to talk to Emma and Morgan when she learned they were representing Alex Giovanni. She told the two lawyers that she and Tessa had previously been good friends and spent a lot of time together in the past. However, after Tessa's miscarriage, she changed and withdrew from her friends. The neighbor said that, recently, she had become very worried about Lindsay and Amber. She frequently saw the girls roaming the neighborhood unsupervised. A few times, she took the girls into her own house and tried to call Tessa but got no answer. She said once she walked the girls home to their house and found the door locked. She rang the doorbell, and, eventually, Tessa answered the door.

This woman told Emma and Morgan that Tessa was obviously intoxicated or under the influence of drugs and very disoriented. The neighbor, on that occasion, offered to keep the girls at her house until Alex got home from work, and Tessa accepted the offer. The neighbor also told them, however, that she had rarely seen Alex with the girls and that he seemed to work very long hours. Nonetheless, after a little cajoling, she agreed to testify on behalf of Alex at the custody trial.

As Emma and Morgan were leaving the neighbor woman's house, Alex pulled into the driveway with his two girls. As they exited the car, Alex greeted Emma and Morgan warmly. "Girls," Alex said to his daughters, "I'd like you to meet a couple of friends of mine, Miss Emma and Miss Morgan. This is Lindsay—she's eleven years old." Lindsay was tall for her age and willowy, with long, straight blonde hair and cobalt eyes. Lindsay greeted the women politely but eyed them suspiciously.

"And this is Amber, my youngest," Alex continued. "She's five years old."

"Hi!" said Amber, bounding toward Morgan. "You're very beautiful!" she said.

"Why, thank you, sweetie," Morgan replied. "That's very nice of you to say."

Amber had mounds of curly blonde ringlets and prominent, dark brown eyes. Her legs were short and stubby, retaining some of the cuddly roundness of her toddler years.

"Well," said Alex, "why don't we all go inside and have something cool to drink and get to know each other?" Amber slipped her hand into Morgan's and led her toward the house. Morgan looked back at Emma, a little anxious.

Emma chuckled. "Morgan hasn't had much close interaction with children," Emma explained to Mr. Giovanni. "She doesn't quite know what to do with them."

"As you can see," Alex said, "Amber is very outgoing, and, sadly, in the past several months, she has latched on to every pretty woman that comes around, clinging to her. I feel as if she's trying to replace her mother, who hasn't been giving Amber the attention she needs. I apologize."

"Not a problem," said Emma. "It's good for Morgan to spend some time with little people."

Once in the kitchen, Lindsay took the hostess role, asking everyone what they wanted to drink and preparing the beverages. She even set out a plate of store-bought cookies. While enjoying their refreshments, they all discussed an animated movie Alex and the girls had seen the previous weekend.

After a short while, Alex said, "If you will all excuse me, I need to make some important phone calls before the end of the business day. Lindsay, Amber, can you entertain my friends for a bit while I step into the den to make my calls?"

"Sure, Papa," said Amber.

Lindsay looked less enthusiastic but obediently replied, "Of course. You won't be long, will you?"

"I'll be as quick as I can," Alex replied. "Why don't you show my friends some of your games?"

As soon as Alex left the room, Lindsay looked directly at Morgan and asked, accusingly, "Are you my father's new girlfriend?"

Morgan was taken aback. "Of course not, honey," she said. "Your father is married to your mother. Miss Emma and I are just doing some work on a project for your dad. We are just business colleagues."

Emma joined in. "Your dad has talked so much about you and Amber and told us how great you were, so Morgan and I asked if we could meet you. And I am so glad we did."

Lindsay appeared to relax a bit and smiled wanly. "I'm glad you wanted to meet us, too. Welcome."

After a short discussion, it was decided that Lindsay would show Morgan her new fashion-design computer game in the adjoining family room and that Emma would play animals with Amber. Amber left the room and returned with a toy-sized, red, plastic lunchbox decorated with characters from "Sesame Street," the children's television show. She brought the lunchbox to the kitchen table and opened it. The box was brimming with an assortment of small, colorful plastic animals. Amber turned the box over, sending the animals scattering across the table. The little girl then began sorting and up-righting the animals, placing them in groups. "The lion, zebra, ostrich, and wart-hog are from Africa," Amber proudly explained. "The elephant and the tiger are from Asia. This white tiger is from Siberia."

"Wow," said Emma, "you know a lot about these places."

"Yep," said Amber, "and someday I am going to go see them all."

"That would be a lot of fun, wouldn't it?" said Emma.

While Emma and Amber were busying themselves with the animals, Lindsay and Morgan were engrossed in Lindsay's game. The object of the program was to pick out the style, type of fabric, trim, and accessories to create an outfit and virtually dress the doll on the screen, which served as the model. Before long, the two were good-naturedly arguing about such decisions as the length and style of sleeves and the proper color of fabric to match the model's hair and skin tones.

In the course of her afternoon with Lindsay, Morgan learned the girls had been very close to their mother, and she had always been the parent who was there for them. However, over the last several months, Tessa had been largely absent, both physically and when present physically, mentally absent. Lindsay defended her mother's actions, claiming her mother was "under a lot of stress" and "dealing with personal issues." At the same time, it was evident that Lindsay resented having to be a mother to Amber as well as to her own mother. Lindsay confided to Morgan that, at times, Tessa would vomit all over herself and pass out. Lindsay didn't want her father to find her mother in such a state and would clean, bathe, and dress her mother, and put her to bed. Then, she'd fix Amber dinner and put her to bed. It seemed Lindsay didn't have many friends. She was embarrassed to have them over to the house, not knowing what state her mother would be in, and was afraid to leave Amber alone with Tessa. Lindsay confessed she wished things would "go back to the way they were before" with her mother.

Similarly, Amber volunteered to Emma that her mother was "sick" and "had to go away a lot to find her special medicine." After a very short time together, Amber climbed into Emma's lap and affectionately stroked Emma's hair and hand, saying, "I like you. You're nice."

Before Morgan and Emma left the Giovanni house, they promised to get together with Lindsay and Amber in the near future and introduce the girls to Emma's children.

The next day, Emma was working at her desk. Kat, her secretary, buzzed her intercom. "There's a woman on the phone named 'Louise.' She won't give a last name. She says she's not a potential client. She won't tell me what it's about but insists you want to talk to her. Do you want to take the call?"

"Absolutely. I think I know who she is. Put her through," said Emma.

Louise explained to Emma that her friend, Maisy, Marvin's ex-girlfriend, had given her Emma's number. Louise told Emma that her twenty-four-year-old son had been injured at work at one of the local plants in Scanton. He had experienced chronic, on-going back pain and had become addicted to morphine. Her son's doctor tried to wean him off the painkiller and had referred him to a methadone clinic. Louise thought her son's addiction was improving, but then Contessa Giovanni came to town.

"I didn't trust her from the beginning," said Louise. "She just seemed too big for her own britches, if you know what I mean. She didn't fit in out here and did nothing but cause trouble. She partied too hard and raised a ruckus in all the local bars. Before long, she stole Maisy's boyfriend, Marvin. Marvin's a good man but kind of simple. He can't see past that hussy's good looks and fancy airs. We have all tried to tell him, but he won't listen. Anyways," Louise continued, "before long, Tessa's dating Marvin, but, at the same time, spending time with my son and other young men like him. Sadly, he's got several buddies in the same spot as him—hurt and hooked on them painkillers. Pretty soon, he's acting all high, like he's on the morphine but worse. The doctor didn't give him no more, and the methadone don't make him act like that. He was all angry and mean, and one day while he was out of the house, I went through his room. I found some stuff I thought looked like drugs. I know a little bit about these things because I watch a lot of those police and crime shows on TV. My boy said they wasn't his but were a friend of his. I asked him what friend, but he wouldn't tell me. I told him I weren't going to allow such stuff in my house. He promised to not bring it home anymore.

"Then, one day, I was in the laundry room, next to my son's room, folding some clothes. Our walls are mighty thin. I wasn't trying to listen in, but my son was talking very loud on his phone. He kept calling the person on the phone 'Abdul.' I heard him getting directions to some bar or club in Washington, D.C., and he was repeating the directions back, I guess to make sure he got them right. The last thing he said was, 'I'll get the money from Tessa, and as soon as I do, I'll come on down.' I didn't want to think my boy was involved in something bad, so I told myself it was something innocent, something with a reasonable explanation."

"We, as mothers, really don't want to believe our child has gotten himself into trouble, do we?" Emma interjected. "Was there an innocent explanation?"

"I so wanted it to be the case," said Louise, "but then, not a week later, my boy came home at five o'clock in the morning. He never stays out that late. The next afternoon, while he was out, I looked through his room again. I found a lot more of them drugs like I found before. I have a nephew in law enforcement, and he did me a favor and got it tested. He said it was heroin. I sent my boy to a rehab place in Mississippi, and he is living with some of my kin down there. My son would never tell me where he got the heroin, but I would bet a million dollars it was from that Contessa Giovanni."

As soon as Emma finished her conversation with Louise, she telephoned Stan. "So Stan, ever hear of a drug dealer, or middle man, or someone named 'Abdul,' who operates out of some club in D.C.?"

Stan laughed. "Hello to you, too, Emma. I'm fine—thanks. You know I can't breach client confidentiality. However, on another topic, I hear there's a really cool, new happening dance club named Electri-City, with a hyphen after the 'Electri.' If you and Morgan were feeling like shaking your groove-things with some Afghanis, you might check it out."

"Wow," said Emma. "That sounds like our kind of place. Want to come along?"

"No way," Stan replied. "Gotta run to an arraignment hearing. Later." Stan hung up the phone.

Emma walked to Morgan's office, and the two agreed to go to Electri-City the following Saturday night.

Friday arrived. Motions Day again. Emma had four motions in three different courtrooms and spent the morning running back and forth, making sure she didn't miss the calling of one of her cases. She returned to the office just before two o'clock.

"Any messages, Kat?" Emma asked as she passed through the reception area.

"Just one, and it looks like a sales call," Kat replied.

"In that case, I'm going to quickly check my e-mail and take the rest of the afternoon off," Emma announced.

"Can I take the rest of the afternoon off, too?" asked Kat, straight-faced.

"Only if you want to work for five hours on Saturday night with Morgan and me, doing an investigation into a club in downtown D.C.," Emma said.

"I'd maybe go to a club in D.C. but not with you guys . . . and not to do an investigation," grimaced Kat.

"You can leave at four today. Have a nice weekend," Emma granted.

CHAPTER ELEVEN

Emma was sitting on the sofa, sipping a diet soda, when the children arrived home from school.

"Mom! What are you doing home?" asked Jasmine. "Are you sick?"

"No. Just sick of work," said Emma. "I thought I'd come home early and spend some time with you guys and maybe take you out tonight to dinner and a movie."

"Yay!" said Justin. "We are going to go down to the river now. Want to bring Sadie and come with us?"

"It's a beautiful day," said Emma. "That sounds absolutely fabulous."

Emma, the three children, and Sadie, the chocolate lab, piled into the car and made the short drive to the jogging and bike path that ran along the Virginia side of the Potomac. It was a pleasantly warm Friday afternoon, and the residents of Metropolitan Washington, D.C. were out taking advantage of the nice weather. Joggers, bikers, parents with babies in strollers, rollerbladers, and handholding lovers all teemed up and down the asphalt path. Old men and young boys dotted the riverbank with fishing poles, trying their luck and sharing conversation. Emma seriously doubted any fish caught out of the Potomac would be safe to eat, given the high level of pollution. No doubt, the act of fishing, rather than the fish itself, was more the point of the exercise for the fishermen. Emma had insisted everyone, including her, leave their cell phones in the car, so they could have some time together free from the interference of all electronics.

Jasmine chattered on about which celebrity was dating whom, which classmates of hers were dating whom, and about how she really, really liked neon-colored nail polish. When they stopped for Jasmine to feed the ducks some stale bread she had brought from home, Jason and Emma sat on a park bench and watched Jasmine and Justin by the water's edge.

Emma and Jason discussed his plan to re-take the S.A.T. test for college admission that fall, as his scores from the summer had not been as high as either of them had hoped. Jason was reluctant to take the arduous exam again, but Emma explained that since Jason's grade-point average was not exactly stellar, he needed to score highly on the standardized test in hopes of gaining admission to a reputable college. As mother and son debated the issue, a dark-skinned, Middle Eastern-looking man walked slowly past on the path behind them. Emma noticed him because, although he did not appear to be old or infirm, he was walking lazily, as if he had nowhere to go and endless time to get there. Less than two minutes later, the man returned from the way he had just gone and walked by again, just as slowly. The man wore blue jeans, a button-front polyester dress shirt, and plastic sandals. Emma thought the sandals a bit odd. It was warm but by no means hot. In addition, the sandals did not seem particularly comfortable or suited for exercise.

Emma's attention was redirected to the river by the sound of a loud splashing noise and Jasmine's squeal of "Sadie!" The chocolate lab was in the river, swimming very deliberately away from the shore.

"Sorry, Mom," said Justin, "she lunged all of the sudden and jerked the leash out of my hand."

Emma ran to the shore. "Sadie, no" commanded Emma. "Sadie, come." Sadie paid Emma no mind whatsoever and continued swimming in a direct line away from shore. "Sadie, come!" Emma called, more sternly and in a lower register. At that moment, Sadie reached her apparent intended target—a long, narrow tree branch, floating in the water. With a quick lunge and snap, Sadie captured the branch, made a U-turn in the water, and as deliberately as she had gone, returned to shore. She scrambled up the bank, trotted to Emma, and dropped the branch at Emma's feet. Emma grabbed Sadie by the collar. "Sit," Emma commanded. Sadie did not sit, but rather, shook herself vigorously, spraying Emma and all three children with smelly river water.

On the way back to the car, Justin described for the others his latest idea for a movie he wanted to make. "You see," he said excitedly, "there's this guy that finds this rare plant. The plant gives him a rash, but he thinks it's just like poison ivy or something. But then, his friends accidentally lock him in a room and forget about him for like a week. But he doesn't die because his body does photosynthesis for food. He turns into a plant zombie. When his friends let him out, he terrorizes the town."

"That sounds very creative," Emma said.

"That sounds stupid," said Jason. "People are physically incapable of performing photosynthesis."

"That's the whole point," Justin replied. "He isn't a person anymore. He's a plant. A plant zombie. Get it?"

"I think zombies are really cool," Jasmine piped in, "but vampires are cooler. Can you make him become a vampire instead of a zombie?"

As Emma was loading the kids and the dog into the minivan, she felt as if someone was watching her. She looked in the side mirror of the van as she was getting into her door and saw the same Middle Eastern man who had walked past them earlier sitting on the curb on the other side of the parking lot, smoking a cigarette. There were no cars parked close to where he sat. Emma thought the man's behavior somewhat strange but was not particularly concerned.

Later that evening, Emma and the children had dinner at a trendy pizza restaurant in a local area featuring many restaurants, shops, and a movie theater. The family was headed from the restaurant to the movie theater but had a few minutes to kill before the movie they wanted to see was going to start. They stopped to listen to a local band performing near the fountain located in the center of the square, in front of the movie theater. Emma and Jason sat on a bench, and Jasmine and Justin trailed their hands in the fountain. Emma casually watched the other people gather around the fountain. Most of them were young couples with small children. Several of the children were dancing around to the music, eating ice cream, or chasing each other around. Emma smiled, remembering the not-so-distant past when her children were young and full of bouncing energy. But then, something caught Emma's eye. On the other side of the fountain, leaning against a tree with his arms crossed, standing all alone, stood the same man she had seen on the path and in the parking lot by the river that afternoon. Emma's heart beat faster, and her breathing became shallow. "You know, Jason," she said, "I remember reading in the paper that this movie is really popular, and it sold out opening night, last night at midnight. We should really go get tickets right now."

"This band's cool, Mom," said Jason. "Can't you go get the tickets, and we'll come inside in a few minutes?"

"No. I don't want to have to find you guys. We are all going together. Now. Go get your brother and sister."

"Mom," said Jason, eyes raised, "what's wrong? Why are you freaking out?"

"I'm not freaking out. I just want to go inside now, please." Emma's jaw was clenched tight.

"OK. OK," said Jason, looking concerned. He called Justin and Jasmine over.

Emma rushed the children into the theater, purchased the tickets, and made them sit with her in the nearly empty auditorium for over thirty minutes until the movie started. She had a hard time focusing on the movie because she kept scanning the audience for their mysterious stalker.

As Emma and the children passed through the movie theater lobby, Emma's eyes scanned every corner, looking, but she did not see the man that had been following them. Emma's blood pressure rose, and she walked briskly on the way to the car, and she tried to hurry the children along. "Come on, kids, get a move on," she said. "I still have some work to do tonight before I go to bed."

In the car on the way home, Emma's cell phone rang. "Quiet, kids . . . please," she said and activated the hands-free feature so the call was transmitted through the minivan's speakers.

"Ms. Parker?" the caller said. "This is Betty, Marvin's mom. Remember we spoke at my house?"

"Of course, Betty. I remember," Emma replied. "What can I do for you?"

"It's Marvin; he's disappeared," Betty said.

"Disappeared?" Emma asked. "What do you mean, disappeared?"

"Nobody has seen or heard from him in four days. Not his friends, not his family. He hasn't even been to his regular bars. That woman seems to have left town, as well. I'm worried."

"Don't you think the two of them just went away together, like on a vacation, or something?" said Emma.

"I guess that's possible," Betty said. "But I just have a really bad feeling about this. Call it mother's intuition or something, but, Ms. Parker, I think my Marvin is dead!"

Emma realized the children were staring at her, their eyes wide. "Betty, let me call you back in a few minutes. I am driving right now, and my children are with me."

CHAPTER TWELVE

Saturday morning was weapons' class at the tae kwon do studio. Emma loved this class. It was easier to feel strong and invincible with a weapon in your hands. Emma's favorite was the bow staff. Her trip to Digger Dan's had shown Emma the value of knowing how to handle a bow staff. The baton lessons she had taken as a child prepared her well for spinning, twirling, and throwing the long, thin wooden staff.

That morning, however, the master was introducing a new weapon: the practice sword. The sword had a cylindrical hilt. It was wrapped in strips of leather. The "blade" of the sword was made up of several thin pieces of flexible wood approximately three feet long, held together at the tip by an elastic band. When the sword made contact with an object or person, it produced a loud, snapping noise as the wooden strips collided together.

"We're going to do some combination moves with the sword," the tae kwon do master called out. "Two chopping moves from above as if striking your opponent on top of the head. Step forward on your lead foot as your swing comes down. Put your back into it!" He demonstrated.

"Then, open your hips by turning your back foot and then swing level, as if hitting a baseball. Swing from your shoulder, not your arm." The class all tried swinging their swords.

"Now, put it together. Chop, chop! Swing, swing! Left side now. Chop, chop! Swing, swing!"

Emma focused and put all her energy into chopping and whacking her invisible foe. She squinted her eyes and pictured her target. It felt wonderful!

After working with the bow staff next, the master led the class in their strength training and endurance exercises. Amazingly, Emma didn't feel tired. Maybe her stamina had improved. After push-ups and sit-ups, the master announced the end of class.

He walked up to Emma and extended his hand. "Congratulations, Emma! You finished the class without vomiting! It's a victory!"

"Wow," said Emma. "You're right. I didn't even feel nauseous at all."

"It's all about sticking with it and beating your body into submission," said the instructor. "I'm proud of you, girl."

"Thanks, sir! I'm proud of me, too."

That evening, Morgan arrived at Emma's house just after 10 p.m. Jason looked up from the computer in the family room as Morgan came in. "Hey, Aunt Morgan," he said. "What are you doing here so late?"

"Your mom and I are going out to a club," Morgan replied.

"What?" Jason exclaimed. "Mom doesn't go out to clubs."

"We're doing an investigation, honey," Emma told Jason.

"Don't you have people to do that for you?" Jason asked.

"They just don't seem to do as good a job as Aunt Morgan and I do," Emma explained.

"Well, be careful," Jason said, "and don't stay out too late."

"Yes, Dad," Morgan teased.

Morgan and Emma traipsed upstairs to Emma's room to choose a suitable outfit for their covert investigation. Morgan plunged into Emma's walk-in closet and rummaged around. She emerged with a barely-there red spandex dress.

"Oh, my, no," said Emma. "I haven't worn that in twenty years. I'm pretty sure it doesn't even fit anymore."

"Just try it on," Morgan urged. Emma took the dress, reluctantly, and went into the adjoining bathroom.

A few long moments later, Emma cracked open the bathroom door.

"Oh, honey," Morgan said, with a grimace, "you were right. You look like a stuffed sausage."

"Thanks for your support," Emma groaned. "I may need the jaws of life to get it off."

When Emma emerged from the bathroom again, Morgan was holding a leather mini-skirt and a leopard-print camisole. "This is perfect," she said. "And they are both bigger than the red dress."

"That's not saying much," Emma replied. "I really think I'm too old to wear things like this anymore."

"If you were planning on wearing this outfit to court, I would agree with you," said Morgan. "And it probably wouldn't play too well at the kids' school functions. However, we are going to a nightclub, and we are trying to talk to some people that are considerably less conservative than you are. Therefore, you need to wear the appropriate costume for the role. Try it on," she commanded.

Emma wrinkled her nose but begrudgingly accepted the garments and re-entered the bathroom. When Emma re-emerged, Morgan let out a long whistle.

"Wow!" Morgan said. "You look fabulous!"

"I feel naked," Emma replied.

"You're supposed to be mostly naked," Morgan said. "It's a nightclub."

"But you're not this scantily clad," Emma pointed out. Morgan was wearing leggings, a long sleeveless silk tunic, and a blazer.

"Not so," said Morgan. "Before we get on the Metro, I am taking off the blazer and the leggings."

"That's not a dress; it's a shirt," Emma objected.

"It's a dress as long as I'm very careful not to reach up, bend down, or sit in an unladylike manner," Morgan said.

"Oh, good grief," said Emma. "Well, I'm also wearing something over this shirt until we get there."

"OK—for now," said Morgan, "but we are *not* riding herd of your extra clothes all night. You need to leave all excess clothing in the car at the Metro station. By the way, who is taking us to the Metro?"

"Jason will drive us," Emma said. "He wants to take the car to go spend the night at a friend's house."

"But what about the other two kids?"

"Claudia's here," Emma explained. "She's mad that she can't go out tonight, but I gave her the afternoon off yesterday. She'll survive."

"Great," said Morgan. "Now on to make-up and hair."

Just before 11:30 p.m., Jason pulled the mini-van into the drop-off zone at the subway station. On the drive over from Emma's house, Morgan had removed her leggings and blazer. Emma glanced nervously at Jason and took off her cardigan sweater. "Mom!" said Jason, "What on earth are you wearing?"

"It's called an animal print, sweetheart," Emma said.

"But, it's so small!" Jason said. "You can't go out in public like that!"

"I promise to tell everyone I meet that my name is Emma Parker and that I'm Jason Parker's mother," Emma said.

"That's not even funny, Mom," said Jason. "Seriously, are you going out in that?"

"Seriously, yes, I am," said Emma. "Bye, honey. Be good."

"I think *I'm* the one that should be telling *you* to be good," said Jason. "Bye."

———

A few minutes after midnight, Emma and Morgan approached the door to Electri-City. Twenty or so adolescent patrons waited in line. Two beefy bouncers checked identification and inspected handbags. From the outside, Electri-City didn't look like much. It was a two-story cinderblock structure painted navy blue. The few observable windows appeared to be covered or painted over from the inside. Surprisingly, the music that must certainly be playing inside could not be heard on the street.

When she reached the front of the queue, Emma unzipped her purse, the one she usually took to cocktail parties, and held it up for inspection. The bouncer looked inside. "I.D.," he said, holding out his hand.

"Are you kidding me?" Emma asked. "I'm practically old enough to be your mother."

"My mother's seventy-five. Everyone shows I.D. No exceptions."

Emma reached into her purse, pulled out her driver's license, and handed it to the man. He examined the card, using a penlight flashlight. The bouncer then looked Emma up and down, lingering on the ample amount of cleavage rising above her leopard-print camisole.

"Looking good, ma'am," he said, handing back her driver's license. "Go ahead."

Once inside the front door, Morgan and Emma encountered a window resembling a ticket booth. A handwritten sign announced, "Cover Charge $25." Two young men were underneath, paying the admission.

As the two men moved forward into the club, Morgan sauntered up to the window and leaned in toward the handsome Black man inside. "Hi, honey," she said to the money collector, "how you doing tonight?"

"I'm doing great . . . how about yourself?" he responded.

"I'm fine," Morgan replied in her most sultry voice.

"You sure are," the young man said.

"Do you need any money from me and my girl?" Morgan asked, cocking her head slightly to the side.

The young man looked over at Emma. "Nah, you're good. Go ahead."

"Thanks, baby," said Morgan. "See you later."

"I sure hope so," the man replied as he watched her go. Emma and Morgan passed down a long hallway. The ceiling, walls, and floor were all painted the same midnight blue as the exterior of the building.

"That's how it's done," Morgan said to Emma.

"So I see," Emma replied.

They heard the thumping beat of the music inside the main room. The farther they went down the hall, the louder the music reverberated in their ears. By the time Emma and Morgan emerged into the club itself, the bass beat caused Emma's collarbone to vibrate. She felt as if her heartbeat aligned with the rhythm of the song. Almost involuntarily, Emma's hips and shoulders began moving with the beat.

The hallway issued into the main bar area. To the right of the doorway, a long, polished wood bar ran the entire length of one wall. The wall behind the bar sparkled with frosted mirrors, rows of glasses, and shelves full of liquor bottles. Five or six bartenders hustled up and down the bar, taking and filling the drink orders of patrons stacked four or five deep in front of the bar. A wooden railing ran the length of the bar area, with the exception of two small entrances onto the dance floor. Several patrons leaned or sat on the railing, both on the bar side and the dance floor side of the railing.

The other three walls of the main floor of the club were ringed with u-shaped booths, upholstered in midnight blue velvet. Each booth surrounded a low, cocktail-level table. The dance floor occupied the bulk of the main floor, and it was already crowded with gyrating partiers.

Across from the bar area, a large, grand staircase, complete with carved wooden banisters, led to the second story. On the second story, a wide balcony ran all the way around the perimeter. Although it was shadowy on the upper level, it appeared to Emma that booths and tables filled the space and looked down onto the dance floor. At the top of the stairs, there was another, much smaller bar area where Emma could see a couple of bartenders. Two large bouncers stood at the bottom of the staircase, blocking the entrance. Emma quickly surmised the upper level must be the V.I.P. section.

Morgan and Emma fought their way to the bar, obtained their drinks, then perched themselves toward the end of the railing, where they had a good vantage point to observe both the dance floor and the bar area.

"Well, it seems like this is the right place," Morgan said loudly, with her mouth close to Emma's ear in order to be heard over the music. "There sure are an inordinate amount of Middle Eastern men here. I have never seen so many in one D.C. establishment at one time."

Emma looked around. Indeed, the vast majority of the male patrons appeared to be Arab, Persian, or from some other Middle Eastern locale. The remaining males consisted of a few dozen Black men and a handful of white guys. On the other hand, there appeared to be no Middle Eastern women. Nearly all the females were Asian. Emma spotted only a few Black women and no white women other than her partner and friend. Upon making this realization, Emma felt more out of place than when she had just felt too "mature" for the venue.

"I hate these women," said Morgan, looking disgustedly at the dance floor. "They are so tiny and cute and delicate and adorable. They make us look like Amazons!"

Emma looked toward the dance floor. The two Asian women dancing near Morgan and Emma were, indeed, quite miniature. They were both significantly smaller than Emma's daughter, Jasmine, who, at thirteen, weighed ninety pounds and was five-foot-four. Emma looked at Morgan and thought that the smaller of the two women could fit entirely inside Morgan's towering five-foot-nine-and-a-half-inch frame. Morgan wasn't fat—by any means—but she was not petite either. Although Emma was only five-foot-five inches, she was pretty sure she had a good fifty pounds on either one of those tiny things. The men in the club seemed to be very enthralled by, and attracted to, the petite women. Three or four men, all vying for her attention, attended each tiny dancer.

"OK.," said Morgan, "time to go to work. I'm going to go gather some information. Let's meet back here from time to time to touch base." Morgan drained the last of her Cosmopolitan Martini, set down her glass on a nearby bar table, and waded onto the dance floor. She was instantly swallowed up by the throng. Occasionally, Emma caught a glimpse of the top of Morgan's platinum-blonde head bobbing above the crowd.

Emma moved to the very end of the bar, near the corner. After a short wait, she managed to obtain a seat on a barstool. She ordered another drink, then turned around to face the dance floor. Because she was facing outward, other patrons were uncomfortable with trying to reach the bartender's attention over Emma's head, causing a cushion of space to form around her. Emma had learned this trick as a much younger woman, in the days when she had frequented nightclubs and bars.

A couple of different men approached Emma and struck up a conversation. Using the same tactic as in Stanton, Emma tried to steer the conversation to inquire about Tessa. She told them she was friends with Tessa and was worried that she hadn't seen her in a while. None of the men admitted to knowing Contessa, and as soon as it became clear Emma wasn't interested in them romantically, each one walked away.

Suddenly, Emma noticed a disturbance on the dance floor. It appeared people were pushing and shoving, and some of the dancers closest to where Emma sat staggered back, as if knocked off balance. Then, a hole opened in the edge of the throng and Morgan burst out. She looked disheveled and perturbed. Morgan's dress was twisted askew, there was a snag in her stockings, and her hair was mussed up. Emma stood up and raised her hand in the air.

"Morgan," she called, but her voice was drowned out by the music. Emma moved to the railing and waved both her arms back and forth. Morgan spied her and rushed through the opening in the railing, pushing past the people in her way, and hurried up to Emma. She plopped down on the stool Emma had just vacated.

"Oh, my word," panted Morgan. "Those guys are complete animals! And the stupid bouncers are worthless. I practically got assaulted on the dance floor. Get me a drink!"

Emma ordered Morgan another Cosmopolitan and Morgan downed half the drink in one slurp. "It was terrible," she said. "First, I was dancing with this one guy. Next thing I know, one of his buddies pushes up against my back, and I was like a sandwich. I could barely breathe. The guy in the back was grinding on me. I was trying to wiggle away, and the next thing I know, he's putting his hand up my skirt. I grabbed his hand and twisted his wrist back and up. He yelled and went down to his knees. His friend started laughing and grabbed me by the hair and tried to kiss me. Ewww! So I kneed him in the nuts. As I was pushing my way off the dance floor, like a hundred other guys thought it was a great opportunity to grab a feel, as well. All these hands were pawing me. The stupid little Asian chicks just watched; they didn't try to help at all." Morgan took another swallow of her drink.

"I am so done with the dance floor tonight. I need another drink. Then I'm going to find the bathroom and freshen up. I'm sure I am a sight. After that, I am going to go over to that side of the room and see who I can chat up."

"Are you sure you don't want to go home?" asked Emma. "You've been pretty traumatized."

"Oh, please," said Morgan, "this isn't my first group groping. I haven't found anything out yet. Have you?"

"No," admitted Emma.

"We can't let tonight be a complete waste of time. We aren't leaving until we get some more information about the lovely Mrs. Giovanni."

"Alright," said Emma, "but be more careful. Don't put yourself in situations where you are completely vulnerable."

"I'll try," said Morgan.

Morgan finished her next drink, and Emma accompanied her to the ladies' room. "Thank goodness I always bring a spare set of hose," said Morgan, pulling a pair of stockings out of her purse.

"Are you serious?" said Emma. "I don't even keep a spare set at work in case I get a snag during the day."

"I know," said Morgan. "You just beg me for my extras. I try to be prepared for every fashion emergency that may arise."

"That's probably why you always look so much better than I do," said Emma.

"Among other reasons," Morgan replied.

"Hey!" Emma protested. "That's not nice."

"I'm sorry," said Morgan. "I'm just playing with you. You know I love you." She attempted to give Emma a hug. Emma pushed her away.

"I'm sure you do," she said.

When they exited the restroom, Morgan headed off to the booths on the side of the room opposite the bar, and Emma returned to her spot at the end of the bar and ordered a club soda with lime. The bartender gave her a look.

"I'm pacing myself," said Emma.

"Whatever," said the bartender, "but that drink costs the same as a beer. Just so you know."

"Thank you," said Emma. "You're too kind."

Emma sat sipping her drink and watching the other patrons. Before too long, a strikingly tall and big-boned Middle Eastern man came and stood directly in front of Emma. Emma's nose almost touched the bulging, straining buttons on the man's ill-fitting, white cotton dress shirt.

"Hello, madam," said the man, loudly. Emma had to lean back and crane her neck to see the man's face. He was sweating profusely, rivulets running across his forehead and down his jowls.

"Hello," said Emma.

"May I buy you a drink?" asked the man.

"I have a nearly full drink here," Emma replied.

"May I buy your next drink when that one is finished?" the man said, stiltedly, with a heavy foreign accent.

"You may if you do me a favor and take three steps back," said Emma, smiling.

"Oh, sorry," the man apologized, stepping back. "I keep forgetting that Americans don't like to be close to other people."

"Yeah," said Emma. "We're funny that way. Thank you for your understanding."

"Not at all," the man said. "By the way," he continued, extending his hand, "my name is Wali."

Emma and Wali sat together watching the people on the dance floor. Emma learned that Wali was Afghani and had lived in the U.S. for over ten years. He said he was in the "import and export" business, was divorced, and had six grown children. When Emma finished her club soda, Wali bought her vodka and soda with lime. "It's the same drink you had before," Wali said, "only more fun."

"And more dangerous," Emma replied.

"We can only hope so," Wali said, suggestively. Emma moved her stool slightly farther away from him.

"You know," Wali said, leaning in to talk in Emma's ear, "we don't see very many women like you in here."

"What type of woman would that be?" Emma asked.

"Beautiful, intelligent, of good breeding and, well, blonde and white," Wali answered honestly.

"I see. And how would you know that?" Emma said. "Do you come here a lot?"

"Almost every night," Wali said.

"Really?" replied Emma. "Then maybe you have seen a friend of mine in here. She's blonde, beautiful, and very outgoing."

"You mean the girl you came in with?" asked Wali.

"No. Another girl . . . similar but not so tall. Her name is Contessa . . . or Tessa," Emma explained.

Wali looked puzzled. "That girl is your friend?" he asked.

"Friend might be a strong word," Emma said. "More like an acquaintance. But I am trying to track her down."

"Why? Do you need something from her?" Wali looked at Emma meaningfully.

"Uh, yes," said Emma, walking into dangerous territory. "I need something from her and have not been able to find her lately to get it."

"Hmmmm," said Wali, leaning back against the bar and taking a slow sip from his drink. He looked Emma up and down slowly. "You don't really look like someone who would need anything that girl has to offer."

"How's that?" said Emma.

"First, you don't look skinny enough."

"Oh, thanks a lot," Emma said.

"That's not an insult," Wali said as he winked. "I mean that you look too healthy."

"Well, all things in moderation. Sometimes, a girl just needs to relax a little, relieve the stress."

"Maybe you should take up smoking cigarettes," Wali suggested. "They're less bad for you."

"Tell that to the Surgeon General," Emma said.

Wali sat silently for a few moments, watching the dancers and occasionally glancing over at Emma. Emma smiled warmly at him.

Then Wali approached Emma, cupped his hand around her ear, and said, "If you really want, I could introduce you to a guy I know that can probably help you out. But I still think it's a bad idea and can't be responsible for any of the results."

Emma gulped. "That would be very helpful of you—if you don't mind too much."

Wali ran the back of his meaty hand down Emma's cheek. The abundance of hair on the hand tickled Emma's skin. "Anything for you, my sweet," Wali said. "Wait right here a few minutes. I'll be right back."

Emma took a big draft of her drink and tried to calm her nerves. It wasn't too late to bolt for the door. But she probably wouldn't get another chance to find out the connection between Tessa and Abdul. Emma anxiously scanned the room for Morgan but was unable to spot her.

Wali shouldered his way across the dance floor and then laboriously made his way up the staircase. He disappeared into the shadowed recesses of the upper level. After what seemed like a decade to Emma, Wali descended the stairs and spoke to the two bouncers stationed at the bottom. He made his way back to Emma.

"OK.," he said. "You sure you don't want to reconsider?"

"I'm sure," Emma replied, although she wasn't sure at all.

"Go up the stairs over there," Wali said, pointing, "I've already cleared you with the security. Go to the bar and tell the bartender you are there to see Abdul."

"Abdul?" asked Emma, a little shakily.

"Yes. Abdul," said Wali. "I'll be here."

Emma battled her way across the crowded dance floor, fending off groping hands with her elbows and knees. Upon reaching the bottom of the stairs, she straightened her clothing and walked up to the pair of burly guardians at the foot of the stairs. As she approached, they each stepped to one side, leaving the way clear. Neither one of the bouncers made eye contact with Emma.

Upon Emma's inquiry, the upstairs bartender gestured to his right. Emma peered into the darkness. At the far end, just before the balcony turned the corner to the far side, Emma could make out a few figures seated in one of the velvet booths. Her knees quivered as she made her way toward the group.

A thin olive-skinned man with unruly curly black hair and a long torso sat in the center of the booth, his arms spread along the back of the cushions on either side of him. He wore a cream silk shirt with green embroidered palm trees all over it. The top three buttons were unfastened, revealing three gold chains nestled in his curly chest hair. He wore black dress pants and a white leather belt, fastened with a substantial gold-tone buckle in the shape of a circle with a crescent moon in the center. An oversized gold Rolex encircled Abdul's left wrist, and each hand sparkled with gold rings adorned with diamonds and semi-precious stones. Two scantily clad Asian girls sat on either side of the man. An additional three girls were spread out along the u-shaped bench.

As Emma approached, the girls eyed her coldly. A giant of a man, whom Emma had amazingly overlooked until then, stepped out of the shadows and directly into Emma's path. Emma stopped. Abdul waved his hand, and the goon stepped back into the shadows, against the wall, from whence he had come.

Abdul smirked. "Well, what do we have here? Hello, sweetheart. How are you doing?" he said to Emma.

"I'm alright," Emma replied. "How are you?"

Abdul laughed. "You know, you are the first person all day to ask me that. No one has any manners anymore. I'm good. Thank you. Come here, honey, and sit by me." He patted the bench next to him. "Move over, woman," he said to the girl to his left. The girl slowly uncrossed her legs, took her time to stand up, and with even less urgency, walked to the end of the booth and plopped herself down with a huffy grunt.

Emma sat down in the spot vacated by the girl. Abdul put his arm around Emma's shoulders and leaned forward to gaze down the front of Emma's camisole. Emma suddenly felt very exposed. "So, why am I granted the honor of your very lovely presence?" Abdul asked.

"A friend of mine said I should meet you," Emma said.

"Is that the case?" Abdul said. "I think I should get to know you, as well." He pulled Emma closer to him and put his right hand on her knee. "What's your name, my princess?"

"Emily," Emma lied.

"A beautiful name for a beautiful lady," said Abdul. The girl to his right sighed and rolled her eyes. Abdul quickly turned to her with a glare.

"Go!" he said, raising his voice and pointing toward the top of the staircase. The girl didn't move, but instead, looked at him, shocked.

"Did you not hear me? I said *go*!" The girl scrambled to get up. The girl next to her pulled in her legs so the exiting girl could climb over her.

"You, too," Abdul said, pointing to the second girl. "All of you, GO!" The other three girls hesitated, but the giant man stepped out of the shadows. He silently held his arm out straight, his open palm indicating the way out. All five girls held their eyes downward but still managed to shoot Emma angry sideways glances as they scurried out.

"Now, where were we?" said Abdul, settling into the cushioned back of the booth and pulling Emma up against his side again.

"So, you want to meet the famous, Abdul, do you?" he said. "I wonder why that would be," he continued, without waiting for an answer from Emma. Still keeping a firm grip around Emma's shoulders with his left arm, he leaned over and trailed the fingers of his right hand across Emma's clavicle. Emma's heart pounded in her chest, and she was afraid she was going to start sweating. She breathed in and out slowly to calm the terror that that has taken root in her gut. Abdul's fingers went lower, grasped the front of Emma's camisole, and pulled it away from her body. He looked down into her shirt.

"Mmmm," he said, "glorious." He released the fabric. Abdul then reached over and ran his right hand down Emma's left side from her armpit to her knee.

"Lovely," he said. Emma squirmed, but Abdul maintained his grip. Then, he ran his hand down Emma's right side in the same fashion.

"Beautiful," he said. "Your curves are wonderful."

"Th-thank you," Emma stammered.

Abdul placed his hand on Emma's knee again. He moved his fingers in slow circles, caressing her kneecap. Smoothly Abdul moved his hand up Emma's thigh, causing her skirt to slide up to a scandalous height. Emma grabbed her skirt, pulled it down, and removed Abdul's hand from her thigh. Abdul chuckled and, releasing Emma's shoulders, ran his open hand down Emma's back and into the waistband of her mini skirt. Emma moved away.

Abdul laughed again and leaned back. "You're exquisite," he said, "and you're not a cop. So why don't you tell me what you want?"

Emma realized she hadn't been felt up; she'd just been searched.

"You know a girl named Tessa, right?" said Emma, ready to be finished with this man.

"If you say so," Abdul replied.

"Well, I want to know what sort of arrangement you have with her," said Emma. Abdul's eyebrows narrowed. "Because, you see," Emma continued, "I think maybe I could give you a better arrangement—better terms."

"That's definitely something we can discuss," Abdul said after a moment's pause. "But first, we party." Abdul snapped his fingers and the giant man lumbered off to the bar and returned shortly after with a tray containing a bottle of Crown Royal, a Liter bottle of Coca Cola, a bucket of ice, and two glasses.

"I'm sorry, I only drink Diet Coke," Emma said. Abdul looked at Emma's mid-section and gestured to the giant again, who returned with a bottle of Diet Coke.

After Emma and Abdul had consumed several drinks and Abdul had showered Emma with an impressive litany of compliments, Abdul said, "Time to kick this party up a notch. Ready for a little smack?" he asked, leaning in toward Emma.

Emma turned her head away, fearing Abdul meant to kiss her. As soon as she made the move, she realized Abdul was offering something else. "Oh, no, thank you," Emma said. "I manage to get myself in quite enough trouble with alcohol; I don't need any other mood-altering substances."

Abdul slowly nodded and pointed his finger at Emma. Emma's blood pressure hit the roof. She didn't know how she was going to get out of the situation. "Smart . . ." Abdul said slowly. "Keep your focus clear. Don't eat into the profits. Very good business. I like you more and more every minute."

Emma forced a smile. "That's me. Miss Smart Business."

"I could probably learn some things from you," said Abdul.

"I seriously doubt that," Emma replied.

A little while later, Abdul leaned forward, peering intently down into the main bar area on the first floor. Emma followed his gaze. Some sort of ruckus had erupted. Emma spotted the top of Morgan's blonde head in what appeared to be the epicenter of the problem. Emma jumped up and went to the railing to get a better vantage point. Just then, Morgan elbowed a Middle Eastern-looking man in the face. His nose spurted blood. Another man moved to backhand Morgan across the cheek. Morgan deftly blocked the blow and delivered a roundhouse kick to the man's left side. He staggered sideways, knocking several other patrons off-balance.

"Oh, crap!" Emma exclaimed. "That's my friend down there! I have to go."

"Absolutely," said Abdul. "We'll talk later. You know where to find me."

"Good-bye!" Emma called over her shoulder, as she raced down the stairs and into the fray. Emma bent forward and ducked under the elbows and pushing arms, worming her way toward Morgan. As Emma caught sight of Morgan, she saw a man behind her with his forearm across her throat, dragging her toward the entrance. Morgan was attempting to elbow the man, but he had Morgan back on her heels, placing his torso out of reach of her elbows.

Emma caught up with Morgan and her abductor at the mouth of the exit hallway. Two bouncers stood on either side of the door. "Hey!" Emma yelled, running up to one of the bouncers. "Help! That guy is kidnapping my friend!"

The bouncer looked unconcerned.

Emma ran behind the abductor and jumped on his back, wrapping her legs around his waist. The man began wiggling, attempting to shake her off. Emma grabbed the man's hair with her left hand and clawed at his eyes with her right. The man roared. A second man stepped up and twisted his hand full of Emma's hair and pulled. Emma released Morgan's abductor and whirled to face her own attacker. The man swung a punch at Emma's head. Emma ducked, spun around, and delivered a snap kick to the man's chin. He staggered back.

Just then, two thick arms went around Emma's middle under her arms, and she found herself lifted off the ground. Emma kicked wildly, but her feet met nothing but air.

"Take it outside!" a gruff voice yelled in Emma's ear. Three other security personnel were hustling Morgan and two attackers down the hallway.

"Wait, wait!" yelled Emma. "They are kidnappers! Don't let them take us! Call the police!"

"Call them yourself," the bouncer said. In the next instant, Morgan, Emma, and the two Middle Eastern assailants were thrust out onto the sidewalk. Morgan, barefoot, her heels lost in the fray, took off running down the sidewalk. Emma's former attacker tackled Morgan, who went to the cement with a sickening thump. Emma looked around wildly. She spotted the metal stand holding the ropes that had formed the admission line. She unhooked the rope hook and picked up the metal stand. The remaining man approached Emma, grinning evilly. Emma cocked back the pole like a baseball bat.

"Get away from me!" she yelled. "I will freaking knock your head off!"

The man kept advancing. Emma swung the pole with all her might, catching the man alongside his ear. The man's eyes rolled back in his head, and he collapsed on the sidewalk.

"Dang, girl!" a voice said behind her. Emma whirled around cocking back the pole again. A lithe, handsome, and muscular Black man, about Emma's age, stood in front of her. He held his hands in the air.

"I'm on your side!" he said. "Take my head off, and I can't help save your girlfriend." He tilted his head toward Morgan and her attacker. They were rolling around on the sidewalk. Morgan broke free, managed to scramble a few feet down the sidewalk, only to be tackled again.

"Stay here and make sure this guy don't wake up," he directed. "I got this." Emma saw a glint of a blade in the Black man's hand. She backed away from him. He turned and ran down the sidewalk toward Morgan. He circled behind Morgan's attacker, wrapped his massive left arm around the man's chest, pinning his arms down, and placed the blade at the man's throat. The Middle Eastern man went limp.

"Hey, man," the Black man said to Morgan's attacker, "why you trying to snatch my girls?" The man whimpered.

"Go, girl, get out of here," the Black man said to Morgan. Giving the men a wide berth, Morgan ran back to Emma. The two women ran the opposite way down the sidewalk, leaving their rescuer and the two attackers behind.

They turned left at the corner and jogged toward the Metro station. Then, Morgan slowed to a walk. "I can't run anymore," she said. "My feet are hamburger. Those were really expensive shoes, too," she moaned.

"Do you think we should call the police?" Emma asked.

"Oh, sure," Morgan replied, "and tell them what? That we came to this nightclub to find some drug dealers, got into a fight with some Arabs, and tried to kill one? And who, pray tell, would be the witnesses? Did you get any names, addresses, and phone numbers? No. Calling the police will only lead to negative publicity for the firm and would not result in the arrest of any of the bad guys."

"I suppose you're right," Emma said. "You don't really think I killed that guy, do you? If I did, I will have to turn myself in."

"You haven't killed anyone before now, have you?" said Morgan. "I highly doubt you're capable."

"I really don't know whether or not to be insulted by that comment."

An old, faded burgundy Toyota Corolla pulled up to the curb next to Emma and Morgan. The women started running.

"Girls! It's me, your Black Knight!" the driver yelled. Emma looked over her shoulder. It was the man who had rescued them. She touched Morgan's elbow, and the women stopped running. The man pulled the car up alongside the pair.

"You ladies need a ride home?" he asked.

"Thanks, but we'll just take the Metro," said Emma.

"Really? It closes in three minutes." Emma and Morgan started running again. The man cruised along beside them. "They don't let people on the Metro without shoes." Emma and Morgan slowed their pace.

"And I kinda doubt you got money or Metro cards hidden anywhere in those skimpy outfits." The women stopped. It was only then they realized they'd lost their purses.

"I guess we'll take that ride," Morgan said.

On the way home, Emma and Morgan's driver introduced himself as Darcy Morris. He said he owned his own plumbing company. He had just happened to be leaving a bar down the street from Electri-City and walking to his car when he encountered the two women and their attackers.

"Um, Darcy," said Emma, "do you think the guy I clobbered is dead?"

"Nah, he's alright. He was sitting up, rubbing his jug last I saw him."

"Well, that's a relief. I just wanted to save Morgan and get away. I didn't want to kill anybody."

It was almost 3:30 Sunday morning when Darcy pulled into Emma's driveway. Morgan got out of the car first and headed up the sidewalk toward Emma's house.

"So, Emma," said Darcy. "Can I get your phone number?"

"Uh," Emma replied. "I'm really not comfortable with giving my phone number out to strangers. I'm sorry."

"If you don't give me your phone number, how are you going to get the opportunity to thank me for saving your life?" Darcy said with a grin.

"You could give me your address, and I could send you a fruit basket, or something," Emma offered.

"I'm sort of between permanent addresses, at the moment . . . unfortunately," Darcy said.

"You're homeless?" Emma asked.

"Oh, I own a home. It's just that I don't live there. I caught my wife cheating on me. I thought about throwing her out, but she's a stay-at-home mom, and I didn't want to take the kids away from their mom or their friends or their home. So she lives in my house, and I've been couch-surfing."

"Wow," said Emma, "you have no idea how refreshing and different it is for me to hear a man say that."

"Why? Are you divorced?" Darcy asked.

"No. However, I am a divorce attorney. But that's another long story. Tell you what, here's my business card. You can call me at the office."

"OK," Darcy said, taking the card "But you have to think of something better than a fruit basket."

Emma smiled. "I'll try," she said and got out of the car. Darcy sat in the driveway until the front door closed behind Emma, and she turned off the porch light.

CHAPTER THIRTEEN

By early afternoon, Emma was several hours into a deposition of one of her clients. Emma, her client, opposing counsel Gretta Firestone, along with her client and associate attorney, and the court reporter were all crowded around a long table in the other lawyer's cramped conference room under the eaves of the top floor of her office townhouse. All the participants were hunched over three-ring binders containing copies of the clients' bank statements and other financial documents. The room was hot and airless.

"Now, Mrs. Wellmont," said Ms. Firestone, "I direct your attention to page seventy-three of Exhibit Number Twelve. About halfway down that page, you will see a withdrawal on March 4 in the amount of $30,000 from your joint money market account. Did you make that withdrawal, Mrs. Wellmont?"

"I don't recall."

"You don't recall? $30,000 is a lot of money. It seems like someone would recall making such a large withdrawal. Are you sure you don't remember taking out that money?" said Ms. Firestone.

Martha sat back and crossed her arms. "I said I don't recall."

"Perhaps I can refresh your recollection. Turn, please to Exhibit Number Thirteen in the book in front of you. Are those copies of bank statements from a money market savings account in your name only, Mrs. Wellmont?"

"They appear to be."

"Do you have any reason to indicate they are not copies of your statements?"

"No."

"Do you have a money market savings account in your name only with this bank?"

Martha glared at Ms. Firestone. "Obviously, you know I do."

Gretta Firestone smirked. "Only because I sent blanket subpoenas to all the local banks. You didn't disclose this account to us in your responses to financial discovery previously propounded on you." Emma willed herself to avoid showing her surprise and displeasure with her client at this revelation.

"Now, Mrs. Wellmont, please turn to page eleven of Exhibit Number Thirteen. Can you please tell me if there was a deposit made to that money market savings account in your name only on March 4th?"

"Yes, there was," said Martha.

"What was the amount of that deposit, please?"

Martha swallowed. "$30,000."

"$30,000? Any idea, Mrs. Wellmont, where that $30,000 came from?" Ms. Firestone looked pointedly at the witness, who squirmed in her chair.

"I don't remember exactly," Mrs. Wellmont said stubbornly.

"Come now, Mrs. Wellmont," said Gretta. "As a matter of fact, you took that $30,000 from the joint marital account, and you put the money in this account in your name only, didn't you?"

"It looks that way."

"Yes, it certainly does," Gretta jabbed. "Now, looking back at Exhibit Thirteen on March fifth, the very next day, there are several withdrawals from that account in your name. Let's look at the first withdrawal, the one for $16,342.52.

Emma had her head bowed and was looking through at her binder when she heard a *thunk*! Emma looked up to see Mrs. Wellmont's three-ring binder in Gretta Firestone's lap and three bright red marks across Gretta's face in regular intervals.

"You are such a monster!" screamed Mrs. Wellmont.

"Let the record reflect that the deponent has just assaulted Ms. Firestone," said the associate attorney.

Emma looked toward the court reporter. She was missing from her chair!

"I am going to have your client arrested for assault!" Gretta yelled at Emma. "And you are going to have to testify against her."

"I didn't see anything," said Emma. "I was looking at my exhibit book. Where's the court reporter?"

A sob emerged from under the table. Everyone bent down to look under the table. The court reporter was curled up in the fetal position on the floor. "I don't have to take this," she sobbed. "My parents beat me, my ex-husband beat me, and I am not going to get beat at work!"

"Oh, for Pete's sake, woman," said Gretta. "No one is beating you. I'm the one who got assaulted. Get back in your chair, or you'll never work in this town again."

"I think this deposition is over for today," said Emma. "Everyone is tired, hungry, and overwrought."

———

Later that afternoon, Emma went to Oakview Terrace Elementary to interview the Giovanni girls' teachers. She met first with Julie Webb, Lindsay's teacher.

"I'm a little concerned about Lindsay," Julie confided. "Through the course of the past school year, she has become increasingly somber. She rarely interacts with the other students and seems withdrawn."

"Has her schoolwork suffered?" asked Emma. "Has there been a decline in her grades?"

"No. In fact, the exact opposite is true. Lindsay has become obsessed with perfection. She gets pretty upset if she gets anything less than one hundred percent on an assignment or test. If she receives less than a perfect score, even if that score is still an *A*, she will re-do the assignment, even though I have told her I can't change the grade."

"Has she said anything to you about her home life?" Emma inquired.

"She doesn't talk much about her family. However, I have overheard her tell other children she cannot play after school or on the weekends because she has to care for her younger sister. I thought that was strange because it is my understanding that Mrs. Giovanni does not work outside the home. I took it as Lindsay simply making an excuse to not socialize. I do have a question for you, though. Do you know anything about the family planning to move away from the area?"

"Why do you say that?" Emma asked.

"Lindsay has told me and the class that she and Amber are going to be moving out of the country soon. She said she is excited about 'seeing the world.'"

Emma became concerned. "When did she say this?"

"She first mentioned it a few months ago, but I heard her make the statement to another child just this week."

"That is very helpful information," said Emma. "Thank you so much for your time."

Emma next interviewed Gloria Felder, Amber's Kindergarten teacher. Mrs. Felder also relayed that Amber had been talking about plans to travel 'far away' to see camels and lions and elephants and monkeys. Mrs. Felder hadn't otherwise seen any changes in Amber's personality or behavior patterns in general.

"However," Mrs. Felder said, "the school recently hired a new custodian. Amber is absolutely terrified of him. When she sees him in the hallway, she runs away. On the two occasions when he has had to come into the classroom, Amber hid—once in the bathroom, once behind a bookcase. I tried to talk to her about it, but she refused to say anything at all."

"Is there a possibility anything happened with Amber and this man?" asked Emma.

"I really don't think so. Kindergarteners are supervised constantly. We have a bathroom in our classroom. I accompany them to and from recess and lunch. I meet them at the bus and see them to the bus. I don't see how she would have any contact with him other than in my presence."

"What does this employee look like?" Emma said.

"Well, he's a Middle Eastern man—olive-skinned, dark wavy hair. He's in his early thirties, I would say. He really seems like a decent, honest, hard-working, and pleasant fellow. None of the other children are afraid of him."

"Very interesting," said Emma. "You have been very helpful. Thank you."

In the car on the way home, Emma called Alexander Giovanni and told him what the girls' teachers had said.

"I can't believe I have been so blind," he fumed. "Tessa is on a path of destruction, and she's taking my daughters with her. I have to stop this. I will call you tomorrow." Alex hung up the phone. Emma tried to call him back several times, but Alex didn't take her calls.

CHAPTER FOURTEEN

E mma didn't hear from Alexander Giovanni for several days. Eventually, he called her at the office. "I finally did it," he announced. "I threw Tessa out."

"You did what?"

"I threw her out. I told her to pack up her stuff and get out."

"You know, you can't legally do that," Emma said. "It's the marital home, meaning it's her home, too. You can't make her leave without a court order, and a judge isn't going to make someone leave unless they pose an imminent threat of harm to you and/or the children."

"Well, she left," said Alex. "And I'm glad. But she called and left me a message today saying she's coming back to get the girls. How can we prevent that?"

"Right now, she has just as much right to them as you do. We need to file an Emergency Motion for Custody and try to get a court order that says you have primary custody. Clear your calendar for tomorrow, and I'll try to get us into court."

The next afternoon, Emma and Alexander Giovanni appeared before Judge Larson on the emergency motion.

Judge Larson could be someone's grandfather. He had pure white hair and large wire-framed bi-focal glasses. "Good afternoon, Ms. Parker."

"Good afternoon, Your Honor."

"Have you given the mother notice of this hearing?"

"Yes, Your Honor," said Emma, holding out a piece of paper for the deputy sheriff to deliver to the judge. "Here is my Affidavit of Service. I had her served in person in West Virginia."

The judge looked at the document. "Very well. As you know, since we are here on the emergency docket, your time is limited. Why don't you proffer to me what evidence you have that this is an emergency."

"Your Honor," said Emma, "the mother has threatened to flee the country with the children."

"OK. To whom did she make this threat?"

"The children told their teachers they were leaving the country."

Judge Larson narrowed his eyebrows. "Ms. Parker, as you are well aware, that is hearsay evidence and not admissible."

"I have the teachers here in the hallway. They are ready to testify."

"As to what the children told them. Still hearsay. Do you have the children here?" asked the judge.

"No, Your Honor," said Emma. "The younger child is only five, and Mr. Giovanni does not want to traumatize his eleven-year-old daughter by forcing her to go through the process or testifying against her mother. He realizes that may be necessary at some point, but we want to limit it to one experience, if necessary."

"I'm not going to hear from the teachers. Do you have any *admissible* evidence to support your claim of an emergency?"

"Your Honor, I also have evidence to indicate that Mrs. Giovanni is using illegal narcotics and, also, that she is most likely distributing drugs."

"That is important, Ms. Parker. What evidence do you have?"

"I have four witnesses here. Two witnesses have, on several occasions, seen Mrs. Giovanni under the influence of some sort of drug. They will say she has a paramour in West Virginia, and she spends days at a time there. In addition, one of the witness's sons received heroin from Mrs. Giovanni. I also have two of Mrs. Giovanni's neighbors here. One will testify that Mrs. Giovanni leaves the children unattended and neglected, and the other will testify to the comings and goings of an individual who has the indications of being a drug dealer."

"Alright, Ms. Parker. I am sure your witnesses would testify as you indicated. While I do have some concerns regarding Mrs. Giovanni's behavior, since the parties are separated, I don't see any immediate danger to the children. We will set the matter down for a full custody hearing in thirty days. That is a very early date, as you well know, Ms. Parker, given this court's heavy docket."

"But, Your Honor, if you don't grant Mr. Giovanni temporary custody, the mother can flee the country with the children!"

"I don't have any admissible evidence of that, Ms. Parker. Is Mrs. Giovanni a U.S. citizen?"

"Yes."

"Does she have any family overseas?"

"No, Your Honor."

"Then I see no reason why she would flee. I am going to grant the mother visitation every Saturday from 1 p.m. to 5 p.m."

"Your Honor, can that visitation be supervised?" pleaded Emma. "Her involvement with drugs puts the children at imminent risk."

"Do you have any evidence that she has used illegal drugs in the presence of the children?"

"No, not at this time."

"Do you have any evidence that she has ever harmed her children?"

"No, Your Honor. But we want to prevent that from happening."

"You will have your opportunity at the full hearing to convince me that Mrs. Giovanni needs to be supervised. Until then, my ruling stands. This matter is concluded." With that, Judge Larson stood up and left the bench.

"What just happened in there?" Alex demanded once he and Emma were alone in the hallway.

"As the judge said, this county's trial docket is so backed up that they don't give full hearings on short notice unless there's an emergency. They don't generally grant temporary custody, except in extreme cases, without a full hearing in order to protect people's constitutional rights to due process. It actually worked in Tessa's favor that she didn't show up today."

"But why wouldn't he listen to the teachers?"

"Because testimony regarding something someone else said, without that person present, is called hearsay. Hearsay isn't admissible because everyone has a constitutional right to confront and cross-examine those who testify against them."

"Well, then why did we even bring the teachers here?" asked Alex.

"Because sometimes, some judges will let the hearsay rule slide when it's a temporary hearing and when the safety of children is involved. It just so happens we pulled Judge Larson, and he is a stickler for the rules."

"That's just great," said Alexander. "So now, I have to give the girls to her on Saturday?"

"Only if she shows up to exercise her visitation," said Emma. "Tessa was given notice of today's hearing. She chose not to appear. It's not my duty to tell her what happened. If she wants to know, and if she wants a copy of the order, she can contact the court clerk herself."

"Let's just hope she continues to care as little about her children as she has in the past several months."

"Let's just hope," Emma agreed.

When Emma returned to the office, Kat was waiting for her with a large stack of pink telephone message slips. "I've prioritized them for you," she said. "The top three are all from Darcy Morris. He actually called more than three times, but I got tired of writing the same thing. I just added the date and time. He seems like a really nice guy. You should call him back."

"He's not a potential client," said Emma. "He's just someone Morgan and I ran into."

"Oh, I know," said Kat. "He told me all about how he rescued you and that he just wants to give you a chance to thank him."

"That's so thoughtful of him," said Emma.

"I think he sounds cute," said Kat. "You should call him."

"How can someone *sound* attractive? For all you know, he could be totally heinous."

"Is he?" said Kat.

"No, he's actually quite handsome," Emma admitted.

"So, call him."

"I'll think about it."

———

It took Emma over an hour to return all the other telephone calls listed on the message slips. It was only then she decided to return Darcy's calls. She didn't want to appear rude or ungrateful for his help.

"Hello."

"Hi, Mr. Morris, this is Emma Parker, returning your call." Emma could hear men's voices echoing and metallic banging in the background.

"Wow. I knew you lawyers were busy, but after leaving five messages, I thought you were never going to call me back."

"I apologize it has taken me so long. I wouldn't want you to think I was rude."

"Never."

"I hope I didn't catch you at a bad time," said Emma. "It sounds like you're at work."

"I am. I'm putting in a new bathroom in a house that's being remodeled."

"Interesting. Don't let me disturb you. You can call me back when you're not busy."

"I'm not too busy. Let me just go to where it's a little quieter." Emma heard the din fade. "I'm back."

"Great," said Emma flatly.

"So, I was wondering," said Darcy, "would you like to have dinner with me tonight?"

"So I can properly thank you for rescuing me?"

"Nah, I just said that so you would call me. I want to take *you* to dinner."

"I don't know," said Emma. "I sort of need to get home to my children."

"OK, when are you next available?"

"I'm not really sure."

"Oh, please. I know you lawyers live and die by your day-timers or whatever your little calendar books are called. You probably know what you're doing next July. It's just one dinner. When will you come?"

Emma realized there was no escape. "You know what? Tonight will actually work. Let's do it tonight." Best just to get her obligation over with. "What time?"

"Eight o'clock. I'll come pick you up."

"No. I don't want the children to get the wrong idea. I'll meet you."

"OK, I guess. Do you know Slick Willy's?"

"The billiard bar near the mall?"

"Yes, exactly."

"Alright. I'll see you there at eight."

"I look forward to it. Really."

The only reason Emma knew where Slick Willy's was is that it was next door to the cake and candy supply store she frequented.

Emma was swamped at the office that afternoon and didn't have an opportunity to go home and change her clothes before going to meet Darcy. As she walked into the bar in her business suit, Emma immediately sensed she was overdressed. The other patrons all wore jeans and T-shirts or sweatshirts. Emma felt as if all eyes were on her as she walked past the pool tables toward the back of the room where the restaurant tables were located. She was relieved to see Darcy stand up and wave at her. He was wearing dusty jeans, work boots, and a dark blue, tight-fitting T-shirt that appeared clean but had a small hole in the left seam. Emma couldn't help but think he looked handsome, despite his casual attire.

"Hi!" Darcy surprised Emma by grabbing her and giving her a hug. Emma's arms hung awkwardly at her sides. "Look at you, all fancy."

"I'm sorry," said Emma. "I didn't have time to go home and change. I was in court today, so had to wear my 'lawyer costume.'"

"You look good. Have a seat."

The cocktail waitress came to their table. Emma ordered a margarita and Darcy ordered another beer.

Darcy sat looking at Emma. "Wow. I can't get over how different you look from the other night. You look so much more . . . serious."

"To be honest, Darcy, this is why I was reluctant to return your phone calls. I am concerned that you got the wrong impression of me. I don't normally dress like I was dressed that night. I don't normally ever go to nightclubs. Morgan and I were doing an investigation for a case. That's why we were at that club and why we were dressed the way we were. You didn't meet the real me."

"You don't think so?" Darcy asked.

"No. I know so."

Darcy thought for a moment. "So, was it the real you or the fake you that beat the feathers out of that guy outside the club? " He took a drink from his beer.

"That's a fair question. I'm not a violent person if that's what you mean. I don't go looking for fights. But in my line of work, unfortunately, I seem to find myself in situations where people are upset with me, and I end up having to defend myself and, sometimes, my friends or family. I'm glad I have learned a few skills to help me do that."

"Skills. I like your skills. I also think it's great that you're tough. You're not afraid to fight back."

"Oh, I'm afraid," said Emma. "I just try to put my fear aside and do what needs to be done. I guess you could also say I'm a natural fighter. That's why I make a good lawyer. People pay me to fight for them, although not usually physically."

"I'm a fighter, too, but I usually get in trouble for it," Darcy said. "Do you want to eat?"

"I'm starving." When Emma ordered a cheeseburger and French fries, Darcy smiled.

"I love it when a girl isn't afraid to eat. I hate these women who only eat salad and crap. I feel like a pig eating real food in front of them."

"So are you going to order salad and make me look like a pig?" Emma smiled.

"Heck, no. I'm having the whole, giant-sized nachos for myself. But, if you want, you can have a couple."

"You're too kind," said Emma.

"On the phone, you said you didn't want me to pick you up because of your kids. How many kids do you have?" Darcy said.

"I have three. Two boys and a girl—ages seventeen, fifteen, and thirteen. My daughter is the youngest."

"I have three boys," said Darcy, "thirteen, ten, and seven. You said you weren't divorced. Are you married?"

"No. Do you think I would have agreed to go on a date with you if I was married?"

"Who said this was a date?"

Emma felt her face getting hot. She took a drink of water. "I am so embarrassed. I totally misinterpreted you. I apologize."

Darcy sputtered a laugh. "No, you didn't. I'm just messing with you. This is a date."

Emma looked at him, miffed. "No. It's not."

"It's not?"

"No." Emma pushed her fries around on her plate.

"But thirty seconds ago you called it a date."

"I was mistaken."

"No, you weren't," said Darcy, smiling.

"This is going nowhere, " Emma said. "I don't want to talk about it anymore."

"Alright," said Darcy. "Were you ever married?"

"First, you think I'm an adulteress, and now, you think I had three children out of wedlock? I see you have a very high opinion of me. Like I said before, I don't normally dress like I was dressed the night you met me."

Darcy chuckled again. "Don't get so defensive. I'm just trying to get to know you. I just asked a simple question."

"Yes, I was married. My husband passed away."

"Oh," said Darcy. "I'm sorry."

"Not nearly as sorry as I was."

"I'm sure. I'm sorry about giving you a hard time."

"It's alright," said Emma. "You had no way of knowing. But, if you don't mind, I don't really want to talk about it now."

"That's cool," said Darcy. "Want to shoot some pool?"

"I don't know."

"Have you ever played before?" Darcy asked.

"Yes, many times. In fact, I played rather recently. It didn't turn out so well. It ended up being one of those times when trouble found me, and I sort of got into a brawl."

"A brawl? As in everybody in the place all jumping into it and stuff?" said Darcy.

"Sadly, yes."

"Miss Emma, you are the most interesting lady I have met in a long time. Come on, let's shoot some pool. I got your back if things get ugly." He looked around the bar. "But these folks are pretty mellow. I come here all the time, and I ain't never seen no brawl. But then, you've never been here before to start one." He winked.

"I'll try to keep the peace," Emma promised.

Darcy and Emma were fairly equally matched at the game. Emma could lay out the geometrical trick shots while Darcy had so much power behind his shot that multiple balls bounced around so much, they eventually found a hole by sheer chance. They each won one game. During the tie-breaking third game, Darcy caught Emma staring at his bicep while he was lining up a shot. "What you looking at, girl?" he said.

Emma flushed. "Uh, I was just noticing that you're really strong."

"You think so?" Darcy said. "I used to play football at Virginia Tech."

"Really? Wow, I'm impressed!"

"Why? Are you surprised that I actually went to college?"

"No. I never thought about it, I guess," Emma stammered. "What did you study?"

"I majored in business. My father was a plumber. He wanted me to take over the family business. I agreed. But he died of a heart attack while I was in college. I felt like I needed to finish my education, and I really enjoyed playing football, so I stayed at Tech. The business went under. I sort of planned on doing something else then, but after I graduated, I moved back up here to help out my mother. I couldn't find a job I liked, so I decided to re-open the business. I like working for myself."

"I know what you mean. I love having my own firm. All the decisions, whether they end up being good or bad, are mine. I take the cases I want to and turn down those I don't. There's a lot of freedom in it. A lot of risks, too, but I think it's worth it."

Darcy won the third game, and they sat down at a table for another drink. "Might I see you again, Emma?" he asked, after a bit.

"You might. It's possible."

"How might that occur?" said Darcy

"You might call me, and I might call you back. And you might ask me out."

"On a date?" Darcy smiled.

"Or something like that."

"And might you say yes?" he asked.

"I just might. Chances are good."

Darcy paid the tab. As they were walking to the parking lot, Darcy took Emma's hand in his. Emma didn't resist. It felt rather good.

———

The next week, Emma called Alexander Giovanni. "Hi, Alex. How are things going?"

"Great," said Alex. "I haven't heard a word from Tessa. Maybe she will just disappear and leave us alone."

"Possibly," said Emma, "but she may also just be laying her plans. In the meantime, no news is good news. The reason I'm calling is I would like to get to know Lindsay and Amber a little better . . . but in a relaxed setting. How do you feel about me taking them to my house this Friday evening to hang out with my kids?"

"That would be fine," Alex said.

"Good. I'll pick them up at your house at 6:00 p.m."

Emma told her children ahead of time that she was bringing home one of her client's children. She also mentioned the girls were going through a hard time at home and that they should be supportive of them.

When Emma entered the house with Amber and Lindsay, Jasmine rose to the occasion. She greeted the girls warmly and invited them to her bedroom. When Amber seemed a little reluctant, Jasmine offered to show Amber her beanie baby collection. Amber beamed.

Emma made meatball subs and oven fries. After dinner, during which Amber managed to get tomato sauce all over the front of her yellow shirt, Jason suggested everyone play a bowling video game. He set the game at different handicap levels for the various players so everyone could play. Before long, Lindsay and Amber were squealing and cheering along with Emma's kids. Emma was glad to see the girls so relaxed. Emma caught Lindsay looking at her on several occasions.

"What's up, Lindsay? Anything wrong?"

"No. You're just really awesome, Miss Emma. Your kids are so lucky."

"Oh, you're very sweet to say that," said Emma and gave Lindsay a hug. "We are lucky to know you."

―――――

The next few weeks were hectic for Emma. She had a custody trial in another case and settled the Wellmont property distribution with Gretta Firestone.

The Giovanni custody case was shaping up well, too. Morgan and Emma had managed to come up with a decent list of witnesses. In addition to the witnesses Emma had taken with her to the temporary hearing, Louise's son agreed to come back from North Carolina to testify that Tessa had sold him heroin. Morgan had located a woman from the tennis club whom Tessa had told she planned to move out of the country with the children. Another mother of one of Amber's friends agreed to testify that she had seen Tessa drive Amber to ballet and appeared to be under the influence of drugs or alcohol. The mother had been so concerned that she called the police, but they didn't respond before Tessa, and then the other mother, had left the studio parking lot.

Emma had seen Darcy several times since their first date. They spoke on the phone nearly every day. If Tessa was in court or with a client when Darcy called, she called him back, and he promptly answered every time. Several evenings, after Emma's kids were in their rooms for the night, Darcy and Emma talked on the telephone for more than an hour, just getting to know one another. Emma was starting to feel quite comfortable with Darcy.

On a Thursday, three weeks after Darcy and Emma's first date, Emma returned to the office from depositions around noon. There was no telephone message from Darcy. Emma asked Kat if he had called. "Not today," she said.

Emma checked her cell phone. No missed call from Darcy. She tried to call him, but he didn't pick up. Emma didn't leave a message.

Later that afternoon, Emma called Darcy again. He picked up on the fifth ring. "Hi, it's me," said Emma.

"I know. I have caller I.D."

"What's up? I didn't hear from you today," said Emma.

"Do I have to call you every day?"

Emma was taken aback. "No, but you usually do."

"Well, I'm busy today."

"OK, well just call me when you have time," Emma said.

"I answered the phone. I obviously have time now," Darcy said.

"What's wrong, Darcy? Did something happen today?"

"Nothing's wrong. What do you want to talk about?"

"Nothing in particular," said Emma. "What would you like to do tomorrow night?"

"I think I have plans tomorrow night."

"Alright. That's fine. Would you like to do something Saturday night or Sunday afternoon?" Emma suggested.

"I don't know if I'm available," Darcy said flatly.

"Oh, OK. Well let's do this, then," said Emma, "when and if you're available, why don't *you* call me. Good-bye."

"Don't hang up on me," said Darcy.

"I'm not hanging up on you. I said good-bye. Our conversation was clearly over," Emma said.

"I didn't think our conversation was over. I'm not busy tonight. Do you want to see me tonight?" Darcy said.

"I'm not sure if I do want to see you tonight. You're acting strange."

"I'm not acting strange," Darcy said.

"Yes, you are."

"No, I'm not."

"OK, you're not. Where and when do you want to meet, Darcy?"

"Six o'clock, the chili place."

"Fine, I'll see you then," said Emma.

"Fine."

Emma arrived at the restaurant at five minutes after six. Darcy wasn't there. He usually arrived before she did. Emma was getting ready to leave at six twenty-five when Darcy walked in. As he approached the table, he gave her a big smile. He bent down and greeted her with a kiss. Emma looked confused.

"Well," she said, "I guess someone is in a better mood now."

"Who? I wasn't in a bad mood."

"Really? So what was this afternoon about?" Emma asked.

"I don't know what you're talking about."

"This afternoon you were acting all stand-offish and aloof. Now you're all warm and fuzzy and kissing. Are you insane?"

Darcy smiled slowly. "I just like to keep you off balance. Now, are we going to eat, or what?"

Emma was too confused and stunned to discuss the matter further. The rest of the evening went smoothly, but Emma couldn't get rid of the nagging thought that something about Darcy was just not quite right.

———

The next day was Friday. The Giovanni custody trial was set for the following Tuesday, just four days away. Emma was ready. She was fairly confident she would be able to win custody for Alexander Giovanni and limit Contessa to supervised visitation.

Emma returned from the Motions Day docket in court to find a strange man in a cheap, ill-fitting suit sitting in her waiting room. She looked at Kat questioningly but didn't say anything. The man jumped up from the sofa. "Emma Parker?" he asked.

Emma shot Kat a glare. "Yes, I'm Miss Parker. Do you have an appointment, sir?"

"I'm not a client, ma'am. William Stewart, Federal Bureau of Investigation." He held out a badge in a thin leather cover for Emma to see. "I need to speak with you."

Emma looked at Kat. "Do I have time? When is my next appointment?"

"Not until three o'clock," said Kat.

"Very well, then. Come into my office," said Emma.

Once they were settled in Emma's office, she said, "So to what do I owe the pleasure of your visit, Mr. Stewart?"

"I understand you represent Alexander Giovanni?"

"I do. That's public record since I have entered an appearance on his behalf in the Circuit Court."

"His custody trial is set for Tuesday?" Mr. Stewart said.

"That also is public record, which you obviously have reviewed," said Emma.

"The Bureau needs you to continue that custody trial hearing to a much later date."

"Why?" inquired Emma.

"I'm afraid I can't tell you that," said Mr. Stewart.

"And I'm afraid I can't do so," Emma said. "Even if I wanted a continuance, for whatever reason, the court wouldn't grant it to me at this late date. Not unless I was in the hospital on my death bed or had a death in my immediate family."

"Well, you're going to have to tell the court that one of those things has occurred," said Mr. Stewart.

"I can't lie to the court. What is this about?"

"We are investigating Mrs. Giovanni regarding her involvement in various criminal activities. Since you have been investigating her, too, I'm sure you have some idea of what those activities are."

"I can't really comment on that one way or the other," said Emma.

"We know what you have been doing, Ms. Parker. We know where you have been and to whom you have spoken. We know whose feathers you have ruffled and what disturbances you have caused," he said.

"Have you been following me? You have no right to follow me."

"Don't be silly, Ms. Parker. We are not following you; we are investigating Mrs. Giovanni, and it seems every time we follow a lead, you have already followed that lead and put the subjects on alert."

"I find that hard to believe, Mr. Stewart. You are supposed to be the professional investigators. I am just a family law attorney preparing a custody case. It would be pretty pathetic if I could find out more information that the F.B.I. could."

"Ms. Parker, if you are making an attempt at humor, it is inappropriate. This is a serious matter and a serious criminal investigation. You need to cease your investigation now."

"My investigation is pretty much done. I go to trial on Tuesday," said Emma.

"You can't go to trial on Tuesday. If you go to trial and put on your witnesses, Mrs. Giovanni and all her co-conspirators will know who the witnesses are and what evidence you have."

"So?"

"So the witnesses will be compromised and the co-conspirators, the ones higher up, the ones we are really after, will be warned. Our investigation will fall apart, and our case will be compromised. So you have to continue your custody trial and cease all investigation until we have concluded our investigation and taken our case or cases to trial."

"And how long do you think that would be?" asked Emma. "For argument's sake."

"I should think we would be able to wrap things up in nine to twelve months," said Mr. Stewart.

"What? That's ridiculous! Absolutely not. You don't understand what's at stake here. There are two little girls whose custody needs to be decided. Until it is, Contessa Giovanni could take those kids and disappear and there's nothing anyone could do about it. You know what this woman is like; you know that would be disastrous for her children."

"If she did that, it would be unfortunate," said Mr. Stewart, "but not as unfortunate as allowing several big-time criminals to remain in operation."

"I don't have an ethical obligation to help catch them. I do have an ethical obligation to help Alexander Giovanni protect the best interest of his children. I can't do that by continuing his custody trial."

"Ms. Parker, I don't want to have to charge you with obstruction of justice," warned Mr. Stewart.

"You ordered me to go tell a lie to the Court. My refusal to do so cannot possibly be against the law. That makes absolutely no sense."

"I'm not ordering you to tell a lie. I'm telling you to get that trial date continued," Mr. Stewart said.

"That's not up to me. It's up to a judge," said Emma.

"Then go ask a judge to continue the case."

"Are you ordering me to request a continuance?" said Emma.

"Yes, I am."

"But you're not ordering me to tell a lie?"

Mr. Stewart sighed. "No, I'm not ordering you to tell a lie."

"Alright," said Emma, resignedly. "I'll request a continuance first thing Monday morning. That is the first available time to make such a request."

Mr. Stewart stood up and extended his hand. "The Bureau appreciates your cooperation, Ms. Parker."

"I'm so glad," said Emma.

Monday morning, Emma was at calendar control. When her name was called she entered the judge's chambers. David Hanson, Contessa Giovanni's recently retained counsel, was there, as well. Emma had given Mr. Hanson notice via facsimile on Friday afternoon. Judge Lillian Allen was handling calendar control that morning. "Good morning, Ms. Parker. What can I do for you this morning?"

"Your Honor, I would like to request a continuance," said Emma.

"When is your case set to be heard?" the judge asked.

"Tomorrow," said Emma.

Judge Allen raised an eyebrow. "Tomorrow? What is your reason for requesting a continuance?"

"Um, I just need some more time," said Emma.

"When was the hearing set?" the judge asked.

"Thirty days ago, Your Honor."

Judge Allen looked at the file. "I see it was set, at your request, Ms. Parker, for an expedited hearing?"

"Yes, Your Honor," said Emma.

"You wanted a quick hearing, and you were given one, and now you are telling me you need more time—is that correct, Ms. Parker?"

"Yes, Your Honor."

"What is your position, Mr. Hanson?" the judge asked.

"I am ready to proceed tomorrow, Your Honor, even though I was just retained two weeks ago," said Mr. Hanson.

"Mr. Hanson is ready, Ms. Parker. I suggest you be ready, as well. I am denying your Motion for a Continuance."

"Thank you, Your Honor," said Mr. Hanson.

"Thank you, Your Honor," said Emma. "May I please get a certified copy of your Order denying my request today?"

"Absolutely," Judge Allen said. "You may check out the file and take it to the Clerk's office for a copy.

"Thank you," said Emma. Agent Stewart had told her to ask. She had asked.

CHAPTER FIFTEEN

E mma, Morgan, Alexander Giovanni, and eight witnesses arrived at the courthouse for the custody trial. Emma had Lindsay Giovanni waiting with Kat at the office. If Emma determined she needed Lindsay to testify, she would call Kat, who would bring the child to court. Emma left the other witnesses in the courthouse hallway and entered the courtroom with Morgan and Alex Giovanni. Contessa's attorney, David Hanson, sat at the defense table. There was no sign of Mrs. Giovanni. Emma looked at her watch. The judge was due on the bench in five minutes. Emma and Morgan set up for trial. They took four three-ring binders of exhibits out of their litigation briefcases and placed them on the counsel table. Morgan set out legal pads, pens, and highlighters. Emma readied her statute book and her handbook on the rules of evidence. As Emma handed Mr. Hanson his copy of the Plaintiff's exhibits, she noticed Mr. Hanson had no exhibit books of his own.

"No exhibits today, David?" she queried.

"Not going to need any," he said.

"That's interesting. Why?"

"You'll find out soon enough," David replied.

"Oooh, a secret," said Emma. Contessa Giovanni had still not arrived.

The bailiff entered the courtroom from the door behind the bench. "The Circuit Court of Exeter County is now in session. The Honorable Harold Larson presiding. Remain standing and come to order." Judge Larson took the bench and sat down. After the judge was seated, everyone else sat down.

"We are here for the final custody and visitation hearing in the matter of Giovanni v Giovanni. Is counsel prepared for trial?"

Emma stood up. "Yes, Your Honor."

David Hanson stood. "Your Honor, I need to request a continuance. My client, Contessa Giovanni, was arrested last night and is currently incarcerated."

"On what charges was your client arrested, Counselor?" asked the judge.

"Well, Your Honor, it is my understanding she has been charged with first-degree murder."

Alexander Giovanni gasped. Morgan elbowed him. "Shh."

"Well, Mr. Hanson, the outcome of that criminal action will undoubtedly impact the custody proceeding. I will remove the matter from the docket for rescheduling at a later time."

Emma scrambled to her feet. "Your Honor, can you please enter an order of Temporary Custody to my client, pending the final hearing, in light of these circumstances? If Mrs. Giovanni is released on bail, she could take the children and run."

"Has your client been granted bail, Mr. Hanson?" asked the judge.

"No, Your Honor."

"She was only arrested last night. She wouldn't have had the chance to have a bail hearing yet," Emma pointed out.

"I'm not going to award custody without a hearing, Ms. Parker. If Mrs. Giovanni is awarded bail and is released, you can file a Motion for Temporary Custody. For now, I will simply remove the matter from the docket." Judge Larson picked up his gavel, rapped the bench twice, stood up, and left the courtroom. Emma was still standing at counsel's table, her mouth hanging open.

As soon as Emma got back to the office, she called Stan and asked him to try to find out what he could about Tessa's charges. He called her back a few hours later.

"Contessa Giovanni has been charged with the first-degree murder of her boyfriend, Marvin Davis. Apparently, she took out a $500,000 life insurance policy on him and was trying to collect the proceeds. The funny thing is until Contessa contacted the insurance company, no one had reported him dead."

"Poor Marvin," said Emma. "Poor Betty."

"I guess it's good news for Mr. Giovanni's custody case, though, isn't it?" said Stan.

"As a matter of fact, no. The trial got continued because Tessa is in jail, and we still have no custody order. Alex and the girls have to live in limbo in the meantime. It's not good at all."

"Sorry, Emma. Let me know if you need anything else."

———

With the delay of the Giovanni custody trial, Emma had time to focus on her other cases. A few days later, Emma met with Mr. Lee, one of her new clients. At their initial meeting, Mr. Lee had told Emma that his wife was having an affair, and she had admitted to him she was pregnant with the other man's baby.

"So, Mr. Lee, tell me what has been going on at home since we last spoke," said Emma.

Mr. Lee, a formal, well-dressed Korean man, moved his chair closer to Emma's desk. "I tell my wife to move out of the house."

Emma massaged her forehead with her thumb and middle finger. "Mr. Lee, I know we talked about this. I told you that you cannot legally force your wife to leave the house."

"I did not force her. I asked her to do so, and she did."

"She agreed to move out?"

"Yes."

"Why?" Emma asked.

"I told her I would give her ten thousand dollars if she would move out and leave our children with me."

"Did you give her ten thousand dollars?"

"I did."

"Where did you get the money?"

"From my savings account."

"Where did the money come from in the savings account?"

"From my business earnings. I own an accounting firm."

"Yes, I remember we talked about that. Were the earnings accumulated during your marriage to Mrs. Lee?"

"Yes, of course."

"Alright," said Emma, "so you really only gave her five thousand dollars. Is she living with her boyfriend now?"

"No," said Mr. Lee. "I gave her the money so she could get an apartment. I made her promise not to live with him."

"If she breaks that promise, there's not a lot we can do about it since she already has the ten thousand."

"I also told her I would pay her another one hundred thousand dollars if she will have an abortion."

Emma looked up from her note-taking. "Excuse me? What did you say?"

Mr. Lee sat up straighter. "I told her if she gets rid of that man's fetus, I will pay her one hundred thousand dollars."

"Mr. Lee! That is unconscionable! You can't pay someone to end a baby's life!"

"She brought dishonor to me, our family, our children. The Korean community is very close. Everyone already knows she was having affair. If they know she is pregnant, I will be ruined. My children will not be able to live in this community. It must go away."

"Mr. Lee, I sympathize with your problem. I know this is very embarrassing and stressful for you. But I cannot condone the manner in which you are dealing with this. You have to tell your wife that you have reconsidered and will not be offering her money to abort her child. If you do not do so, I cannot be your attorney." Emma stood up. "Our meeting is done for today. Please reconsider your offer to your wife, and let me know what you decide to do."

Mr. Lee still sat in his chair, frowning at Emma. "Ms. Parker, I don't think you understand my situation."

"Maybe not, Mr. Lee. Maybe your way of thinking and mine on this matter are just too different. I understand people sometimes choose to have abortions.

But I don't think you are really giving your wife a choice. You are putting too much pressure on her and giving her too much incentive to make it a real choice. Furthermore, that baby's life is precious, and I can't be any part of your plan to encourage abortion. You need to choose whether or not you want me as your attorney. If you do, you can't continue with this plan." Emma gestured toward the door. "Please, call me next week, Mr. Lee."

Mr. Lee picked up his briefcase and slowly moved toward the door. "I am sorry if I upset you, Ms. Parker. I will think about it and will call you."

———

After the comment about "keeping her off balance," Emma didn't hear from Darcy for almost a week. Then, one evening, as Emma was leaving the office for the day, Darcy was waiting for her in the parking lot. As she spotted him, Emma's heart skipped a beat, and she couldn't help but think how handsome Darcy looked, leaning casually against Emma's minivan. As Emma approached, Darcy stood up, took his hand out of the pocket of his jeans, and looked at Emma sheepishly.

"Hi, counselor," Darcy said, "I would like to make a confession."

Despite Emma's irritation with Darcy's recent strange behavior, she smiled. "Oh, really?" she replied, "What would you like to confess, sir?"

"I confess that I am a lily-livered snake," Darcy pronounced, raising his chin.

"Really," Emma queried, "How's that?"

At this Darcy dropped his eyes to the ground and returned his hands to his pockets. He hesitated. "I know that when I last saw you, I didn't treat you right."

"I would agree with that statement," said Emma.

"I apologize for being mean. My mama taught me to not make excuses for my bad behavior, so I won't do that. But I would like to explain if I can," Darcy said, still looking at the ground.

"By all means," Emma prompted.

"Well," Darcy began then paused. "I have been having such a good time getting to know you and am starting to really feel, um strong feelings about you."

"And, I am starting to feel that way, too," Emma said, gently. "So . . ."

"So, I got scared. I love, or loved, my wife so much. I thought everything was good. I was happy. I thought we had this beautiful life and a wonderful family. And then she just blew up my world by cheating on me. I was completely destroyed . . . I can't go through that again. So I acted like a big fat chicken and pretended like I didn't care." Darcy raised his head and looked Emma in the eye. "For that, I am sorry."

Emma looked back at Darcy through tear-filled eyes. "I accept your apology," she said. "I know it wasn't easy for you to tell me that. I completely understand your fears. I have been hurt, too. I am afraid, too." Emma walked up to Darcy and wrapped her arms around his waist. Looking up at him, she continued," But I am not your wife and our relationship is not that relationship."

"That's for sure," said Darcy, smiling wryly.

"Can we make a pact to not play games and to tell the other what is going on in our head, no matter how crazy?" Emma asked.

"Yes, ma'am, I'll try," Darcy said. Then he bent down and kissed her slowly, sweetly, and sensuously.

After their heart-to-heart chat, things improved between Emma and Darcy. They chatted on the phone every day. Emma enjoyed Darcy's sense of humor and common-sense way of viewing the world. Emma had to increase her exercise routine, however, because Darcy shared her love for high-calorie foods, such as hamburgers, pizza, nachos, and buffalo wings. Their six children got along well. Emma was touched by the way Darcy seemed to truly care for and enjoy her children.

As summer descended and the days turned warm, Darcy and Emma took the children on picnics, bike rides, and day trips to the beach. Darcy's boys idolized Justin and Jason. Emma was pleasantly surprised to see how nurturing and kind Jasmine was to Darcy's seven-year-old.

One evening, Darcy and Emma enjoyed dinner at an actual restaurant—not a sports bar or pool hall. As they waited for their dessert order to arrive, Darcy reached across the table and grabbed Emma's hand. "I'm really having a good time with you, Emma."

"I'm having a good time with you, too."

"But I feel like you know a lot more about me than I do about you. I talk to you all the time about my marriage and the hurt and pain my wife caused me. And you're a really great listener. I appreciate that." Emma smiled.

"But," Darcy continued, "I feel like there's this part of you that's blocked off from me. You never talk about your marriage or your husband or what happened. I feel like I can't know all of you unless I know your history."

Emma looked at the table. "It is just really, really hard for me to talk about him. It hurts less if I don't think about it."

"OK. If you're not ready, I understand. But I hope eventually you'll feel comfortable enough with me to share that part of your past."

Emma looked up at him. "Thanks for understanding."

"No problem. Hey, here comes our big, nasty, chocolate thingy." Emma looked up to see the waiter approaching.

"You make it sound so appetizing," said Emma.

Over coffee, Darcy and Emma laughed and talked about the upcoming football season. "I just feel like this year is finally the year for our Washington football team," Emma said. "I think they're going to turn it around."

"People say that every year, and every year they get their hopes up. And every year, they stink up the place," said Darcy.

"Without hope, we have nothing," laughed Emma.

"Too true," Darcy agreed.

Once the two were settled in the car, just as Darcy was about to put the car in reverse and back out of the parking space, Emma put her hand on his knee and looked at him solemnly. "I think I'm ready."

Darcy glanced at Emma's hand, resting on his knee, and then looked at her. "For what?" he asked.

"To tell you about Jeffrey."

Darcy turned off the engine and turned toward Emma. "Shoot."

"We met when we were in high school. We started dating our senior year and went to college together and dated throughout college. We got married the weekend after graduation. Jeffrey joined the Foreign Service, and I went to law school. Emma realized she sounded like she was stating the facts of a case, but was afraid to open the floodgates of her emotions.

She continued, "After I got out of law school, I started my career. Jeffrey traveled a lot for his work. Once we had children, the kids and I went with him whenever we could. We have been very fortunate in that we've been able to see a lot of the world. Fortunately, I am a pretty independent and self-sufficient girl because he was gone a lot. I sometimes felt the children suffered a little by not having their dad around all the time, but they, too, are very independent."

"Then, almost three and a half years ago now, Jeffrey had been out of the country for three weeks. When he came back, he had to attend a conference in Boston before he could come home. A huge ice storm had shut down the airport. When he called to tell me his flight was canceled, and he wouldn't be home that night as planned, I gave him a hard time. I cried and told him I missed him . . . the children missed him." Emma was wringing her hands together. Darcy reached over and placed his big hand, calmly over hers.

"He decided to rent a car and drive from Boston to Virginia so he could get home. " Emma paused, took a deep breath, and looked out the side window, trying to maintain her composure.

When she felt in control again, she continued, "There was a huge multi-car pileup just outside of Boston." Emma pulled her hands away from Darcy's and turned toward the side window again. She took another ragged breath. "He was killed. A State Trooper called my house and told me the news. The children and I never got to say good-bye. We never got to tell him how much we loved him."

Darcy had gone completely silent and even appeared to be holding his breath. When Emma finally looked back to him, she saw that tears were running down his cheeks.

"And that's my sad story. Probably much less gripping than you imagined. One day we were living this busy, hectic life, trying to pursue our careers and raise our children, and the next day it just ended. Except that I had to keep on raising our children and pursue my career so I could support them . . . and me."

Darcy reached over and hugged Emma. She leaned into him and, after what seemed to be a very long time, Emma's shoulders relaxed.

Darcy pulled her in tighter. After a moment, Darcy held Emma back at arm's length, and gently wiped a tear from Emma's face with one large, calloused thumb. "Thanks for telling me. It means a lot to me."

———

Morgan and Emma shared conversation and drinks after work one evening. "Tell me about your boyfriend *de jour*," Emma said.

"His name is Ian. You wouldn't believe how unbelievably good-looking he is. He used to be a model. He's ten years younger than I am. I can't believe he's interested in me."

"You're a very attractive woman, Morgan. You know that. Is he good to you?"

"So far. But there are a few little red flags," said Morgan.

"Oh-oh. If you see little red flags, that usually means there are actually great big red flags . . . maybe even warning sirens that you're missing," Emma commented.

"Don't be so negative, Emma," said Morgan.

"Tell me about the red flags."

"Well, for one thing," said Morgan, "his job seems a little bogus."

"Why? What does he do?"

"He's a professional hypnotist."

"You mean, like the comic kind that performs in Vegas?" said Emma.

"No. He's not funny at all. He works for companies doing marketing. He holds these informational meetings and claims to hypnotize the audience members so they will buy the company's product or services."

Emma laughed. "Are you kidding? Companies actually *pay* him to do this?"

"Apparently."

"That's ridiculous," said Emma. "That *is* a red flag."

"There's another little flag, as well," said Morgan.

"Do tell."

"Well . . . he recently told me he has had serious relationships in the past with other women *and* with men."

"He's bisexual?"

"That's what I said to him, but he said it's only bisexual if you are involved with men and women at the same time. He says he's currently only interested in women."

"And how do you feel about that?" asked Emma.

"I guess I'm willing to overlook things in the past, as long as he isn't interested in men anymore."

"Anymore or currently?" Emma asked.

"Does it matter?" said Morgan.

"I would think so. 'Currently' seems transitory; who's to say whether next week or next month he will 'currently' not be interested in you and will be interested in men again?"

"Maybe next week or next month I won't 'currently' be interested in him any longer and will be interested in some other man," said Morgan.

"Fair enough. Given your romantic history, I guess that is a distinct possibility."

"For now, we are having a good time," said Morgan.

"Well, here's to your good fortune holding out," Emma held up her glass in a toast.

———

One afternoon when Emma came back from court, she passed Morgan's office door, and Morgan called her into her office. "Shut the door," she said.

Emma was puzzled. Kat was at her desk in the reception area, and no one else was in the office. Morgan had an Internet browser pulled up on her computer. She pointed at the screen. "Remember we were talking about red flags?" she said. "Well, I was checking out this website: 'don'tdatehim.com,' and I found Ian. There are a ton of women on here saying what a freak he is."

"I'm sorry, Morgan," said Emma.

"You're going to be even more sorry in a minute. Guess who else is on there?"

"Who?"

"Darcy."

"Are you sure it's my Darcy?"

"There's a picture," said Morgan. She clicked the mouse, and a picture of Darcy came up. "That looks like the guy you introduced me to as your boyfriend." Emma gaped in dismay.

"How many women?" asked Emma.

"It looks like just one," Morgan said. "But she is *really* ticked off."

"I don't know that I even care to know what she has to say," said Emma.

"You don't want to know? What is it you said about ignoring the red flags?"

"It's just basically gossip, and I make a point of not listening to gossip."

"Alright," said Morgan. "Be an ostrich. Or, maybe it's better to know what you're getting yourself into," said Morgan. "Just read it. I'll send you the link to the website."

"This is ridiculous," said Emma. "I have work to do." She headed toward her office.

"Just read it," Morgan yelled after her. "Knowledge is power!"

By mid-afternoon, Emma's curiosity got the best of her. She looked up the website.

Clearly, the relationship had not ended well between Darcy and the writer of the entry. "This guy's a complete narcissist. Doesn't care about anyone but himself. One day he's in love with you, the next he's gone." That was it. No other entries from other people. No further information.

Emma, by nature, was a skeptic. Furthermore, she was not one to believe everything she read on the Internet. Anyone could post anything, and the information was rarely verified, if ever. Emma tried to shrug off the ranting of one scorned woman. However, her thoughts kept returning to the matter.

She spent the next few days ruminating.

Later that week, as Darcy was driving her home after a bowling date, Emma said, "Am I the first woman you have dated since separating from your wife?"

"Why?"

"I was just curious."

Darcy was silent for a moment. "I guess you could say I sort of dated one other girl, but it was very short-lived . . . about three weeks."

"What happened?" said Emma.

"Nothing happened. It just didn't work out," Darcy said shortly.

"Why didn't it work out?"

"Emma, there doesn't have to be a reason. You date someone to see if you are compatible. If you're not, you stop dating them. If you are, you continue. It's not that complicated."

Neither of them spoke for a minute. Emma looked at Darcy's profile. His teeth were clenched, and she could see a muscle pulsating along his jawline. In spite of the fact that Darcy was clearly angry, Emma pressed forward. "What happened between you and your wife?"

Darcy sighed. "I told you before; I caught her cheating."

"I know. But before that, how was your relationship? Were you happy?"

"I thought we were. Apparently, she wasn't. But rather than say anything to me, she just went out and found someone else."

"Did you have any clues? Like, for example, were you having trouble with your sex life?"

"Emma, I really don't want to discuss my sex life with my wife with my girlfriend. It's just too weird."

Emma inwardly agreed and didn't pursue the issue any further.

———

Although Alexander Giovanni's custody case had been quiet since the arrest of Contessa, Emma continued to have regular contact with Alex and his girls. Jasmine had become close to Lindsay and the Giovanni girls were frequent guests at Emma's house. Emma was becoming attached to both girls, as well, but was particularly fond of Amber. Emma missed the days when her children would slip a little hand into hers or sit on her lap and asked to be read to. Amber always had her lunchbox of animals with her, and the minute Emma walked in the door when Amber was there, Amber would run and get the animals and beg Emma to play with her.

Lindsay frequently joined Emma in the kitchen. She was very interested in cooking and asked Emma non-stop questions about cooking, such as what made things rise and how could you thicken a sauce. Emma's own children were more interested in eating the food than they were in the process of preparing it, so Emma enjoyed having a curious helper.

Over the past several months that Contessa Giovanni had been out of the family home, Emma had seen Amber and Lindsay calm down. They seemed less anxious and more relaxed. She was sure they still missed their mother, but they mentioned her less and less as time passed. Occasionally, Lindsay made a comment, such as, "My mother used to do that with us . . . before she got sick." Emma did have to agree, in her mind, that Tessa Giovanni's substance abuse was, indeed, an illness. However, she also had made choices that had caused her children grief, loss, and emotional harm.

CHAPTER SIXTEEN

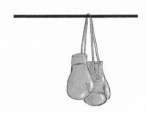

O ver the next few months, Emma focused on her other clients. Morgan stopped seeing Ian the hypnotist and began dating a local politician. Lindsay and Amber spent a lot of time with Emma's children.

Then, one afternoon Emma was working at her desk when Stan called her. "You busy, Emma?"

"Not really. I'm just going over some opposing party bank records I just received. What's up?"

"The jury is back in the Giovanni murder case. Courtroom Five-F."

"I'll be right over."

Emma and Morgan slipped into the back of the courtroom just as the judge took the bench. The jury was already seated in their box. Contessa Giovanni and her criminal defense attorney sat at one counsel table and two prosecutors sat at the other.

"Mr. Foreman," the judge asked the jury foreman, "have you reached a verdict?"

A pale, thin man wearing a cardigan sweater stood up. "Yes, Your Honor, we have." The bailiff took the piece of paper the foreman was holding and delivered it to the judge. The judge opened and read the paper, giving away no indication as to the contents.

"The Defendant, please rise. On the first count of murder in the first degree, how does the jury find?"

"Guilty." The few people in the gallery inhaled a collective breath.

"On the second count of attempted fraud, how does the jury find?"

"Guilty."

"I will set this matter down for sentencing next Friday at 10 a.m. The Defendant is remanded to the custody of the sheriff until then. This matter is concluded." The judge rapped his gavel twice. Everyone in the courtroom stood up, and the judge departed.

A few mornings later, Morgan and David Hanson, Mrs. Giovanni's custody lawyer, appeared before the scheduling judge.

"Your Honor, the mother has been convicted of murder and insurance fraud. We need to immediately schedule a custody trial in this matter," Morgan said.

"The earliest date I have is in sixty days," said the judge.

"Your Honor, please. This matter needs to be expedited," Morgan pled.

"Your Honor, my client is currently incarcerated. There is no emergency. Furthermore, we have filed an appeal of the criminal convictions, and argument is set in approximately forty days," said Mr. Hanson. "We anticipate the convictions will be overturned."

"Success on appeal is highly unlikely, Your Honor," Morgan pressed. "May we please have the earliest possible trial date for the custody matter?"

"The earliest available date is in sixty days. Would you like that date, Ms. Price?" The judge peered at Morgan over the top of his glasses.

"If there isn't any possibility of an earlier date, then, yes, I'll take that date," sighed Morgan.

"Very well. We'll see you then."

Alex Giovanni was surprised by his wife's conviction. "I can't believe she would actually kill someone. She can be crazy and selfish and demanding, but I don't see her killing a person for the insurance money. It just doesn't seem like Tess."

"When people are under the influence of drugs, they often do things they would never do otherwise," said Emma. "As far as the custody issues go, the girls are safe as long as your wife is in jail. If she gets out, though, for whatever reason, there is currently no custody order, and she could just pick up the girls. I really wish, Morgan, you could have got an earlier trial date."

"I tried, Emma. I really did."

"Tessa's in jail now. Even before she went to jail, she never once attempted to contact the girls or come to see them," said Alex. "She's just not interested. There isn't anything to worry about."

"Let's hope not," said Emma. "I just like to have all the possible contingencies covered when I can. Unfortunately, this is the best I can do right now."

"I appreciate everything you've done, Emma," said Alex. "Lindsay and Amber are so happy now, and they really love your kids."

"We love the girls, too," said Emma.

———

Emma and Darcy fell into a comfortable routine. They often went out together on Friday nights. On Saturday, they spent time with their children. If it was Darcy's weekend to have his boys, he often brought them to do things with Emma and her kids. Darcy introduced Emma's brood to NASCAR racing, fishing, and skeet shooting. Emma took Darcy's boys to the opera and the ballet. The kids seemed to love it all.

Late one Saturday night, after Emma had spent an evening alone with her children while Darcy went out with his brothers, Emma received a telephone call.

"I have a collect call from the Adult Detention Center. Will you accept the charges?"

Emma supposed one of her clients had done something stupid and somehow landed in jail. She accepted the charges.

"Emma. It's me, Darcy. I need you to come bail me out."

Emma was silent.

"Emma?"

"Why are you in jail?" asked Emma.

"I don't really want to talk about it right now, honey, with the whole world listening. Can you just come bail me out?"

"I don't know," said Emma. "I'm not sure I'm comfortable with that."

"Are you kidding me?" said Darcy. "I'm really sorry, but I don't have anyone else to ask."

"What about one of your brothers?" said Emma

"They don't have any money."

"What about your wife?"

"Oh, sure. You know better than that. She'd leave me here. *And* she'd use it as an excuse to keep the boys away from me. I'll pay you back, Emma. Just please come get me."

"Claudia has the night off. I can't leave the kids alone for too long. I will go see a bondsman I know, will give him the money, and he will come get you. It can take several hours to actually get released once the bail is paid."

"Thanks, honey, you're the best," said Darcy.

"Hey, Darcy,"

"Yeah?"

"I'm disappointed in you."

"I know, Emma. I'm disappointed in me, too. We'll talk things over after I get out. I'll call you tomorrow."

Emma's seventeen-year-old son, Jason, was still up watching television. She told him she had to go bail a client out of jail and would be back shortly.

Jake Dubrowski's bail bonds office sat in the same office complex as Emma's office. Jake and Emma were acquaintances but not friends. Emma regularly asked Jake to remove at least one of his five garishly painted S.U.V.'s advertising his company from the parking lot so other people in the complex had room to park. Emma also frequently asked Jake and his employees to refrain from blocking the entrance to the building while smoking. Emma's clients had complained that they felt intimidated by the men when coming to see Emma or Morgan. The individuals Jake hired looked like the criminals they served. For all Emma knew, they were criminals—or at least former criminals. In a pinch, Emma had also hired Jake to serve process on people who she either believed to be violent or thought would attempt to avoid service.

As Emma approached Jake's office at 11:49 p.m. that Saturday, the neon sign advertising "Bail Bonds" lit up the entire parking lot, the red and blue lights reflecting off the puddles and oil slicks on the black asphalt. The only cars in the parking lot were Jake's ad cars. When Emma walked in, Jake was tilted back in his chair with his feet on his grey metal desk, drinking a beer. He sat up when Emma entered the room and quickly shoved the magazine that rested in his lap under the desk in front of him.

"Darlin'," Jake said, a little too loudly," what on earth brings you here late on a weekend night? It'll be Sunday in a few minutes, and you know Sunday service ain't good service . . . unless it's a church service, hah!"

"Actually, Mr. Dubrowski," said Emma. "I am here because a friend of mine has found himself in the Adult Detention Center, and I need you to go get him out."

"A lawyer friend?"

"No, of course not," said Emma. "Just a friend."

"How much is the bail?"

"Twenty thousand dollars," said Emma.

"Wow. What's the charge?" asked Jake.

"I don't know," said Emma.

"I need two thousand from you. I will put up the rest. The ten percent is my fee. If he fails to show up for his court date, you will have to pay me back the other eighteen thousand."

"Two thousand seems steep for a few hours of your time," said Emma.

"It's not the time so much as that the court comes after me for the eighteen grand. I have to have the funds available to secure the bond. Think of it as a cash advance from your credit card."

"What is the alternative?" said Emma.

"You go down to the jail with twenty thousand dollars yourself and put it up as security."

"Fine. I'll pay you the two thousand. I assure you he will pay me back."

"That's between you and the gentleman," said Jake. "Sign this stack of papers." He pushed a grungy, slightly wrinkled stack of yellow papers toward Emma.

When Darcy called Emma's cell phone at 3:35 a.m., she didn't answer. After getting three more messages from him on Monday, Emma called Darcy back and asked him to meet her for a drink after work.

That evening, Darcy stood up and gave Emma a hug as she approached the table where he was seated in the bar. "Hi, honey," he said. "I really, really appreciate your helping me out the other night."

Emma didn't respond but sat down and leaned back in her chair. "So tell me what happened," she said coldly.

"My brother and I were chilling at my sister's house all afternoon on Saturday. Her husband brought out the moonshine he makes, and we all started drinking."

"People still actually make moonshine?" said Emma. "Don't you know that if it is not exactly right, it can kill you or at least cause brain damage?"

"My brother-in-law definitely got the brain damage from it," Darcy chuckled.

"I'm serious, just so you know," said Emma.

"Anyway," Darcy said, "after we'd been boozing it up for a couple of hours, my brother and I got in a dispute. Before we know it, we're pushing and scuffling and carrying on. He pushed me back, and I fell over a chair. That made me see red, so I jumped him and pounded his face pretty good. Then his wife and my sister got real upset with me and screamed at me to get out. I tore off in my car and was driving pretty fast when I got pulled over."

"Were you drunk?" said Emma.

"Maybe a little."

"Did they arrest you for drunk driving?" Emma asked.

"Nah." Darcy pulled a wrinkled, yellow, carbon copy paper out of the back pocket of his jeans. It had been folded over several times.

Emma unfolded the paper and read it. "It says here you were charged with reckless driving for going more than twenty miles an hour over the speed limit . . . and with an illegal lane change. Did the officer make you take a Breathalyzer test?"

"No."

"Did you have to walk a straight line or touch your nose or anything?"

"No."

Emma placed the paper on the table and looked at Darcy. "You are so lucky. What were you thinking?"

"I wasn't thinking, honey. I was mad," said Darcy.

"I see. And do you often get so mad that you don't know what you are doing?"

"It's not like that. I just had a bad day," Darcy said.

"A bad day. I would say you actually had a good day. It could have ended a lot worse. Anyway, you have a court date next week, and you have to appear. This isn't like a speeding ticket where you can just pay the fine in the mail. You have to go to court," Emma explained. But that doesn't explain the bond. What else did you get charged with?"

Darcy pulled out another yellow piece of paper. "Assault and battery of my brother, the bum."

Emma sighed. "Anyway, you have to go to court. If you don't go to court I lose $20,000. So you absolutely must go to court."

"Will you go with me?" asked Darcy.

"No," said Emma. "I don't do criminal law. I can give you a referral, though."

"I don't have any money to pay a lawyer," said Darcy. "My wife is sucking me dry."

Emma looked at him for a moment. "Then I will call a friend and see if he will represent you as a favor to me."

"I don't want that," said Darcy. "I want you to go with me."

"No, you don't. I don't know what I'm doing."

"You're a lawyer. You go to court all the time. You can figure it out. Please!" Darcy leaned forward and took Emma's hand. "I want you to be my lawyer."

"I'll think about it," said Emma.

———

On the morning of the criminal court appearance, Darcy assured Emma his brother was not going to show up and testify against him. As they approached the courthouse, Emma reminded him, "I am your lawyer, not your girlfriend. You will not touch me in any manner. You can't call me any term of endearment. You have to act as though we have nothing other than a professional relationship. Got it?" said Emma.

"Got it, ma'am," said Darcy. "Thanks, baby." He winked at Emma.

"Not funny. Here we go."

After going through the security screening, Emma and Darcy headed to the traffic court area of the courthouse. Emma pointed to a bench. "Sit there. Wait for me." Darcy sat.

Emma walked past several attorneys and their clients sitting along the hallway, awaiting the start of court. "Hey, Parker!" Emma looked to see an attorney, whom she knew had a general law practice. He would take any case that made it to his door. On occasion, he would stumble into a divorce case and promptly be decimated by the lawyers that focused solely on family law.

"What are you doing down here in traffic court?" the attorney asked.

Emma smiled. "Slumming."

The attorney smiled weakly. "Nice."

Emma walked over and sat down by him. "Say, Thompson, what judge is sitting in Courtroom B today?"

"Judge Sutherland," he said.

"Lisa Sutherland?"

"Yep. That's her. You been before her before?" said Mr. Thompson.

"No," said Emma, "but I know her socially. She's pretty cool."

Mr. Thompson leaned back and looked at Emma. "I don't know about socially, but as a judge, she's definitely not 'cool.' She's really tough."

"Hmmm," said Emma. "Good to know. Who's the prosecutor in this courtroom today?"

"Peter Townsley."

"How's he?" Emma asked.

"He's alright. He's young. He hates to try cases. He likes to work out plea bargains."

"Also good to know," said Emma. "Where does he hang out after docket call?"

"In that conference room over there," said Mr. Thompson. "I'm waiting for him, too."

"Where's your client?" asked Emma.

"Incarcerated. They'll bring him out later."

"Thanks," said Emma. "Talk to you later."

"Good luck!"

Emma walked back over to Darcy. "I'm going to go tell the prosecutor you are here and that you have an attorney. Then I am going to come back and wait for him to come out and try to work out a deal for you. Just stay here."

Emma was standing in a long line of attorneys waiting to speak with the prosecutor. The good-looking white-haired gentleman next to her was wearing an expensive suit and highly polished shoes. "Haven't I seen you around the courthouse upstairs?" he said.

"Yes," said Emma. "I normally stay up in Circuit Court. I have seen you, too. What brings you down here?"

"I practice mainly criminal defense. I appear here a lot, and also upstairs, for the appeals and the felonies. And what type of practice do you have?"

"Mostly family law," said Emma.

"Ugh," the man said. "I don't have the stomach for it."

"That's how I feel about criminal work," said Emma, smiling.

"So what are you doing here?"

"Favor for a friend," said Emma.

"Ah. That's usually how I find myself in a divorce case."

"So you understand," said Emma. "Can I bounce my case off you?"

"Sure," the man said.

"Assault and battery of his brother, who we don't think will show up today. Also, reckless driving for more than twenty over the limit and an illegal lane change."

"How much over the limit?" the man asked.

"Twenty-two."

"An accident?"

"No."

"Any prior record?"

"No."

"Any witnesses that you know about?"

"No."

"I'd say you can get Townsley to agree to nineteen over the limit, big fine, go to traffic school, and drop the lane change."

"Really? That would be awesome," said Emma.

"Just act tough and say you're willing to try the case. He'll cave," the man said. "And if he doesn't, just try the case, and if you lose, appeal it. You can't get a meaner judge upstairs."

"Thanks a lot. What do you have today?"

"DUI. Third offense. I have my work cut out for me."

When it was Emma's turn, she entered the conference room. She extended her hand. "Emma Parker."

"Peter Townsley. So you represent Darcy Morris?"

"Yes."

"On the assault, the victim did not appear. I am going to ask for a continuance. However, Mr. Morris is a very naughty boy. He was going very fast and driving quite recklessly."

"Mr. Morris has no prior record and denies changing lanes at all. I think it would be appropriate to *nol pros* the illegal lane change. He will agree to nineteen miles over the limit, pay the maximum fine, and agree to attend the safe driving one-day class."

"I think we should suspend his license for six months, he should attend the five-day safe driving course, and I'll drop the illegal lane change."

"He won't agree to suspend his license . . . or even to reckless."

"Or what?" said Mr. Townsley.

"Or I'll just try the case," said Emma. "I don't think you can meet your burden of proof."

"Based on what?"

"Based on information I have," said Emma.

"Have you ever tried a case before?" said Mr. Townsley.

"Just a few hundred," said Emma.

"I've never seen you before," Mr. Townsley pushed back.

"That's because I'm too busy trying cases upstairs in grown-up court. I am a trial lawyer. That's what I do. I have been practicing for more than a decade. If you want to go to trial, let's go."

"We have a really big docket today, you could be here all day waiting to try it."

"I got nothing but time," said Emma.

"Your client may not want to pay you to sit around all day."

"I'm doing this case *pro bono*."

"OK. Nineteen over the limit. Maximum fine. One-day traffic school. We drop the lane change."

"Deal," said Emma.

"Sign here. We'll present it to the judge. You better hope she agrees."

Emma and Darcy slipped into the back of the courtroom. Judge Lisa Sutherland was in the middle of hearing a case involving a run stop sign and an accident. She looked up as Emma and Darcy were climbing over seated individuals to get to an empty spot.

"Ms. Parker," said the judge. All eyes in the courtroom turned to Emma. "Are you lost?"

Emma felt her face get hot. "No, Your Honor. I have a case before you today."

"I didn't think you deigned to darken the halls of general district court," said Judge Sutherland.

"It's true, Your Honor, that I rarely have the privilege of appearing before you." All eyes turned back to the Judge.

"Well, we will get to you in due time. Welcome, Ms. Parker."

"Thank you, Your Honor." Emma sat down. Judge Sutherland resumed her hearing.

Darcy leaned over and whispered in Emma's ear, "Well, that was embarrassing."

"I told you I don't do this kind of law," Emma whispered back.

When the case was called, Judge Sutherland accepted the plea bargain but gave Darcy a lecture on safe driving. The prosecutor asked for a continuance of the assault charge based on Darcy's brother not showing up.

"Did you subpoena the witness?" the judge asked Mr. Townsley.

"No, your Honor," the prosecutor stammered. "He said he would appear voluntarily."

"Continuance denied."

As they walked back to Emma's office, Darcy proclaimed, "You are awesome! You are amazing! You rock! You owned that young prosecutor!"

Emma stopped walking. "No, I was lucky. You were lucky. You were very lucky you didn't get arrested for drunk driving. And you were lucky your brother didn't show up to testify against you. We are *not* doing this ever again!"

Darcy smiled guiltily. "Yes, ma'am."

Morgan walked into Emma's office later that afternoon. "I heard you were slumming it today."

"Sort of."

"I also heard you were representing your boyfriend."

"Just on a couple very minor matters."

"Bad idea, Emma. Bad idea. You should never mix business with your personal life. You don't have good judgment when you have a personal relationship with the client."

"Morgan. It was a few stupid misdemeanors," said Emma.

"Which you know nothing about," said Morgan.

"It was in general district court. If I lost, I would have appealed and made him hire a real criminal defense lawyer."

Morgan stood up. "It's also just low-class. Only bottom-dwelling attorneys represent friends and family members."

"Whatever," said Emma. "It's over."

"I hope so," said Morgan and left the room.

———

A few weeks later, Emma and Darcy were sitting on the sofa in Emma's family room, watching a movie. Jason and Justin were out with friends and Jasmine was spending the night with a classmate. Darcy had his arm around Emma. Emma was running her index finger up and down Darcy's arm, over his round, hard bicep, through the soft crook of his elbow and up over the swell of his forearm. "Your skin is so soft," said Emma. "Except for your hands. They are really rough."

"I'll tell you a secret, if you promise not to repeat it," said Darcy.

"I promise," said Emma.

"I use lotion. Twice a day. Otherwise, I get flaky. But I make sure I don't use the girly smelling kind." Emma pressed her nose to Darcy's bicep and sniffed.

"Nope. Not girly smelling." She snuggled closer to Darcy's arm. "This feels good," she said.

"It does, doesn't it?" Darcy said. "Maybe someday I won't have to go home when the movie is over."

Emma crooked her head to look up at him. "Maybe someday. But you and I aren't married. I know this sounds terribly old-fashioned, but I don't believe in sex outside of marriage. I want to 'practice what I preach' and set a good example for my children. And not to presume anything, but our getting married is not even a possibility while you're married to someone else."

"I'm not married now."

"Legally, you are. I certainly can't have your wife claim we are committing adultery."

"Wow. Adultery. That's a scary Ten-Commandment kind of word."

"It's also a law kind of word. As long as you are still legally married, we can't even give the impression of wrong-doing."

"I don't think it would be so wrong if we were together," said Darcy.

"I would like that, too," said Emma. "But first you have to take care of your business with your wife. Where are you at with the divorce, anyway?"

Darcy pulled his arm back from around Emma's shoulders. "I thought you didn't want to discuss the details of my case."

"I don't want to discuss the details. I just want to know where you are in the process. Do you have a settlement agreement? Has anyone filed for divorce?"

Darcy sat silent.

"Darcy? What, if anything, is happening? We can't just live in limbo indefinitely."

"It's complicated," Darcy said.

"I'm very well aware that it's complicated. I deal with divorces every day. But even though it's complicated, you have to resolve things one way or another."

"I know. It's just so hard. I don't want to hurt the kids, and it seems all she wants to do is hurt me."

Emma got on her knees and put her arms around Darcy's neck. "I know, baby. But you have to get through it."

"I will," he said, "but it might take some time."

After the movie, Emma walked Darcy to the door. He reached down and gave her a long, slow, sweet kiss. "Please be patient with me," he said.

"OK," said Emma. "Good things are worth waiting for."

———

Emma was busy the following week at work. She had a custody trial, a property distribution trial, and two briefs due. It wasn't until Thursday when she realized she hadn't heard from Darcy since their movie night on Saturday. Emma checked with Kat, and Darcy hadn't left any messages with her, either. Emma called him and left a voicemail message. He didn't return her call.

Emma left two more messages for Darcy over the weekend. When she still didn't hear from him by Monday, she started to worry. Maybe he was in a car accident? Maybe he got arrested again and was too embarrassed to call her? Monday evening Emma called Darcy four times in succession and the call went right to voicemail. Then she called a fifth time. Emma heard the line pick up, and loud background noise, as if in a restaurant or bar, came through the phone. Then the call was disconnected.

Since Emma now knew Darcy was not in the hospital or in jail, she felt angry. She couldn't believe Darcy's behavior. If he was upset with her, why didn't he talk to her about it? Why would he just ignore her and not take her calls? Emma decided not to call Darcy any more but, rather, wait for him to contact her.

Three more weeks passed. Then one Saturday evening, Emma was spending the night at Morgan's house. Emma's parents had taken Emma's three children away to the mountains for the weekend. Since Emma was free of responsibility, Morgan asked Emma to bring her dog, Sadie, and have a grown-up "sleep-over." The two of them had consumed one bottle of wine while cooking dinner, another bottle soaking in the hot tub on Morgan's deck, and were finishing off a third bottle while watching bad reality television.

"I really don't understand why Darcy would just drop off the face of the earth," complained Emma. "It's not as if we had some big argument. I asked about the status of his divorce, and he got a little testy, but everything seemed alright when he left that night."

"I think," said Morgan, "he liked things the way they were. If he's still married to someone else, he doesn't have to make any sort of commitment to you. He's separated from his wife, so he doesn't have to be committed to her, either. As they say, he's 'having his cake and eating it, too.'"

"He has definitely not been eating any of my cake," slurred Emma. "I told him we couldn't do that unless we were married."

"Well, that could certainly explain why he lost interest," said Morgan.

"And what makes you such an expert, Morgan?"

"That's obvious—I have dated thousands of men and married four of them."

Emma ran her hand through her hair and looked at Morgan. "Maybe those statistics indicate that you're the opposite of an expert on men; but, rather, you don't know anything about men, which is why none of your relationships with them work out."

Morgan rubbed out her cigarette in the ashtray. "That was just mean."

"I'm sorry. You're right. You really do know much more about men than I do. I'm just so hurt by Darcy's behavior. I was really starting to wonder if I love him."

"Maybe he realized that and that's why he ran."

"That's really a chicken response on his part," said Emma. "He told me before he was afraid of being hurt, but I thought we worked through that." Emma picked up her cell phone and started tapping buttons.

"What are you doing?" said Morgan.

"I am texting Darcy and telling him exactly what I think of his falling off the face of the earth."

"Don't do it! Never, never, ever let them see you cry, either in reality or in text!"

"I'm not crying," said Emma. "I'm giving him what for."

"No, no, no! Then he knows he's hurt you. Don't give him the satisfaction."

"He should know that he's hurt me. I don't want him to think he can get away with being inconsiderate."

"You're not his mother. Of course he can get away with being inconsiderate. What are you going to do, send him to his room?"

"I just want him to understand," said Emma.

"Fine. You can do that tomorrow if you still want to. But I learned the hard way to never call or text or e-mail a guy when drunk. You are apt to say things you will regret."

"I'm not drunk," said Emma.

"Yes, you are. You drank a bottle and a half of wine by yourself."

"I don't care," Emma stated as she juggled her phone in her hand. "I'm pushing 'send.'"

Morgan lunged for Emma's phone, but Emma held it above her head and out of Morgan's reach. The two were struggling when they heard the 'swish,' indicating the message had been sent.

"You just wait," said Morgan. "You are going to be so mortified tomorrow when you read what you just sent. Trust me on this one."

Emma still had not had any contact whatsoever with Darcy two weeks later. Even though it was clear that Darcy was broken and had a lot of issues regarding trust and commitment, Emma was inexplicably drawn to his good characteristics. Darcy was fun, caring, a good father, and a great companion.

Emma had almost convinced herself to call Darcy to try to resolve his disappearing act when Stan called her at the office. "You are not going to believe this, Emma," he said. "I was just reading online the latest appellate opinions that came out yesterday. Contessa Giovanni's murder conviction was overturned by the appellate court based on insufficient evidence."

"Please tell me you're joking," begged Emma.

"No. Go check it out yourself. Sorry. Gotta go."

Emma then had the unenviable job of breaking the news to Alexander Giovanni.

"What? What does that mean?" he demanded. "The jury found her guilty."

"The law says that even if a jury finds a defendant guilty, on appeal, the appellate court can overturn the verdict if they find that no reasonable jury could have made a finding of guilty based on the evidence put before them. In other words, they found the jury acted unreasonably. "

"I can't believe this!" said Alexander. "So now what do we do?"

"I will, once again, go in and try to get a custody hearing set as soon as possible. In the meantime, let's hope Tessa stays away from the girls."

"I think now would be the perfect time to take the girls away on a short vacation. I can't be away too long, and they can't miss too much school, but I think we can go for a week," said Alex.

"I think that would be alright," Emma said. "Just make sure I know where to contact you in the unlikely event I get us a trial date in the next week."

Emma was drafting the paperwork necessary to schedule the custody trial when Kat buzzed her over the intercom. "That guy from the F.B.I. is on the phone."

"William Stewart?"

"Yes, that's him."

"Put him through," said Emma.

"Ms. Parker. William Stewart, Federal Bureau of Investigation."

"I know, Mr. Stewart, you gave your name to my assistant."

"Right. I'm calling to let you know that Contessa Giovanni was just arrested on drug trafficking charges."

"Already? Didn't she just get out of jail yesterday?"

"Yes. And we don't want her to slip away. What is the status of your family law case?"

"I am getting ready to set the custody case again for trial in light of the fact that the murder conviction was overturned," said Emma.

"That won't be necessary. She is currently incarcerated."

"What if she makes bail?"

"That is highly unlikely. Furthermore," said Mr. Stewart, "we can't have you poking around and stirring up witnesses and jeopardizing our narcotics case. You need to hold off on scheduling that hearing."

"Mr. Stewart, I am done investigating. I am not going to be doing any poking around. This custody case needs to be resolved."

"We have been through all this before. Your handling of this minor civil matter is obstructing the prosecution of a federal crime. You need to cease and desist."

"I'll tell you what, Mr. Stewart. I'll give you one week. Then, I am going to move forward," said Emma. "I suggest you get your investigation wrapped up and your witnesses lined up by then."

"I guess that's a start. Keep in touch, Ms. Parker."

"I have no doubt you will keep in touch with me, Mr. Stewart."

Three days later, Kat rushed into Emma's office, out of breath. "Guess who I just saw leaving Jake Dubrowski's bail bond office?"

"Who?"

"Alex Giovanni's wife."

"Are you sure it was her?"

"I'm positive," said Kat.

"That's just fabulous." Emma had told Mr. Stewart she wouldn't go to the calendar judge until Monday. Alexander and the girls were scheduled to get back in town on Friday. What could go wrong over the weekend?

Emma was in kickboxing class Friday after work when Alexander Giovanni showed up at the door of the studio. "Sorry, Emma, to bother you. Your boys told me you were here. We have a problem."

Emma led Alex into the parking lot. "What's going on?"

"Tessa was just at the house. She said she's coming tomorrow to take the girls for her Saturday visitation the judge gave her when we first went to court. She can't do that, can she?"

"Let me think for a minute." Emma sat down on the curb and rubbed her forehead. "The judge just took the case off the docket—the schedule. He didn't dismiss the case. So the temporary visitation order is still valid. I can withdraw your custody petition, and since Tessa didn't file a cross-petition, the case would go away. However, I can't do that until Monday morning. The courthouse is closed now for the weekend. I'm afraid she can see the girls for her Saturday visitation if she insists on it."

"I'm not going to let her," said Alex. "It's crazy."

"As your lawyer and an officer of the court, I cannot tell you to disobey a court order. In addition, I do have to tell you that I have seen cases where one parent withholds the visitation, thinking it is in the best interest of the child, only to have the court deal with that parent harshly. I have even seen a judge give the other parent custody. Now that I think of it, that case was Judge Larson, the judge who made the temporary visitation order in your case. The court doesn't like people substituting their own judgment for that of the court when there is an order. It would be dangerous to deny her visitation. It would be one thing if you were still out of town. But Tessa knows you're here, and if you leave town now, it will be obvious you did so to disobey the court order. I'm sorry."

"Why didn't you get us into court before this happened? Why did you tell the F.B.I. you'd wait?"

"Of course, Alex, now I wish I had not agreed to wait. But even if I had gone in on the day Tessa's murder conviction was overturned, you and I both know they wouldn't have given us a trial before this Saturday. Tessa hasn't shown much interest in the girls before now. She probably just misses them and wants to touch base. She has a lot on her plate right now. I doubt she wants to deal with the added responsibility of taking care of two children."

"I don't know, Emma. I am just sick about this," said Alex. "But I am a law-abiding citizen. I follow the law, even if I disagree with it. And I don't want to take even the slightest chance that the judge would give Tessa custody of the girls. I will let her take the girls."

"It will be alright, Alex. Try not to worry too much," said Emma.

On Saturday afternoon, Emma was uneasy. Tessa's visitation with her daughters was set for 1:00 p.m. to 5:00 p.m. Alex had called Emma at 1:20 to tell her Tessa had shown up fifteen minutes late. He said Lindsay and Amber were happy to see their mother and ran to her and hugged her. Alex told Emma he had made sure Lindsay had her cell phone and that it was fully charged. He instructed her to call him if she felt uncomfortable at all for any reason during the visitation.

Everything seemed to be going according to plan, but Emma just couldn't shake a feeling of anxiety. Maybe it was because Lindsay and Amber had become so much a part of her family that she was starting to feel maternal toward them. Or maybe Alex's anxiety was rubbing off on her.

Alex called Emma at 5:15. She picked up on the first ring. "Are they back?" Emma asked anxiously.

"No."

"Are you at home?"

"Of course. Tess was supposed to bring the girls back here at five o'clock."

"Right. I'm coming over. If she gets there before I do, call me."

Emma pulled into Alex's driveway at 5:27. Alex was standing on the front steps of his house. Emma knew from his face that Tessa hadn't returned. "I'm sure she's just deliberately being late to make you worry," said Emma.

"Well, it's working," said Alex. "What do we do now?"

"Let's wait until she's an hour late," said Emma. "Then we will call the police and tell them she's in violation of a court order. It's sort of hit or miss as to whether they will actually do anything, but they definitely won't get excited about it until she's at least an hour late. Let's go inside and make some coffee or something."

"I'm so jittery right now, the last thing I need is coffee," said Alex.

"You've got a point there. Do you have any herbal tea?"

At one minute after six, Emma called the police. After a short conversation, she hung up the phone.

"What did they say?" asked Alex.

"They wanted to know where Tessa was. When I said we didn't know, they asked how they were supposed to go remove the girls from their mother? I suggested they go out looking for her. They wanted to know where I thought they should start their search. They want me to call back with a description and license plate number of the car she was driving. Do you have that information?"

"She came in a cab," said Alex.

"Do you remember the company?"

"It was yellow," said Alex.

"I guess that's something. I'll let them know."

At 7 p.m., Emma called William Stewart. "Mr. Stewart, Emma Parker. Do you, by chance, currently have a tail on Contessa Giovanni?"

"You know I can't share that information with you, Ms. Parker. Why?"

"Mrs. Giovanni got out on bail. Do you know that?"

"Yes."

"She took her children on visitation this afternoon. She was supposed to be back by five o'clock. She still hasn't returned."

"Do you know where she went?" asked Mr. Stewart.

"If I knew that, would I be calling you?" said Emma shortly.

"I will see if we can locate her. I will get back with you. If she returns, please let me know."

Emma called Morgan and advised her on the situation. Morgan insisted on joining Emma and Alex in their vigil. When Morgan arrived, she brought Chinese carry out with her. The food went cold, basically untouched.

At 8:10, Alexander's cell phone rang. He looked at the caller identification. "It's Lindsay!" he said.

Alex put the phone on speaker mode and picked up the call. "Daddy?" Lindsay said in a whisper.

"Yes, baby. Where are you?"

Lindsay started to cry. "Daddy, we are on an airplane."

"What? Baby, where are you going?" said Alex

"The sign on the desk by the tunnel to the airplane said 'Cairo,' Daddy. Isn't that in Egypt?"

"Lindsay, honey, get off the plane right now!"

"Daddy!" Lindsay yelled loudly. The line disconnected. All of Alex's return calls went directly to voice mail.

CHAPTER SEVENTEEN

"I thought you said Tessa was involved with some Afghani guys," said Alex. "So why, on earth, would she be going to Egypt?"

"It's not like you can just go on the Internet and book a flight to Kabul," said Emma. "You have to get permission to go there—a visa ahead of time—unless, of course, you sneak across the border from Pakistan or some other neighboring country. On the other hand, Egypt is a big tourist destination, and you can easily get tourist visas there and commercial flights in," Emma thought out loud. "Now, what Tessa intends to do once she's in Egypt, I haven't figured out yet. My guess is that she will meet up with her Afghani contacts and exchange money and merchandise in Egypt, or they will help her go somewhere else from there."

Emma's mind was whirring and she was speaking her thoughts aloud. "I also can't figure out why she wanted to have the children with her. The only explanation I can come up with for that one is too terrible to even think of."

"What?" Alex demanded. "What is too terrible to think of?"

"I have no indication that Tessa would actually do such a thing, but your young girls would bring a hefty price on the human trafficking market," Emma said quietly.

"You mean sell her children? Tessa could never do such a thing," said Alex.

"She probably killed Marvin," said Emma.

"She was found innocent of that charge."

"No. Her conviction was overturned. That does *not* mean she was innocent. It just means the prosecutor didn't do a thorough job of *proving* she did it. Do you think it was a coincidence that she bought a life insurance policy on her boyfriend, he turned up dead, and she tried to claim the proceeds, all within a two-month period? The jury didn't think so," said Emma.

"How did she get the girls out of the country? I have the girls' passports in my safe at the office?"

"She probably either bought fake ones on the black market or got someone to pretend he was you and sign the paperwork to get new ones, claiming they were lost or something. It's not that hard."

Alex slapped his hand on the kitchen table and stood up. "We have to get Lindsay and Amber back before she can do anything crazy with them. When can we get into court?"

"Alex, even if we get a court order giving you custody and demanding the girls be returned to you, Egypt is not going to give that order any credence. They do not have treaties with the U.S. regarding the reciprocity of family law."

"How do you know so much about Egypt?" asked Alex.

"My deceased husband did a lot of work there, and the children and I traveled with him as often as we could."

Alex paced around the table, thinking. "Let's call the F.B.I. and have them help us," he said.

"I might decide to talk to them, in spite of the fact they have ordered me to butt out," said Emma, "but even if they have the authority to arrest and detain Tessa, I don't know if they would be willing or able to bring the girls back."

"What can we do, then?"

"I can't legally advise you to do so, but if I were you, I would hire someone to go retrieve them," said Emma.

"Like a mercenary? These are my baby girls. I'm not going to have some slimy gun-for-hire go snatch them. The girls would be scared to death. What if you go get them, Emma?"

"Me? I can't go get them. I am a lawyer, not a bounty hunter."

"You're perfect. You just said you know the country; the girls trust you; you know all about Tessa and what she's up to. No one can do the job better than you. Please, Emma. Go get my children! I will pay all your expenses and pay for all your time at your exorbitant hourly rate."

Emma thought for a moment. "We would have to take Morgan with us, I think, to help out."

"Really?" said Morgan. "I am so in."

"What do you mean by 'we' and 'us?'" asked Alex. "I can't go."

"You have to go," said Emma. "You are their father. I don't have any authority to get them."

"I don't have a passport," said Alex.

"Who doesn't have a passport?"

"I never wanted to go anywhere outside the country," said Alex.

"So why do the girls have passports?" Morgan asked.

"Tess took them to France and Italy," said Alex. "It was more of her trying to be sophisticated. Can't I sign something saying you have my permission to get the girls?"

"I guess we could try that," said Emma. "But I really think you should come with us."

"You need to leave tonight," said Alex. "I'm pretty sure I can't even start working on the process of getting a passport until Monday morning. By then the girls might be lost forever!"

"I know I'm going to regret this," said Emma.

"Thank you! I love you!" cried Alex.

"Yeah, yeah," said Emma. "Prove it by transferring twenty-five-thousand dollars into my client trust account right away. I have to get online and get us plane tickets. You also need to go get me the girls' passports."

———

Emma booked two economy seats on the 2:00 a.m. Egypt Air flight from J.F.K. airport to Cairo. Before Emma left to go home and pack, she gave Morgan instructions.

"You need to pack carefully, Morgan," said Emma. "Egypt is a conservative country. No short skirts, no low-cut or spaghetti-strap shirts, and definitely no shorts," she lectured.

"All my shirts are low-cut," said Morgan.

"Then bring something to wear under them, like a camisole or tank top. No cleavage."

"Are you going to follow that rule, too?" asked Morgan.

"To the best of my ability," said Emma.

Once at home, Emma made arrangements for Claudia to stay with the children and packed her own suitcase.

"Mom, you are so lucky," said Jason, "I love, love Egypt. I wish I could go."

"I'm not going to sight-see, honey. I'm going to try to get back Lindsay and Amber."

Jasmine sniffled. "Are they going to be OK, Mommy?"

Emma gave her a hug. "I hope so, baby. I'm going to try very hard to make sure they are. You need to pray that God will protect them and make them not feel afraid. Also, pray that He will help me find them."

———

Morgan and Emma deplaned the commuter flight to New York a few minutes before 11 p.m. "If we hurry, we can catch the flight to Cairo." After checking in and checking their bags, Emma and Morgan went through security. They followed the signs to the designated gate. There was an additional security screening, and then the women found themselves in a large waiting room. The waiting area was crowded already with Egyptian families. Nearly all the women wore hijabs covering their heads, and most of them wore long, floor-length garments hiding their clothing. Emma and Morgan felt curious eyes on them.

"We don't exactly blend, do we?" Morgan whispered in Emma's ear.

"This was the cheapest and soonest flight I could find," said Emma. "It's alright; I've flown this airline before. It's just sort of no-frills."

An hour before their flight was due to take off, Morgan stood up. "I'm going to go have a cigarette before we leave."

"No, you can't," said Emma. "You would have to go back through security at least once, maybe twice. They are going to start boarding soon. You're just going to have to wait."

"The plane doesn't leave for an hour," Morgan protested.

"Why do you do this every time, Morgan? You act as if you've never flown before. It's too late."

Morgan plopped down into her chair with a sigh, took out a piece of gum, and chewed it vigorously.

"We will now begin pre-boarding of Flight 9701 to Cairo. We welcome our first-class passengers, those traveling with small children, and anyone needing special assistance to board at this time. We will begin regular boarding shortly."

Nearly every other passenger in the large waiting room leaped up from their seats and rushed toward the gate. Young, able-bodied men were pushing and shoving small children and senior citizens aside to reach the gate first.

The young American airline employee stood in the middle of the causeway and extended her arms. "Only first-class passengers, small children, and those needing special assistance at this time!" The young men closest to her began jostling and attempted to push past her.

"Step aside!" the young woman said firmly. "It's not your turn to board!" The men in the front of the crowd took a few steps back but did not step aside. A young mother with four small children was attempting to reach the front of the crowd, but she kept getting pushed back.

The airline employee held her arm in the air. "This way, ma'am," she called. "Let those with young children through, please." The crowd begrudgingly let the mother through. An elderly woman with a three-legged cane struggled through behind her. A few well-dressed men in business attire, carrying briefcases called out that they were in first-class and the crowd let them through.

After scanning the crowd, the young woman picked up the intercom microphone again. "Now, we will board rows forty-five and higher only. Forty-five and higher." The crowd all surged forward again. The airline employee was asking to see individual boarding passes and refused to allow anyone through who was not in the group she had called. Passengers shouted and jostled back and forth.

"What is wrong with these people?" Morgan asked Emma.

Emma looked amused. "Most Middle Easterners don't believe in standing in line or taking turns. In their culture, you simply push your way to the front, as these folks are doing. Waiting in line is for suckers. What is interesting is that I would guess that many of them live here in the U.S. now—or at least visit frequently—and you'd think they would have accepted the system by now."

"This is ridiculous. It's complete chaos."

A few more minutes passed. The crowd was not listening, and the airline employee was looking more and more frazzled. When one more surge of the crowd nearly knocked her off her feet, the young woman lost all patience. She fastened the nylon rope across the entrance to the causeway, climbed up on the counter, and stood above the throng of people. She grabbed the loudspeaker and shouted, "This plane is not going ANYWHERE until we get it boarded. And we are not going to get it boarded unless you all FOLLOW INSTRUCTIONS!" The crowd grew a little quieter.

"Everyone BACK AWAY FROM THE GATE, and go sit down!" she shouted. No one moved. "NOW!" she shouted, even more loudly than before. People slowly edged a little bit away from the gate.

"Not one person is getting on this plane until you all take a seat!" the airline employee threatened. The passengers looked at each other in consternation. It was occurring to them that perhaps the young woman actually meant what she said. Like slow-moving lava, and grumbling all the while, the passengers backed up and perched on the edge of the closest seats.

"Thank you," said the young woman. "Now, when I say, 'come ahead,' I want the passengers seated in rows forty and higher, and ONLY rows forty and higher, to board. If you all come rushing again, I will call airport security, and this plane will absolutely NOT leave on time. Rows forty and higher come ahead." This time, a reasonable number of passengers gathered their carry-on bags and approached the gate.

As the boarding process continued, Emma's cell phone rang. "Emma, this is Alex. I was just checking online, and I saw that Tessa used my credit card at the Four Seasons Hotel in Cairo. That seems a good place to start, so I made reservations for you and Morgan. Is that alright?"

"That's fantastic, Alex. Thank you. Even if Tessa's not there anymore, at least we may pick up some leads there. Do you have the address?"

"The website says it's on The Corniche. No street address."

"I know exactly where that is. All the big hotels are on that same strip. Our plane is boarding, Alex. I'll call you when we get there, in about fourteen hours." Emma hung up and turned off her phone.

Once Morgan and Emma were settled into their seats, Morgan said, "Well, that was painful. Let's hope the rest of the trip is easier going."

Emma stared at her. Morgan laughed. "Just kidding. I'm sure this is only the beginning. I'm going to take a sleeping pill and put myself in a coma for the next eight hours, so I am ready to tear up Cairo and get those babies back!"

"Excellent idea," said Emma. "I think I'll join you."

Emma woke up when the cabin lights came on. Sunlight was streaming in through those windows that had their shades up. The cabin attendants asked passengers to raise the remainder of the shades. Emma looked around. Her fellow passengers were waking up, their hair in various states of disarray, and their clothing askew and lint-covered from the airline blankets. There was an odd intimacy between hundreds of total strangers that had just spent the night together. Under normal circumstances, only their closest family members see them immediately upon waking. Emma took her comb out of her purse and tidied her own hair.

Emma shook Morgan awake. "Rise and shine, 'Sleeping Beauty,'" she said. "Time for breakfast."

Morgan lifted her nightshade blindfold from one eye. "I'm not hungry," she said.

"You should eat," said Emma. "It could be a while before we can find something edible."

"Let me know when breakfast gets here," sighed Morgan as she replaced her eye covering.

Before long, the attendant and her cart reached Emma and Morgan. She placed the foil-covered containers on the tray tables in front of them. Emma elbowed Morgan. Morgan groaned. Emma slowly peeled back the foil from her breakfast. Malodorous steam hit her in the face. "Oh, yuck!" said Emma. "It's fish!" Emma peeled back the corner of Morgan's food tray. Also fish.

Morgan stirred and removed her nightshade. "What is that horrendous smell?" she asked.

"Your breakfast," said Emma. "Here, have a roll." She handed Morgan the dinner roll off her tray.

As the plane landed, the passengers applauded. "I guess they're as happy as I am that the flight is over," said Morgan.

After passing through passport control, Morgan said, "I need to use the bathroom."

"You should have gone on the plane before we arrived," said Emma. "Egypt is not known for its fine public accommodations."

"I really need to find one," said Morgan.

After a bit of searching, the women located a sign that said 'W.C.' Morgan ran toward the door, and then froze once she reached the entrance. As Emma caught up, she saw the entire bathroom was in some sort of remodeling or construction and consisted of nothing but rubble. The floor had been jackhammered to bits and remnants of toilets, sinks, and stalls lay scattered on top of the heap.

"I think it's out of service," said Emma.

"Really? You're very intuitive," said Morgan.

After a thirty-minute wait at baggage claim, Morgan and Emma secured their bags, albeit a little dusty and scratched up. "Let's go find a taxi," said Emma.

As they walked out of the airport, a hot wind slapped them in the face.

"Oh, my!" Morgan exclaimed, "It is HOT! And it smells terrible!"

Emma smiled. "Welcome to Egypt!"

Emma hailed a taxi and negotiated the fare to the Four Seasons Hotel before they loaded into the car. As the cab driver put their suitcases in the trunk, Morgan eyed the cab critically and whispered to Emma, "I hope this piece of crap can make it all the way to the hotel. I thought the cabs in the Caribbean were bad, but this one makes them look fancy."

"Don't worry. If we break down, we will just catch another cab," said Emma. "Happens all the time."

"I don't doubt that a bit," said Morgan, wryly.

The cab driver left the airport area and merged onto a major road. The traffic was heavy. The closer they inched to the city center, the heavier the traffic became. Before long, the drivers crammed six or seven cars wide into three lanes. Morgan gasped as a large delivery truck came within centimeters of the side of their cab. Horns were beeping wildly and constantly. "Why is everyone honking?" Morgan asked.

"My theory is that because there are so many cars and because most of them have their side mirrors torn off, the drivers let each other know where they are by beeping. It's kind of like car sonar," said Emma. "However, my personal view is that once you get to a certain point, where everyone is honking constantly, everyone tunes it out."

Their taxi driver and everyone else around them ran through a red light. The traffic waiting to cross honked and waved their arms to no avail. "So they don't stay in their lanes, and they don't obey traffic lights?" asked Morgan.

"As I told you earlier," said Emma. "Middle Easterners aren't so much about rules. It's more of a dog-eat-dog way of life. If you want something, take it. If you hesitate or give way, the next guy will get ahead of you."

"Why is it that it's the Americans that have a reputation for being aggressive and obnoxious?"

"To tell the truth," said Emma, "I can't figure that one out, either."

Their cab battled and nudged its way onto The Corniche. "The Nile," said the cab driver, pointing to his left.

"Wow," said Morgan. "It's not as wide as I thought it would be."

"What you see is not the other side," said Emma, "but an island, of sorts."

The Nile was busy with boats of all types: small fishing boats, big fishing boats, cargo barges, yachts, tour boats, and small Faluka sailboats."

"It looks pretty dirty," Morgan commented.

"Very," said Emma. "But probably not much more so than the Potomac. I wouldn't swim in, or eat fish from, either one."

The traffic slowed to a stop. A young boy, around seven or eight years old, crossed in front of their cab. He carried above his head, like a waiter with a tray, a large square made of plywood. Stacks and stacks of pita bread were neatly balanced in rows on the board. The boy moved quickly and kept his load perfectly level.

"That's impressive," said Morgan. "I hope he doesn't step in a pothole or have a cat run in front of him."

A block further stood a white donkey. He did not seem phased by the beeping cars surging dangerously close to him. The donkey was laden with aluminum pots and pans, dangling from ropes and ties across his multi-colored blanket, which covered his back.

Even though the weather was hot and humid, the Corniche River Walk was busy with foot traffic. Older men slowly strolled arm in arm, chatting. Mothers with baby strollers and children scampering back and forth enjoyed time out of the house. Young couples maintained a respectable distance between them while slowly walking and shyly conversing.

The cab pulled up in front of the Four Seasons. A bellman opened the cab door. "Welcome to the Four Seasons," he said. Emma and Morgan climbed out. After paying the driver and handing their bags over to the bellman, the ladies walked into the hotel lobby. Four wide marble steps led up to the reception level. The reception desk was to the right. After a landing, three more steps led to the main lobby. Low, silk-cushioned sofas surrounded large coffee tables and were scattered about under the sunny atrium. A mosaic fountain gurgled in the center of it all. To the side of the lobby, next to a highly polished bar, was a shiny black grand piano.

The women made their way to the reception desk. A massive floral arrangement in a giant vase took up the center of the floor. Morgan reached out and touched a bloom. "These are *real*!" she said. "This is incredible!"

The desk clerk told them Alex Giovanni had booked two connecting mini-suites for them and had arranged for payment on his credit card. The bellman showed them to their rooms. As she walked in, Morgan said, "Wow! I am *so* glad Contessa picked this great hotel to hide out in!" The floors and countertops gleamed with copper-collared marble. Each spacious room boasted a king-sized bed, sitting area with a loveseat, chair, and coffee table, as well as a bistro table and two chairs in the corner. The balconies overlooked the Corniche and the Nile.

Emma looked at her watch. "Let's take an hour to shower and get fresh clothes. We need to go down to see a man I know that owns a gold shop near the pyramids. Dress comfortably and, of course, modestly."

"Can't I just stay here and go to bed?" Morgan asked.

"No. You need to adjust to the time zone by making yourself stay up until it's time to go to bed here. Plus, it is not appropriate, or probably even safe, for a woman to go out alone here. You are going with me. I will make you a cappuccino in this fancy little machine while you shower."

"Fine," said Morgan. "Thought it was worth a shot."

Emma knocked on the adjoining door, two cappuccinos in hand. Morgan answered the door dressed in jeans, a t-shirt, flat sandals, and a black Starbucks coffee baseball hat. Her long, blonde ponytail sprouted out of the back of the cap. "The t-shirt is a little tight, but otherwise, you look good," said Emma.

After the women enjoyed their coffee, they headed off in another cab to Giza. After the hot, dusty ride through the traffic, the cab driver pulled up at the end of a short street lined with jewelry stores and souvenir shops. Morgan stepped out of the cab and pointed down the street. "Look, Emma! The pyramids are right there! We have to go see them!"

"You'll get a chance to see them," said Emma. "We just need to talk to this man first."

As Emma and Morgan entered the small gold shop, the wrinkled man behind the counter struggled to pull himself up off his stool. "Emma, *habiibitii* [my dear]!" he cried. "Why did you not tell me you were coming?" He came around the counter and grasped Emma's right hand with both of his hands.

"Hello, Gamal," Emma said warmly. "I am sorry I didn't let you know ahead of time. I came on short notice."

"Come, come," Gamal said. "Have some tea with me." He waved at a young man in the doorway, who hurried into the back of the store and returned quickly carrying two more dusty stools, both with peeling paint. He set them down near the end of the counter. Gamal pulled a few pieces of tissue from a box and brushed off the tops of the stools.

"Sit, sit," he said. "The tea will come soon." He waved off the young man again, who disappeared into the back room.

"Tell me," said Gamal, "how is your husband? I have not seen him in a long time."

"I am sorry you have not heard, Gamal," said Emma. "Jeffrey passed away in an auto accident three years ago."

Gamal gasped and placed his right hand over his heart. "Oh, Emma, *habibbitii*, that is terrible, terrible news! I am so very sorry for you and your children. Mr. Parker was a very good friend of mine."

"I know he was, Gamal," said Emma. "He considered you a good friend, too."

"And the children?" asked Gamal.

"They are doing well. They miss their father, but they young are resilient," said Emma.

"Thanks to God; the children heal quickly," said Gamal.

Gamal's helper returned with three glasses of tea in containers that resembled shot glasses. He placed a small bowl of sugar and three spoons on the counter. Gamal served the ladies, and the three sipped tea in silence for a moment. Emma inquired about Gamal's family and learned about the marriages and births of his various children and grandchildren. After an acceptable period of small talk had lapsed, Emma told Gamal about Tessa Giovanni and her search for Lindsay and Amber.

"I know you know everyone and everything that goes on in Cairo," said Emma. "If anyone can find her, you can, Gamal."

"It is true," said Gamal. "I will see what I can find out. Come back in three or four hours, and I will tell you what I can."

Emma thanked Gamal profusely and took her leave of him. "Now we can go see the pyramids," she told Morgan, as they exited the shop. They walked the few short blocks to the entrance of the area housing the pyramids. As they reached the grounds, the shops, houses, streets, and sidewalks abruptly ended and the desert began. Once they paid their entrance fee at the booth, nothing but sand lay before them. The three pyramids, made of stone the same color as the desert, seemed to grow up out of the earth. Immediately before Emma and Morgan, in front of the Pyramids, lay the Sphinx. They headed toward the massive paws stretched before it, now somewhat eroded with the passage of centuries. On the way, several children accosted them, selling postcards and plastic replicas of the

Pyramids and the Sphinx. After shooing several away, Emma bought one strip of postcards from a particularly cute girl around three years old. After making the purchase, every time other children approached them, Emma flashed her postcards to tell them she already had some.

Morgan looked up at the Sphinx. It had the head of what appeared to be an Egyptian Pharaoh mounted on the body of a lion. "What happened to his nose?" she asked.

"The most popular explanation is that it was shot off by Napoleon's troops engaging in target practice after they conquered the area," Emma explained, "but some historians say it appears to have been removed by a hammer sometime between the Eleventh and Fifteenth Centuries. The former explanation makes more sense, though."

"I thought it would have been bigger," said Morgan.

"It really is quite large," said Emma. "It just seems small compared to the Pyramids."

The women walked the length of the Sphinx and then traversed the causeway leading up to the ruins of Khafre's Funerary Temple. A young man approached them. "You want a guide? I give you very special price," he said.

"That's alright," said Emma. "I'm the guide."

"You are a guide?" the young man said. "Do you have a license?"

"Do you?" said Emma. "Can you tell me about this path we are walking on?"

"It is very old and important," said the young man.

"Yes. It also used to lead to the banks of the Nile, at the time it was built," said Emma.

"But the Nile is way, way over there," said Morgan, pointing behind them.

"Rivers have a tendency to move and recede over time," said Emma.

"OK, have a nice day," said the want-to-be guide and walked toward a Japanese couple headed toward the Sphinx.

The women walked around the Funerary Temple and approached the middle pyramid, Khafre's Pyramid. It loomed above them, casting a giant shadow across the sand. Morgan craned her head back and looked toward the top. "Wow! Now that's much bigger than I ever imagined!"

"Isn't it amazing?" said Emma. "And this isn't even the biggest one; that one over there is the Great Pyramid and is a little bit bigger."

"I think it's hard to tell in pictures how big they are because there is nothing around to compare them to," said Morgan.

"If you look way up at the top," said Emma, "you can see the smooth limestone covering that all three pyramids used to have. Imagine how impressive they were fully covered and smooth all the way down, like marble."

"I cannot even imagine how long, and how much manpower, it took to build one of these, especially without modern machinery. A guy's got to have a pretty big ego to build this kind of tribute to himself."

"Or maybe just be really afraid that he'll be forgotten," said Emma.

A man rode up on a horse. He was leading another horse. "You want to ride a horse?" he asked.

"No, thank you," said Emma. "I have a horse."

"You have a horse?" said the man.

"Actually, I have four horses," said Emma.

The man looked at Morgan. "You want to ride a horse?"

"No, thank you," she replied, "I always ride her horses."

The man eyed Morgan's Starbucks Coffee hat. "I like Starbucks," he said.

"Who doesn't?" said Morgan

"Can I have your hat?" the man asked.

Morgan looked surprised. "Oh, I'm sorry, but I really need it to keep the sun off my face."

The man took off his dirty, sweat-stained canvas hat. "You can have my hat," he said.

Morgan wrinkled her nose, ever so slightly. "You are very kind," she said, "but I prefer to keep my own hat."

The man looked dejected and slowly rode away.

After the women walked halfway around Khafre's Pyramid, Emma pointed to the small pyramid to their left. "Do you want to go see the little pyramid before we go see the Great Pyramid?"

"No, it's really hot. I can see it well enough from here," said Morgan.

As Morgan and Emma walked toward the Great Pyramid, they again ran the gauntlet of souvenir salesmen and potential "guides." "Good Grief," said Morgan, "it's kind of hard to enjoy history while being harassed."

"Apparently, it's not a new phenomenon," said Emma. "Mark Twain visited in the mid-1800s and later wrote about the pushy salesmen." They approached the Great Pyramid and looked up at its grandeur.

"Can you believe this behemoth has endured nearly four thousand years?" said Emma. "Yet, the rock wall I built in my backyard ten years ago is falling down. Clearly, the ancient Egyptians knew a lot more about these things than I do."

As they headed across the sand, back toward the city street, Morgan and Emma passed a man who had five camels lined up. They were bedecked in colorful blankets and multi-colored pom-poms had been tied to their reins. "You want to ride a camel?" he called out to them.

"No, thank you," said Emma.

"I don't want to ride, but I want my picture taken with your camel," said Morgan.

"No, you don't," said Emma.

"Yes, I do," said Morgan.

"Don't go there," said Emma. "Once you open the door, it's very hard to get it closed."

The man looked at Emma quizzically.

Morgan approached one of the camels reclining on the ground and stood by it. She turned around to Emma. "Take my picture," she said.

"Wait, wait," said the man. "You should sit on the camel."

"No ride," said Emma. "Just a picture."

"No ride," said the man. "Just sit on camel for photo."

"Good idea," said Morgan.

"Bad idea," said Emma.

Morgan climbed on the camel. The man very quickly unwrapped his headscarf from his head and reached toward Morgan's head with it. Morgan saw him coming at the last second and screamed, stiff-arming him. "No! Touch my hair with that thing, and I'll break your arm!"

The man looked startled and the camel bellowed a loud, angry complaint. Morgan looked at Emma. "Take my picture, quick!" she said.

"Wait, wait," the man said and grabbed the camel's reins, pulling him forward.

"No, no!" said Morgan. "Just a picture. No ride!"

The man ignored her and pulled on the camel's reins. The camel bellowed again and stood up on his back legs first, causing Morgan to pitch forward. She screamed.

"Hold on very tightly!" called Emma. "Lean back!" Morgan grabbed the horn of the saddle with both hands and leaned back as the camel struggled up on his front legs, as well.

"OK, now take the picture," said Morgan. Emma snapped a picture.

The man started to lead the camel across the sand. The other four camels struggled to their feet and started to follow. "No! No ride!" said Morgan. "Stop! Let me off!" The man kept walking, his small caravan following. Emma, laughing and shaking her head, trudged through the sand, trying to catch up.

When Emma reached the plaza near the ticket booth, Morgan and the man were arguing over the fee. He was demanding an outrageous fee for a "camel ride," and Morgan was insisting that all she was paying for was a picture. Emma gave the man twenty dollars, grabbed Morgan's hand, and walked briskly toward the exit. The man continued to complain for all those around to hear but did not follow them.

Emma looked at her watch. "I'm hungry," she said. "Let's eat and then go back to see Gamal." Emma headed across the street. Morgan followed. They entered Pizza Hut. Morgan laughed, "This is so juxtaposed! A symbol of modern culture is across the street from these symbols of antiquity."

"Wait until you see the best part," said Emma. After the women placed their order, they went upstairs to the dining room area. A large picture window overlooked the Pyramids. The red Pizza Hut logo was stenciled on the middle of the window, making it appear as if the Great Pyramid itself bore the trademark.

"I have to take a picture of this," said Morgan.

After eating, the women went back to Gamal's shop. Gamal was with a customer when they entered. Emma and Morgan browsed until the woman left.

Gamal beckoned them to the counter. "I believe this woman you seek is here in Cairo. A woman meeting her description, along with two young golden-haired little girls, has been seen around the more, uh, unsavory people about. They say she is under the influence of drugs and very confused. She is also taking the children to bars and nightclubs and drinking alcohol in front of the children. This is very, very shameful, and dangerous, as well. There are many people that could hurt her and the children. She should not be doing these things, particularly as a mother."

"I agree," said Emma. "That is why we want to get the children and return them to their father."

"That would be the very best thing," said Gamal. "Please, tell me where you are staying. I will try to find out this woman's current location and let you know."

"Thank you so much, Gamal," said Emma. "The children's father appreciates your help so much!"

"I will do anything for you, Madam Emma," said Gamal. "You and Mr. Jeffrey have been a friend to me and my family for many years."

Emma and Morgan took a taxi back to the hotel. After freshening up, relaxing a bit, and changing clothes, they met in the hotel lobby. The hotel was offering "Happy Hour" drink and appetizer specials. They were enjoying a drink and some hummus when a voice behind them said, "What a small world! What brings you ladies to Cairo?"

Emma and Morgan turned around. "Oh, hello, Mr. Dubrowski," said Emma. "We're just here on a little vacation. How about you?"

"Yeah, me, too," Jake said, "just a little *R* and *R*."

"Wow, what a coincidence," said Morgan flatly.

"It really is," said Jake. "Gotta go. See you around."

"Not if I can help it," Emma said under her breath.

Morgan looked at Emma. "Guess he got word that Tessa jumped bail."

"And, more importantly, he also got word that she came here," said Emma. "I wonder where he gets his information."

After Happy Hour, Emma and Morgan took a walk along the Nile. They didn't last very long, however, because mosquitoes swarmed them. "Do you know how many diseases are mosquito-born?" inquired Morgan.

"More than I'd care to know, I'm sure," said Emma.

When Emma got back to her room, she had a message from Gamal. She called him back on the number he left. "Emma," said Gamal, "I found her. She just left Cairo with the girls on a yacht headed for Upper Egypt. The yacht is owned by rich, young Saudi playboys. I don't feel good about those little girls being around those guys. If you fly up there in the morning, you should arrive at about the same time. I have family there. You can stay with my sister, and we can find out where the woman and the girls are staying. I will call you in an hour or so with your travel details."

CHAPTER EIGHTEEN

T he small propeller plane made a bumpy landing at the Luxor airport. The passengers, the majority of whom were, clearly, excited Western tourists, pushed and shoved their way off the aircraft and down the stairs. The tarmac was so hot that waves rose from the surface, distorting the view of the shuttle bus. The sweaty passengers pushed their way onto the bus, jockeying one another with carry-on bags. Some of the more observant travelers nervously eyed the young soldiers standing on either side of the stairway, holding machine guns.

As they surged into the small, dusty terminal, they heard a woman's voice calling, "Morgan! Emma!" They followed the sound of the voice and spotted a round, middle-aged woman in an abaya and hijab, waving her arm in the air. Emma and Morgan walked over to her. The woman had a friendly, spherical face to match her body, with rosy cheeks and big, liquid brown eyes.

"*Ahlan*, welcome!" she said, warmly. "My name is Maha. I am Gamal's sister." Maha grabbed Morgan and kissed her on both cheeks. Morgan stood stiffly, looking startled. Emma stepped forward.

"Hello, Maha. I'm Emma," she said, leaning in and kissing Maha on either cheek. "It is so nice to meet you!"

"And I am so happy to finally meet you," said Maha. "Gamal speaks about you and your dear husband all the time. You have been so generous with Gamal over the years. I am so sorry to learn about your husband's passing. I, too, lost my husband recently."

"Thank you so much," said Emma. "I am sorry to hear of your loss."

"Let's get your bags," said Maha. "My son is waiting outside with a taxi."

As they emerged onto the street from the baggage claim area, an Egyptian man in his late thirties jumped out of the back seat of a waiting taxicab and hurried toward them.

"Please, let me take your bags," he said eagerly. "My name is Abdul-Rahman, Maha's son." The three women squeezed into the back seat of the taxi and Abdul-Rahman climbed in front with the driver.

"How was your time in Cairo?" he asked. "Did you see many demonstrations?"

"No," Emma replied. "Surprisingly, we didn't see any. Of course, we didn't go anywhere near Tahrir Square and stayed mainly in the tourist areas. Have you had much turmoil here in Luxor?"

"When the 'Arab Spring' first broke out, there were a few demonstrations here. However, things have, for the most part, calmed down in this part of the country. The local people are very dependent on tourism for their livelihoods and are not anxious to do anything that would scare away business. They all remember 1997—too well."

"What happened in 1997?" asked Morgan. Maha glared at her son, willing him to keep quiet.

"It was very unfortunate," said Abdul-Rahman. "Almost sixty tourists were gunned down at Deir al-Bahri, the Temple of Hatshepsut. For years afterward, tourism was way down because the tourists were afraid to come here. The Egyptian government greatly increased security and was very harsh on anyone who did anything to jeopardize the tourist industry. It took a long time, but the level of tourism eventually regained its previous level. However, we all remember those terrible days. I am afraid Cairo tourism is now suffering."

"Now that you mention it," said Emma. "The hotel area and the pyramids were a lot less crowded than I have ever seen them."

Abdul-Rahman shook his head. "It is very difficult. People want reform and change, but they cannot afford to lose their means of income in the process. The children must be fed. Politics is a luxury."

Once they reached the town of Luxor, the cab wove its way through narrow, littered; streets of modest houses. They eventually stopped in front of a small, one-story, stucco sand-colored building. "This is our house," said Maha.

As they entered the front door, the sturdy stone house with its shuttered windows provided respite from the sun and the marble floors were cool. "Please, just leave your bags here by the door," said Maha. "My son will see they get to your room." Maha showed them into the living room. Several low-cushioned sofas were covered with floral-designed cotton fabric. The sofas surrounded a low wooden table that stretched half the room in length. Emma and Morgan sank into the sofas. Morgan folded her long legs, but her knees still rose to nearly level with her chin. Emma giggled, and Morgan tilted her knees to one side, lowering them to a less ridiculous height.

Maha excused herself and disappeared into an adjoining room. She returned shortly after with a round plastic tray holding four glasses. "Please," she said, "I have made some lemonade with mint. I hope you will find it very refreshing." Emma and Morgan sampled their drinks as Abdul-Rahman re-entered the room.

"My mother makes the best lemon mint in town," he said, picking up a glass. "I hope you like it."

"Lemon mint is one of my very favorite things about Egypt," said Emma.

"I can see why," said Morgan. "This is fabulous."

"I thought you ladies might be hungry after your trip," said Maha. "I have made you a small lunch."

"You really didn't have to put yourself out, Maha," said Emma.

"Mother likes nothing more than cooking for guests," said Abdul-Rahman.

"It's no trouble at all," said Maha.

"Well, then, we would be happy to have some lunch," said Emma.

Maha brought in another tray bearing four small pottery bowls. She set the tray on the table and distributed the bowls.

"This is kusherie," said Abdul-Rahman. It is a very traditional, everyday food made of lentils and rice, topped with a tomato sauce, and garnished with caramelized onions."

"It smells delicious," said Morgan.

After they finished eating, Maha suggested Emma and Morgan take a little rest. "I hope you don't mind sharing a room," she said. "Our house is a modest one, and we have a large family."

"It is not a problem at all," Emma assured her. "We are so appreciative of your generous offer to host us. We really could have stayed at a hotel."

"Oh, no," said Maha. "Only strangers stay at a hotel. You are like family to us. When Gamal told us you were coming, I insisted you stay here."

Maha showed Morgan and Emma to a small clean room. It held two twin beds, neatly made up in a similar floral fabric as the sofas, a small wooden dresser, and a wooden straight-back chair. After Maha left the room, Morgan flopped down on one of the beds.

"Why aren't we staying in a hotel?" she asked.

"Because Gamal and his family are helping us. They would be offended if we stayed in a hotel. We don't want to offend them because I like them, but also because they know a lot of people and have a lot of connections. If we are with them, we will be closer to the information. Also, we are less conspicuous here and less likely to run into danger."

"We chased drug dealers to a Middle Eastern country," said Morgan. "It seems sort of likely we will run into danger."

"Which is precisely why it makes sense to limit that danger when possible. You will survive the accommodations."

"I know I will. I just have to whine a little in the process," said Morgan. "It's my nature."

The women had been resting about forty minutes when Maha knocked on the door. "Miss Emma," she said, "I am sorry to bother you, but Gamal is on the telephone. He has some information for you."

Emma learned from her telephone conversation with Gamal that his cousin, a cab driver, informed him some Saudis had arranged for him to pick up six passengers from their yacht anchored in the Nile and take them to the West Bank area. Apparently, the cab driver was on his way to make the pick-up.

Emma asked Abdul-Rahman why he thought the Saudis and Tessa would be going to the Valley of the Kings area.

"It's a desolate area," he said. "Because there are tourists walking around in the area, people don't look suspicious being there, as you would if out in the barren desert. On the other hand, because it is so spread out, the guards and tourist police are rarely close enough to really hear or see what is going on. It is the perfect place for a clandestine meeting."

Emma roused Morgan and told her to dress for sand and heat. Abdul-Rahman told them where to catch a launch boat from the East Bank to the West Bank of the Nile. When Maha learned where they were going, she objected.

"It is the hottest part of the day!" she said. "You will wilt in this heat! Wait until later to go see the tombs."

"If we were sight-seeing," said Emma, "that would be an excellent idea. However, we need to find these little girls before they are lost forever. We are tough; we will survive."

"At least let me send some sweets and ice water with you," said Maha.

As Morgan and Emma were heading out the door, Abdul-Rahman told them he had called his cousin, Yusef, who was a cab driver in the tourist area on the West Bank. "He will be waiting for you at the launch parking lot," said Abdul-Rahman. "He is willing to drive you wherever you need to go. You will know him because he will be waving a gold scarf."

The sun beat down on Emma and Morgan as they struggled up the hill from the dock toward the taxi lot. Morgan repeatedly dabbed her forehead with a tissue. Emma noticed the tissue was becoming a tan color. "Are you wearing foundation?" she asked.

"Of course," said Morgan. "I don't leave the house without my face properly made up."

"It's one hundred and ten degrees!"

"Which is why I am going to have to touch up in the cab," said Morgan.

As the group of tourists approached the taxi lot, the drivers were calling out and waving their arms. "You want a good price?" one man yelled as they walked by.

"I have very special car!" promised another.

"Remember, don't make eye contact," Emma told Morgan.

After dodging around several drivers and telling a few flat out to leave them alone, Morgan spotted the driver waving a gold scarf. "Look, Emma, there's our guy," she said. Emma waved back at Yusef.

Introductions were made and the women slid into the back seat. Mercifully, Yusef had the air conditioning turned up full blast, and the cab was blissfully chilly. Yusef twisted around in his seat to face Emma and Morgan.

"Abdul-Rahman told me that you are looking for two Saudi men with a blonde woman and two little girls. While I was waiting for you, I was driving around. I saw a group that sounds like you describe. They were walking down the road between the tombs of Ramses II and the Sons of Ramses II. However, there were two other men with them. Not Saudis. Not Egyptian. Maybe Persian or Afghan. I think they are planning something not honest. I worry about the woman and the daughters."

"We worry, too," said Emma. "Can you take us near that area but where we won't be seen by them?"

Yusef quickly maneuvered his taxi out of the crowded parking lot and headed up the dusty main road. The landscape before them was rolling hills of sand, going on for as far as they could see. The sides of the hills were dotted with black patches, indicating the entrances to tombs or other cave-like formations.

"Wow!" said Morgan. "Look at those guys!" The taxi was passing two enormous stone statues of pharaohs seated on thrones. Time had eroded their faces, and the one on the right looked as if it had been smashed to pieces at some point and reassembled, giving a jigsaw-like appearance.

"Those are the Colossi of Memnon," said Yusef. "They are thought to be built by Amenhotep III, but the Graeco-Roman travelers thought them to be statues of Memnon and his mother, Eos." Yusef made a quick stop so Emma could purchase entrance tickets for the tombs.

As the taxi continued on, they passed more tombs on the main road. Morgan saw they were marked by small, unassuming placards on short posts. Each placard bore the name of the inhabitant and a number.

Yusef turned left onto a side road, just before a large mound of sand. He pulled the taxi over to the right and stopped. "The place where I saw them is just up the main road behind us. He handed them a tattered guidebook.

"Cover your light hair," Yusef said. "That way you won't be so noticeable. Wear your sunglasses and hold the book up, as if consulting it. Maybe you can come upon them unnoticed. I will wait for you here."

Morgan and Emma wrapped their heads in the silk scarves Maha had given them. Emma picked up the backpack containing their water, snacks, flashlight, and other supplies. She handed the guidebook to Morgan. "Let's go."

As the women crested the hill on the main road, they saw a group of people gathered in front of one of the tombs. As they approached, they discerned it was a group of elderly tourists. No sign of Tessa or any of her companions.

"Excuse me," said Emma. "We have managed to get separated from the rest of our group. I wonder if you might have seen them. We are looking for my sister, a pretty blonde woman, and my two young nieces, also blondes. They have local tour guides with them, as well. Have you seen such a group?"

A gray-haired woman wearing a flowered skirt and high-topped sneakers nodded. "As a matter of fact, we did pass them just a while ago. We were coming down the hill and they were going up. I saw them just up there, between those two tombs." The woman indicated an area approximately fifty yards up the hill. "I have to tell you, though, those guides were not being very gentlemanly. They were hurrying your family along and were speaking in very unkind voices. I heard the little girl ask for water, and one of the men told her to 'Shut up.' I would make sure they do not get a good tip, if I were you."

"Do you know which tomb they entered?" asked Morgan. "Because they are not on the road now."

"I'm sorry, honey," said the elderly woman. "Once they were behind me, I did not look back. I don't know where they went."

"You have been very helpful," said Emma. "Have a wonderful rest of your trip."

Emma and Morgan hurried up the road. Morgan's scarf slipped back on her head and her pale blonde hair fluttered in the hot breeze. The tomb on the left had a sign indicating "Number 6," the tomb of Ramses IX. A young guard lounged on a folding chair, tipped back on its back legs. He languorously chewed on a drinking straw. As the women approached, he shamelessly ran his eyes up and down the full length of Morgan's form.

"I got this," Morgan quietly said to Emma. Morgan sauntered up to the guard and stood so close to him that he couldn't put the front legs of the chair down unless he bumped into Morgan. He remained tipped back.

"Hello," said Morgan. "Do you speak English?"

The guard smiled widely. "I do. Do you speak English?"

"Of course," Morgan replied. "I was wondering—could you possibly help us out? My friend and I have become separated from our group and perhaps you have seen them. There is a woman, blonde, like me, two young blonde girls, and some Arab men."

The guard said nothing for a moment, drinking Morgan in. "What do you want with those guys?" he finally responded. "They are not Egyptians. Egyptian men are gentlemen. We know how to treat a lady."

"Great! You have seen them, then," said Morgan.

"I did not say I have seen them."

"How did you know, then, that the men were not Egyptian?" Morgan retorted. "I merely said they were Arabs. You would have had to see them to know they weren't Egyptian."

"Oh, you are a smart one, aren't you? But not so smart; two of them are not Arabs. I think they are Afghani. Afghanis and Saudis together. I think they are not good men. You beautiful ladies should stay away from them."

"We totally agree," said Morgan. "We are actually trying to convince our friend, the lady with them, to come with us instead."

"I think that is a very good idea. But perhaps the men will not be happy about that."

"I don't really care if those guys are happy or not," said Morgan.

"I would be very happy if you were with me," said the guard. He held out his hand. "My name is Mohammed."

Morgan placed her hand in his. "My name is Morgan. I am pleased to meet you."

"The pleasure is all mine," gushed Mohammed, continuing to hold onto Morgan's hand.

"So, Mohammed, can you tell me where our friend and her daughters are?"

Mohammed thought for a second. "I know they went into this tomb here." He indicated toward the entrance behind him. "But I don't remember if they came out or not. There are so many tourists . . ."

Emma stepped forward. "Thank you so much, Mohammed." She handed him two entrance tickets and a crumpled, dirty Egyptian bill. "You are too kind. Come on, Morgan."

Morgan extracted her hand from Mohammed's clasp. "I'll see you soon, my friend," she purred.

"I will be anxiously awaiting your return," said Mohammed.

Emma and Morgan had to stoop over to fit through the doorway. The way before them was a narrow, steep, downward-sloping passageway. The walls and roof appeared to be dusty rock. The floor was packed sand. Horizontal strips of narrow wood had been placed in regular intervals to prevent slipping underfoot. The women's figures blocked the bright sunlight from outside and cast long, dark shadows down the tunnel. The end of the passageway was not visible from the top. Emma pulled a small flashlight from the backpack and switched it on.

"It looks like there is only one way in and one way out," said Emma. "If they are down here, we have to run into them."

"Won't that be a fun encounter," commented Morgan.

The two worked their way slowly downward, Emma leading the way. After a bit, the passage narrowed slightly, and they could hear voices coming from below them. Morgan's breathing became heavier and faster.

"How long is this tunnel?" she asked.

"It shouldn't be too much longer," said Emma. "The pharaohs intentionally hid their burial chambers in hopes of thwarting grave robbers. Unfortunately, it usually didn't work. Nearly all of the burial chambers were robbed not long after the pharaohs died."

The voices grew louder, and a small group of tourists appeared, making their way up the sloping passageway.

"They aren't really going to try to pass us, are they?" said Morgan worriedly.

"It would appear so," said Emma.

"Oh, heck no!" said Morgan. "I can't do this, Emma. I will wait for you at the top." Morgan turned around and headed up the ramp.

"Morgan! You can't just leave me to face them alone!"

"I'm sorry, Emma. I have claustrophobia. I can't stay in here!" she called over her shoulder. Morgan moved quickly toward the entrance.

"At least I didn't let her hold the flashlight," said Emma, to no one in particular.

As the approaching tourists moved upward, Emma squinted to make out their faces. Tessa and the girls were not in the group. When the group met Emma and was squeezing by, Emma asked, "Is there anyone else down there?"

"Oh, yes," a ruddy-faced portly woman replied. "There are scores of people still below."

Emma continued downward a few minutes more. Suddenly, the tunnel ended and opened to a large antechamber. The walls were colorfully decorated with ancient depictions of snakes, a variety of animals, and some scary, demonic-looking creatures. A small group of tourists was clustered at the far end of the antechamber, listening to their tour guide. Emma quickly ascertained that Tessa and the girls were not in the group. Emma squeezed past that assembly and entered a small hallway. At the end of the hallway, a tour guide was explaining to a young European couple that the symbols on the wall were the cartouche symbols of Ramses IX.

As Emma approached the stairway leading down beyond the hallway, she could hear voices coming up from the burial chamber below. She listened closely. She could hear the voices of men, women, and even what sounded like a young girl. Emma's heart beat faster. Emma felt around in her pants pocket and wrapped her fingers around a small pocketknife. She wasn't sure what good it would do her against four men, but it felt better than being completely unarmed.

Emma stealthily descended the stairway. She reached the entrance to the burial chamber. Concealing herself to the side of the doorway, Emma peeked her head around the opening. The burial chamber was beautiful! Emma had never visited this tomb before. The ceiling was painted a deep blue and then covered with thousands of tiny gold stars. A large depiction of a goddess stretched over the ceiling, resting in the "sky," as if hovering over the earth.

Emma forced her attention back to the inhabitants of the burial chamber. Immediately, her eyes were drawn to a petite, blonde woman. Her back was toward Emma. In front of the woman, also with their backs to Emma, were two young, blonde girls. Emma started to breathe faster. But then, Emma spied a pale, bearded, European standing in profile next to the woman. The other individuals in the group also appeared to be European, not Middle Eastern. The group was facing a tour guide. As Emma listened closely, she realized the guide was speaking French, as were the individuals in the group. Tessa and the girls were not there!

Emma turned around and ran back toward the entrance of the tomb. She realized she had just wasted precious time on a false assumption.

Emma burst out of the tomb entrance into blinding sunlight. As her eyes adjusted to the light, Emma saw Morgan sitting on Mohammed's folding chair. Mohammed was patting Morgan's shoulder. Morgan was breathing heavily and taking sips from a bottle of water.

Emma looked annoyed. "Are you still that upset from your bout of claustrophobia? You need to get over it because they are not in there. We need to move on."

Morgan shook her head but said nothing. Mohammed spoke up. "Something happened while you were gone," he said. "Miss Morgan came out of the tomb and was walking around up the road, trying to calm herself. I was distracted by a large group of tourists asking me all sorts of annoying questions. When they finally moved away from me, I looked up the road, toward the turnoff to the tomb of Merneptah and saw a man dragging Miss Morgan toward a sand dune. Miss Morgan was kicking the sand all around and screaming. I yelled at him, grabbed my gun, and ran that way. The man pushed Miss Morgan to the ground, kicked her in the side, and ran up around the curve. I called on my radio for help, and the tourist police are looking for him."

"Did you see Tessa or the girls?" Emma asked Morgan.

Morgan shook her head. "I didn't even see that guy until he jumped me from behind and wrapped his arm around my throat."

"I cannot believe he was so bold as to attack her here, with guards and tourist police all around," said Mohammed.

"No one said they were smart," said Emma. "Are you alright, Morgan?"

Morgan rubbed her side. "I think my ribs are a little bruised, and I am shaken up a bit, but I am fine."

Emma looked at Mohammed. "Thank you. You are our hero." Mohammed beamed. "We can be sure they aren't around this area any longer, knowing that security is looking for them. Let's get you back to Maha's house. You can take a little rest, and we will try to figure out what to do next."

———

Back at Maha's house, the women took showers and Morgan lay down for a nap. Emma and Abdul-Rahman sat in the parlor, enjoying a cold drink. She filled Abdul-Rahman in on the whole story about Tessa Giovanni.

"I suspected she was getting her drug supply from some Afghanis," Emma explained. "What I don't understand is the connection with the Saudis and how they ended up here in Egypt."

"When the Taliban was in control in Afghanistan, they were also in tight control of the poppy market and the drugs derived from poppies. That's the main way they funded their political and terrorist activities," said Abdul-Rahman. "However, after the U.S. invaded Afghanistan, the poppy trade continued but was less controlled. Different players got involved and are now selling wherever they can. Afghanistan is not that easy to get into unless you have internal connections. Therefore, the growers and their agents take the drugs out of Afghanistan and transfer them to other traffickers. Relatively recently, rich Saudis have been getting richer by trafficking drugs. They have the connections and resources to travel freely throughout the Middle East. Egypt depends heavily on tourism for income. Visas are easy to get, and a lot of tourists are coming and going. It's easy for foreigners to conduct black market business in Egypt without detection. I would suppose that this woman, Tessa, either originally planned to meet these Saudis and use them as middlemen, or she intended to meet up with the Afghanis but enlisted the help of the Saudis when she felt she was being threatened or pursued. Another possibility is that the Saudis didn't have anything to do with the drug business, but she just used them to further her purposes, and they were happy to be used, hoping to gain some sexual favors in return."

"But how would Tessa know how to make all these connections?" asked Emma.

"You said she was previously married to a Saudi and lived there. She was probably a shady individual back then and learned how the underworld worked. Also, she obviously had the Afghani connections back in the U.S. Somehow, bad eggs always seem to manage to find each other."

"How do you know all this?"

"In my younger days, some of my cousins got involved in some bad business and tried to pull me into it. Fortunately, I decided very early on that I did not want to go down that path. I went to the U.S. for college to get away from them."

"Now what do you think we should do?" asked Emma.

"Let's hope they didn't make the connections they hoped to make out at the Valley of the Kings today. If that's the case, they will be looking to plan another rendezvous. Popular tourist places seem to be their locales of choice. I guess they are hoping to get lost in the crowd, and since they have a blonde woman and two young girls with them, they can't move unnoticed among the local neighborhoods. I propose you go into Luxor tonight and look around Luxor Temple and the Temples of Karnack. Maybe you'll get lucky," said Abdul-Rahman.

"It seems as if luck is the only way we are going to find them," said Emma.

"We will also keep asking around the members of our very large family for any news," he said.

After dinner, Morgan seemed revived and agreeable regarding a trip downtown. It was decided that Abdul-Rahman would drop Maha and the women off at the Temple and that he and Yusef would go hang around the coffee shops with the local men to see if they could pick up any gossip about Tess and her entourage.

As the taxi drove past the Temples of Karnak and approached the Luxor Temple, Emma was awe-struck. She had seen both landmarks several times during the day but had never seen them at night. The mammoth structures were backlit by hundreds of orange- and gold-tinted lights. The buildings loomed up out of the sand and cast long shadows over the surrounding village. The recesses and shadows seemed particularly dark and eerie, while the brightly lit surfaces seemed almost festive.

The taxi dropped them off at the entrance to Luxor Temple. Maha kissed and embraced the ticket-seller, another nephew, and he waved the group in without payment. Maha and Emma walked arm-in-arm, while Morgan strode ahead. All three of them tried to appear nonchalant while scanning the faces of the tourists for signs of Tessa or the girls.

Morgan stopped in front of an epic pink granite obelisk. "I absolutely love this!" she said. I have never seen *pink* granite before! This is fabulous!"

"Pink granite is naturally found here in Egypt," said Maha. The ancient Egyptians obviously thought it was wonderful, too. They used it to carve out their most precious monuments."

Behind the pink obelisk loomed the colossal statues of Ramses II, standing guard between three massive pillars. "These pharaoh guys just couldn't get over themselves," said Morgan. "They had such big egos they had to make all these mammoth monuments of themselves to match their egos."

"Or, maybe," said Morgan, "they realized how tiny and insignificant they were in comparison to the gods and in the big scheme of things. In a world where dynasties could last for hundreds of years, maybe they were afraid of being nothing but a tiny blip on the timeline, so they exerted such effort to be remembered."

"These statues and monuments have survived thousands of years," said Maha, "so, in some way, their efforts were rewarded. We know today who they were. They have not been forgotten."

The three entered the temple, all the while looking for signs of Tessa. They entered the great court of Ramses II. They looked behind the double rows of lotus-bud capital columns to see who might be lurking in the shadows. Maha pointed out the remains of the thirteenth-century mosque of Abu al-Haggag on one side of the great court.

Similarly, they wove in and out of the papyrus columns of the colonnade of Amenhotep III, looking each tourist in the eye. Maha waved at the security guard who gave them curious looks. He slowly waved back. The group passed through the hypostyle hall and was in Amenhotep III's birth room, examining the scenes depicting his deified conception and birth, when a voice behind them said, "What are you doing here?"

All three women spun around. Jake Dubrowski stood with his arms crossed, a sarcastic grin on his face.

"Probably the same thing you are," said Emma.

"I seriously doubt that," said Jake.

"We want to get the Giovanni girls back to their father, where they belong," said Morgan.

"You see—we are not here for the same thing. I have no interest in the children. I am only here to get Contessa Giovanni and bring her back to custody, so I don't lose the bond I posted," said Jake. "Have you seen them?"

"We tracked them earlier today to the Valley of the Kings but didn't actually lay eyes on them," said Emma.

"Well, they're not here in the Luxor Temple. I've searched it thoroughly," Jake stated.

"Don't be offended if we don't take your word for it, Jake," said Emma. "Come on, Morgan, Maha." Emma headed out of the birth room and Morgan and Maha followed.

Once Jake was out of sight and earshot, Morgan said, "Emma, obviously, Jake wasn't lying about them not being here. If they were here, he would be chasing them, not standing around chatting us up."

"I know," said Emma. "But I just don't trust him. He's a weasel."

"He gives off a bad spirit," said Maha. "I can feel it."

"That's just his cheap cologne," said Morgan.

"Let's take a taxi up to the Temples of Karnak," Maha suggested. "There's going to be a sound and light show there later; maybe the people you are looking for will try to hide in the crowd in the dark." Emma and Morgan agreed.

After getting out of the taxi, the women walked the path to the ticket booth between two rows of massive, ram-headed sphinxes. "Everything in this town is gigantic!" said Morgan. "For the first time in my life, I feel short."

The three followed the flow of the crowd heading toward the seating area for the sound and light show. They passed through the Great Court and through the Great Hypostyle Hall. The latter was a forest of enormous columns, each one covered in hieroglyphics, cartouche symbols, and depictions of scenes of Egyptian life and the fantastic deeds of the pharaohs.

"This doesn't make any sense," said Morgan. "I always thought columns were erected for the purpose of holding something up. No roof could have been heavy enough to warrant so many columns."

"I think someone just thought columns were really cool and provided an interesting blank space on which to do artwork," said Emma.

As Emma, Morgan, and Maha passed out of the temple to the open area around the Sacred Lake, Morgan grabbed Emma's elbow and pulled her to a stop. "Emma, look! Over there, under the giant bug! Isn't that Lindsay and Amber?"

"Quick, come here!" said Emma, gesturing behind a broken obelisk lying on its side. Morgan and Maha followed her. The three peered around the end of the piece of granite. On the edge of the lake was a huge statue of a scarab beetle. Huddling underneath the back legs of the beetle were the Giovanni girls, holding on to one another. The girls were looking toward the lake. Emma followed their gaze. Although several tourists stood between Emma and the lake, she could make out two men struggling with a thin, blonde woman. Tessa!

Contessa Giovanni was staggering as she walked and talking loudly. The two men were trying to subdue her and steer her toward the edge of the lake. Tessa broke free and tried to run but almost immediately fell backward and sat on the ground.

Just then, a male figure ran toward Tessa and the two men. Emma realized the man was Jake Dubrowski. Jake grabbed Tessa under the arm and tried to bring her to her feet. One of the men ran toward Jake. Jake punched the man in the jaw with his free hand and the man staggered back. The second man jumped on Jake's back, bringing him to the ground on top of Tessa. The first man then returned and pried Jake's hand from Tessa's arm. He then placed his heel on the front of Jake's shoulder and rolled him off Tessa. The second man rolled to the side, taking Jake with him. He grabbed Jake by the back of the shirt and banged his face repeatedly into the ground. The first man was dragging Tessa around the edge of the lake. Tessa looked dazed and confused and her efforts to resist were ineffectual. The second man got off Jake and ran to join the first man and Tessa.

Emma and Morgan left their shelter behind the obelisk and began to run toward the girls. They had covered half the distance when Jake saw them and then spotted the girls. He leaped up from the ground and grabbed each girl by the back neck of the shirts, dragging them to their feet. The girls screamed. Many of the bystanders stopped and watched disapprovingly, but no one moved to stop him. Before they could reach him, Jake pushed through the crowd, steering the girls into the temple. Emma and Morgan gave chase. Maha trailed behind.

Emma caught sight of Jake and the girls as they disappeared into the maze of columns in the Great Hypostyle Hall, which they had recently passed through. "Lindsay! Amber! It's Emma! I'm coming to save you!" Emma yelled.

"Help, Emma, help!" the girls called out. The girls' cries were suddenly muffled.

"If you hurt them, Dubrowski, I'll cut your balls off!" Morgan screamed.

Emma and Morgan tried to ascertain Jake's whereabouts by the sounds of running feet and the reaction of the tourists as he stampeded by them. "Stop that man!" called Emma. "He's a kidnapper!"

Some helpful people pointed toward the Great Court and the exit. Emma and Morgan dashed into the Great Court. No sign of Jake and the girls. As they emerged from the temple, Emma saw a blonde ponytail disappear behind one of the sphinxes.

"You go down the right side, Morgan. I'll take the left," said Emma. The two split off.

Emma and Morgan rejoined each other at the ticket booth, out of breath. "Did you see them?" asked Emma.

"I caught sight of them a couple times but couldn't catch up," Morgan puffed.

"Me, too. How did he get those girls to move so fast?"

Maha came straggling up to them. She, too, was winded. "I will talk to the tourist police and get them to put out a call," she said. "You two go look in the village and see if you can catch that bad man."

Emma and Morgan began jogging again. The street with lined with sidewalk cafés and souvenir shops. The women slowed at each establishment, looking inside for signs of Jake or the girls. As they jogged past one café with several men sitting outside, who were drinking coffee and smoking shisha, a voice called out, "Morgan!"

The women slowed. The voice belonged to Mohammed, the guard from the Valley of the Kings. Morgan quickly explained about Jake taking the girls.

"So this is another guy? An American?" he asked.

"Yes. It's a long story, which we don't have time to tell," said Morgan.

"I will help you look," said Mohammed. He tossed some bills on the table and took off down the street with Morgan and Emma.

After thirty minutes of weaving in and out of the streets around the Temples, Emma and Morgan were worn out. "I think we can safely say we lost them," said Emma.

"I thought Jake said he didn't want the girls," Morgan said.

"Like you said, his word can't be trusted," said Emma.

While the three were sitting, drinking several bottles of water, and having a snack, Emma and Morgan filled Mohammed in on the latest events and Jake's involvement. "Tomorrow's my day off," said Mohammed. "Let me do some asking around. Tell me where you are staying, and I will meet you there in the morning and help you look for the girls."

"We are staying with our friend, Maha," said Emma. "Maha! She must be worried sick! We forgot all about her! We need to get back to the ticket booth. When they returned to the ticket booth, the Temples were closed, but the security guard told them Maha left a message for them to meet her at the house.

Emma was sure she would be unable to sleep, due to her worry for Lindsay and Amber. However, as soon as she lay down in her bed, she passed out and did not stir until morning. When she awoke, she felt a little guilty about having slept so soundly. Although she was angry with Jake for snatching the girls, she was pretty sure he did not intend to hurt them. He was probably using them to gain some sort of leverage or advantage, which was still despicable but not imminently dangerous.

Emma noticed Morgan was missing from her bed. Emma got dressed and went to the kitchen. Maha was standing at the stove. Morgan sat at the kitchen table, drinking a tiny cup of Turkish coffee and staring into a pottery bowl before her. Emma peeked into the bowl. "Fuhl! My favorite breakfast!" said Emma. "Any left for me?"

"I have a whole big pot," said Maha. "I don't think Miss Morgan is very fond of fuhl, though."

"She's probably just never had it," said Emma. "It's basically the Egyptian version of refried beans, Morgan. It's very bland. Each person adds whatever spices or vegetables they desire. I, personally, like mine spicy." Morgan merely looked at Emma with slitted eyes and took another sip of coffee.

As Emma was eating her breakfast, there was a knock on the door. Maha went to answer it and returned with Mohammed and another young man. "This is my brother, Magdi," said Mohammed. "Magdi has a good friend that works down at the port. He says the American man and the two little American girls took the first train this morning to Aswan. If we hurry, we can catch the next one in an hour."

On the train, Morgan dozed and Emma filled Magdi in on the status of the search for Tessa and the girls. "You know, in Egypt," said Magdi, "if a couple gets divorced, the father always gets custody of the children. No one in Egypt will question you returning the children to their father."

The group was met at the train station by a taxi driver who was yet another relative of Maha and Gamal. On the ride to the hotel, the road followed the Nile. Emma noticed there were many more trees and vegetation there than in Cairo, or even in Luxor. The water of the Nile was blue and dotted with hundreds of rocky cataracts. Despite the obvious obstacles, the river was decorated with the fluttering white sails of a plethora of felucca boats and other pleasure craft.

The hotel was small and plain but clean. As they checked in, the desk clerk, a cousin of Mohammed and Magdi, told them he had head Jake and the girls had gone to the Temple of Isis on the Island of Philai. Mohammed called the taxi driver on his mobile phone and asked him to return to the hotel. They quickly dropped their bags in their rooms and returned to the street where the driver was waiting.

As they piled into the taxi, Morgan said, "Where does Jake get the energy to run all over the place like this? And how does he manage to drag two unwilling little girls with him?"

"I suspect Jake's job entails a lot of running around with unwilling travel companions," said Emma.

"Well, I'm exhausted," said Morgan. "We need to put an end to this nonsense today. I have enjoyed this lovely tour of Egypt, but I am done."

"You really need to come back, Morgan, when I can show you my country at a much more leisurely pace," said Mohammed.

"That would be nice," said Morgan. "But for now, I am ready to head back to the States."

"I will miss you," said Mohammed.

"I know."

The taxi driver dropped them off in the small village of Shellal. As they exited the taxi, Magdi pointed toward the river. "The boat launch is over there."

"What?" Morgan exclaimed. "We have to take another mode of transportation?"

"You did hear Mohammed say we were going to an *island*, didn't you?" said Emma. "How else are we going to get to an island other than by boat?"

"I don't know. Bridge?"

"There's no bridge. The boat will be fine," said Emma.

The weather was spectacular. The sky was bright blue, spotted with puffy white clouds. A breeze kept them cool. The island was so beautiful and idyllic, Emma could almost believe gods once dwelled there. Small clusters of tourists strolled about, chatting happily and soaking in the nice day and the history around them.

Emma, Morgan, and their Egyptian companions were met by double rows of colonnades leading to a giant pylon decorated with reliefs of Cleopatra's father, Ptolemy XII, battling his foes. As they entered the Temple of Isis, Emma and Morgan scanned the faces of the visitors for signs of Jake or the little girls. The group was exiting the northern end of the temple when Magdi pointed to the Temple of Augustus, on the tip of the island.

"See those two little blonde girls up there. Are they perhaps the children you are seeking?" Emma and Morgan peered ahead. The two girls Magdi indicated were certainly the right sizes and ages, but they couldn't tell from that far away if it was, in fact, the Giovanni girls.

"Let's go around to the side, so Jake and whoever else he's with don't spot us," said Emma. The four hurriedly skirted the edge of the ruins, bending down to be obscured by the various pieces of rubble. They rounded the edge of the Temple of Augustus just in time to see two blonde heads disappear behind a pillar in the Temple of Hathor, back the way they had come from, next to the Temple of Isis. All four broke into a run in pursuit of the girls.

They burst into the Temple of Hathor, only to find it abandoned. Not a single person was inside. The reliefs of the musicians that covered the walls and columns seemed to mock them with their silent music. "They obviously didn't come back our way," said Mohammed, "so they have to have gone the other way."

The four jogged to the unfinished pavilion known as "Pharaoh's Bed." Lindsay and Amber were not there, either. However, Jake Dubrowski sat peacefully on a step, looking out onto the water. Morgan rushed forward and jumped on his back and began hammering him with her fists. "Where are they, you pig?" she said.

Jake grabbed Morgan's wrists, restraining her from hitting him. He chuckled. "I am happy to see you, too, darling," he said.

"What have you done with the children, Jake?" Emma demanded. Mohammed and Magdi moved closer, looking to Emma for guidance.

"They're fine," said Jake. "They're enjoying their Egyptian vacation."

"You said you weren't after them," said Emma.

"I wasn't, and I'm not," said Jake. "I'm just using them as bait to snare the mama bear."

"You're despicable!" Morgan hissed in Jake's ear. "They are innocent children. They don't have anything to do with Tessa's dirty games."

"Nor do I," said Jake. "I just need to get my customer back into custody, so that I don't lose my money. Now get off me!" Jake suddenly thrust backward, sending Morgan sprawling across the marble floor of the pavilion.

Just as quickly, Magdi pounced in behind Jake and wrapped a thin piece of wire around Jake's throat. Jake started to thrash, grabbing for Magdi, who stood just far enough back that Jake couldn't reach him. Jake tried to arch his back, and Magdi gave him a quick kick to the kidney. Jake sunk to the floor and began to turn red.

"Don't kill him, Magdi," Emma pled.

"Go ahead and kill him, Magdi," said Morgan, now on her feet and standing in front of Jake.

"I won't kill him . . . *if* he tells us where the little girls are." Jake couldn't speak, so he nodded. Magdi released the wire ever so slightly. Jake let out a low whistle. A hulking, bald, pockmarked man, who looked like Sinbad the Sailor, came out from behind a pillar. He had one Giovanni girl under each arm. The girls were shaking and pale.

The big man looked at Jake and released the girls. They ran to Emma. Magdi released the wire around Jake's neck. Jake scrambled onto his hands and feet and lunged in the direction of the girls. Morgan let out a yell and landed a roundhouse kick squarely in Jake's nose. His nose made a crunching noise and began spouting blood. Mohammed and Magdi attacked the giant bald man, who was trying to recapture the children.

Emma picked up Amber. Morgan grabbed Lindsay by the hand. "Run!" Morgan shouted. The women and girls took off toward the boat launch. Emma looked back when she heard footsteps gaining on them. It was Mohammed and Magdi. Jake and his goon were nowhere in sight.

The group bypassed the line of tourists waiting for the boats. The tourists issued indignant protests but did nothing to stop them. A security guard with a gun stepped out from the front of the line. Mohammed yelled something at him in Arabic. The guard yelled into his radio and took off running toward the spot where they had last left Jake and his cohort. Mohammed approached the ticket collector and greeted him by name. After exchanging quick kisses on either cheek, Mohammed cupped his hand behind the ticket-taker's neck, pulled him toward himself, and murmured something in his ear. The ticket-taker nodded almost imperceptibly and Mohammed smoothly deposited a bundle of bills into the man's opposite hand. The man fluidly deposited the money in the pocket of his trousers as he extended his other hand in a welcoming gesture to Mohammed's party.

"*Ahlan wa Sahlan* [Welcome]," he said.

Emma, Morgan, the girls, Mohammed, and Magdi jumped onto the boat. They maneuvered themselves to the rear of the crowd on the deck and nervously watched the boarding of the remaining passengers.

CHAPTER NINETEEN

Just as it appeared boarding was nearly complete, there was a disturbance in the boarding queue. Mohammed and Magdi stepped between the females and the crowd and stood on the balls of their feet, hands at their waistbands, poised to rebuff any attack. However, it turned out to be a tattered, weathered woman who was upset the ferry staff didn't want her to bring her goat on board. There was no apparent sign of Jake or his minion. As the vessel cast of its lines and pushed off, Emma and Morgan finally breathed a collective sigh.

After debarking the ferry, Mohammed was able to talk the ticket agent into booking all six of them onto the fancy sleeper train to Cairo. Emma, Morgan, and the girls were in one car, and the men were in another. Having expended so much adrenalin in escaping the captors, the group of females boarded the train as if in a trance. It was only after settling into their private car, with the door safely latched, that they began to process what they had just been through. Completely exhausted and depleted from the drama, the two young girls promptly fell asleep, even before the train left the station. Emma sat nervously watching the door of the sleeper car until she lost consciousness. Morgan sat staring emptily out the window.

Just as morning dawned, there was a soft knock on the door. Emma jolted awake. She went to the door and placed her ear close to the opening. "Emma. It's Mohammed. I need to talk to you."

Emma opened the door quietly and stepped into the passageway, closing the door behind her. "There is a problem," said Mohammed. "My friend, who is a police officer in Cairo, just called me. I asked him for information before, when we were trying to locate the girls and their mother. He said a notification just came into the office. It appears you and Morgan have been reported to the police as kidnappers and drug traffickers. All officers are alerted to arrest and detain you and the girls if you are spotted. It has been distributed to all the hotels and the airport. You can stay at my cousin's flat until we can figure out how to get you and the girls back to America."

"You've got to be kidding! What else can go wrong?" Emma wearily exclaimed. "Is your friend going to turn us in?"

"No. He wouldn't have warned me if that were the case. He can't help us, but he will just be quiet, I am sure."

"This is just great. Tessa is really the drug dealer and a kidnapper, and the authorities did nothing. Now they are coming after us? Don't you think we could just turn ourselves in and explain the real situation?"

"Absolutely not. That is a terrible idea," said Mohammed. "Whoever got this warrant issued has connections within the police force. That means the police will do whatever they want them to do. It doesn't matter what the truth is; it only matters who pays the bribe first."

"Fabulous," said Emma. "So how are we going to get out of the country?"

"We are going to have to pay off the airport employees, of course," said Mohammed. "How much money do you have with you?"

———

Mohammed's cousin lived in a modest, second-floor flat close to the Khan al-Khalili *souq* in Cairo. Mohammed's cousin, Hala, was young, slender, and beautiful. Her dark eyes sparkled playfully and her braid reached halfway down her back. She warmly welcomed them into her apartment. As soon as introductions were made, Mohammed and Magdi left to make travel arrangements.

Lindsay and Amber were seated in front of the television, watching American cartoons dubbed over in Arabic. Hala, Emma, and Morgan reclined at the kitchen table, drinking tea. "The girls must have been terrified," said Hala. "They don't look too bad, though, except for the fact they are filthy."

"Lindsay told us they lost their suitcases soon after they arrived in Egypt," Emma explained. "They have been on the run the entire time, and their mother was obviously too distracted to care whether or not the girls got bathed."

"We are going to need to get them some clean clothes," said Hala. "You can't walk into the airport with them looking like they do. You probably should also buy some extra clothes and suitcases, so you don't raise any suspicions either."

"You have a very good point, Hala," said Morgan. "But how will we find the mall?"

Hala laughed. "I live right next to Khan al-Khalili, one of the biggest, most famous *souqs* in the Middle East. You can buy anything and everything there."

"What's a *souq*?" asked Morgan.

"Think of a really big, really crowded flea market," said Emma. "Only most of the goods are new, not used."

"That sounds tiring," said Morgan. "I'll stay here with the children."

"And just in case the police are looking for you, Emma, you should wear some of my clothes," Hala said.

Emma and Hala emerged from Hala's flat, looking like thousands of other Egyptian women. They both wore long skirts, long-sleeved hip-length tunics, headscarves, and sunglasses. Hala carried a large cloth bag to hold their purchases.

As they neared the edge of the *souq*, the crowds became thicker. The air rang with the sounds of the vendors hawking their goods and became thick with the aromas of coffee, shisha, fried falafal, and incense. Shoppers jostled each other in the narrow alleyways, and merchants vied for the attention of the passers-by.

Emma had been to Khan al-Khalili several times in the past, and she loved it. She loved the colors, the smells, and the bustling activity. Unlike the shopping malls or downtown shopping areas in the U.S., most Middle East *souqs* are conveniently organized so that all the merchants selling goods of a similar type are together in the same general area. This organization makes it easier to find what the shoppers are looking for but also allows for price comparison, leading to competitive rates.

Emma and Hala quickly passed by the restaurants and food vendors, the household goods vendors, and the blocks and blocks of souvenir shops. Eventually, Hala led them to the street containing clothing stores. Emma honed in on one store that displayed a large variety of cute outfits for little girls. She picked out three outfits for each girl and let Hala do the negotiating. Hala drove a hard bargain, including one moment when she and Emma headed for the door as if they intended to leave. Although the quality of the clothing was clearly not the best, Emma was amazed at how little she ended up spending. A few streets over, Emma picked up two small pink suitcases with wheels and handles with the word "Princess" stitched on the front. Before heading home, the women picked up some chicken kabob, pita bread, hummus, and salad to bring back for lunch.

All four of the travelers took baths and dressed in fresh clean clothes. Emma worked Amber's curly hair into two cute pigtails. They were all sitting down to lunch when Mohammed and Magdi returned. The men accepted the invitation to join them. Over lunch, Mohammed described the travel plans. Amber finished and wandered to the living room. She was drawing with some paper and a pencil Maha had given her. Lindsay stayed at the table with the adults.

"I got you on a flight to JFK in New York, connecting to Washington Dulles," said Mohammed. "I listed you, Emma, as the mother of the two girls."

Emma looked at Lindsay. "I really hate to tell you that you might have to tell a lie, honey. But if anyone asks you who I am, you need to say I am your mother. We need to do this to get you out of Egypt and back to Virginia with your daddy. Do you think you can do that if you have to?"

Lindsay nodded solemnly. "I don't want to stay here. I want to go home. I don't know what my mom was thinking when she brought us here. It wasn't a fun adventure at all." Her eyes began to well up.

Emma put her arm around Lindsay's shoulders. "I know, honey. We're going to get you home. You just need to be brave, and we'll get through this." Lindsay nodded again.

Mohammed handed Emma four airline tickets. "Here are your tickets," he said. He then showed Emma a roll of Egyptian bills. "And here are your exit visas."

When the taxi dropped them off at the airport, Mohammed led the way, and Magdi brought up the rear. As they approached the open area before the ticket counters, Mohammed told them to wait a moment. With a big smile on his face, Mohammed strode toward the security guard standing at the entrance to the security checkpoint. The guard had a machine gun slung over his shoulder.

"*Habibi* [Beloved friend]!" said Mohammed. He placed his hands on the guard's upper arms, leaned in, and kissed him on each cheek. After the second kiss, Mohammed lingered a few seconds, whispering in the guard's ear. He then pulled back and heartily clasped the guard's hand in a vigorous handshake. Emma just barely glimpsed the corners of a few bills peeking out of the men's clasped hands.

When they got to the front of the ticket line, Mohammed chatted it up with the ticket agent for a minute. He then handed the agent the travel folder containing the four tickets. Emma could see that under the tickets lay several large denomination Egyptian bills. The agent looked up at Mohammed and held his gaze for a moment. Emma's heart leaped into her throat. The agent then offered a big smile and said, "Passports, please." The agent checked their bags and gave them their baggage claim tags and boarding passes.

Mohammed and Magdi walked Emma, Morgan, and the girls to the security checkpoint entrance. Magdi kissed the guard on each cheek. The guard indicated for them to pass and leaving Mohammed and Magdi behind, the four females passed through the security checkpoint.

Emma's blood pressure remained elevated, and her heart beat loudly in her ears. They purchased snacks, browsed in the gift shops, used the restroom, and waited at the gate area without incident. Morgan didn't even comment on the unorganized stampede for the gate when the flight was announced. The party settled into their seats on the plane. No official came on board to drag them off. When the plane pushed off from the gate, Emma relaxed a tiny bit. When the wheels left the ground, she took a big, cleansing breath. They were safely out of Egypt.

CHAPTER TWENTY

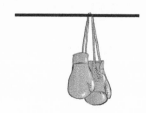

JFK Airport

The group sprinted out of the restroom and for the outside door. They made it to the door unhindered and emerged onto the street. A line of taxis stood in the queue. Miraculously, no other passengers were in the taxi line. Emma, with Amber glued to her side, ran to the first cab, yanked open the back door, and stuffed the girl inside. Next, she hurried in Lindsay, followed by Morgan. Emma shut the back door and climbed into the front seat of the cab.

The cab driver, a Caucasian, looked to be in his mid-thirties, was clean-shaven, and, most oddly, wore a suit. In addition, the car smelled like cleaning chemicals—new, even. Emma immediately realized that something was not right. At that moment, she noticed the pistol holstered on the cabbie's hip.

"Oh, no!" she exclaimed, "I forgot one of my suitcases at the baggage carousel. We have to go back! Get out of the car, everyone!" As she reached for the door handle, the door locks simultaneously clicked. The doors refused to open. Morgan started to pound on the window of the back door.

"What are you doing? Let us out!" she yelled.

The driver calmly sat with his hands on the steering wheel. "Ms. Parker, Ms. Price, welcome to New York," he stated in a near monotone. "A lot of people have been spending a lot of time and a lot of resources looking for you and your little friends. It's time to stop running."

No one said a word during the ensuing cab ride. After what seemed an interminable amount of time, the driver finally started down a cement ramp. He stopped, the garage door opened, and he drove into a concrete room. The driver stepped out, opened the back door, and gestured to a metal door. Emma, Morgan, and the girls walked up to the door.

After securing the "taxi," the man led them down a sterile hallway, into an elevator, and finally into a room that very much resembled the interrogation room at the airport. This time, however, there was no adjoining room for the children. After depositing his charges in the room, the man left.

"What's happening, Emma?" asked Lindsay.

"I honestly don't know, honey," said Emma. "We will just have to wait and find out."

After fifteen minutes or so, a man dressed in a cheap, navy blue suit entered the room. He took out a badge and showed it to Emma. "My name is F.B.I. Agent Jackson." He sat down on the table and glowered down at Emma and Morgan.

"I am not very happy with you two at the moment," he said.

"That seems a little odd, seeing that you've never met us," said Morgan.

"Oh, but you have made my life a living nightmare for the past several weeks," he said. "I haven't been home in days. I haven't seen my wife or children. I have been surviving on coffee and vending machine food. All because of you two."

Emma and Morgan said nothing.

"Our agency, along with the D.E.A. and some other entities, have been investigating Contessa Giovanni for quite some time now. We have invested a lot of time and resources into building a case against her. If you recall, Ms. Price, you were specifically told to cease your investigation of her and her activities because you were interfering with our own investigation. You refused to cooperate. You plunged on with your civil case.

It seemed things were going to resolve themselves, when the subject got herself arrested and convicted for, um, other charges." Agent Jackson glanced at the children. "But the reversal on appeal messed things up again."

Agent Jackson rubbed his eyes. "I cannot believe you actually decided to run off to Egypt after her. What on earth were you thinking? That was the worst move ever. You spooked our informants in Egypt, alerted her associates that someone knew what she was up to, kidnapped her children, and could have been killed. You are lucky you are not in an Egyptian prison!"

"We didn't break any Egyptian laws," Emma protested.

"Whether you actually did or not is sort of beside the point. The Egyptian police had a warrant out for your arrest, based on allegations that you were kidnappers and drug traffickers."

"Why would they think that?" asked Morgan.

Agent Jackson consulted a tiny notebook he pulled from his back pocket. "Based on a sworn affidavit by someone named Jake Dubrowski."

"That rat!" yelled Morgan. "Dubrowski took the children from their mother. We just rescued them from him."

"Well, that's an interesting story," said Agent Jackson.

"It's true," Lindsay piped up. Jake stole us from our mother. "He said if we didn't be good and do what he said that he would throw us in the Nile with the crocodiles!"

Agent Jackson did not respond to Lindsay's comment. He turned his attention back to Emma and Morgan. "Now, not that I'm not sympathetic with your motives, let's get back to the charges against you in the United States," he said. "First of all, you are charged with kidnapping. What right did you have to take those children?"

"Their father specifically retained us to go get them, and we did so on his authority," said Morgan.

"The problem being, their father doesn't have legal custody," said Agent Jackson. "Their mother does, although I can't imagine how that happened, given her behavior."

"By what court order?" asked Emma.

Agent Jackson consulted his notebook. "By a West Virginia court order."

"West Virginia never had jurisdiction to decide the custody of these children," said Emma. "The children never lived in West Virginia. Under the Uniform Child Custody Jurisdiction and Enforcement Act, a state has to meet certain requirements to obtain jurisdiction and under the facts of this case, West Virginia could not have done so. That order is void."

Nonetheless, these children were reported kidnapped five days ago," said Agent Jackson.

"Their father reported them as kidnapped when their mother violated the visitation order and failed to return them," said Emma. "Contessa Giovanni was the kidnapper, not us."

"But the mother cannot, legally, be the kidnapper if she had a court order giving her custody, right?" Agent Jackson said, looking and sounding less confident.

There was a knock on the door, and a young agent poked his head into the room. "Ms. Price's and Ms. Parker's attorney is here and demanding to be present during the interrogation," he said.

Morgan leaned toward Emma. "We have an attorney?" Emma shrugged.

A moment later Emma's friend, Stan, strode into the room. He was wearing a grey suit, white shirt, and red tie and carrying a briefcase. He confidently strode up to Agent Jackson and held out his hand. "Stanley Valentino, counsel for Parker and Price." Agent Jackson gestured to an empty chair.

Stan sat down, opened his briefcase, and took out a legal pad and pen. Emma and Morgan exchanged a look.

"Now, tell me, if you will, what my clients are being charged with," Stan said.

"I was just going over that with them," said Agent Jackson. "The first charge is kidnapping. They claim they had the father's authority to take the children. However, the mother has legal custody, pursuant to a West Virginia Court order."

Stan reached into his briefcase and pulled out a document. He handed it to Agent Jackson. "Here is a certified copy of a court order issued yesterday vacating the previous order to which you refer, based on the fact that West Virginia never had jurisdiction to enter that order in the first place." Emma shot Agent Jackson a smug smirk.

He handed Agent Jackson a second document. "This is a certified copy of a court order issued this morning granting Alexander Giovanni sole legal and physical custody of the minor children and revoking the mother's visitation rights, based on her taking the children and fleeing the country."

Agent Jackson reviewed the two documents. He rubbed his temples and thought for a moment. "Well, everything appears in order here," he said. "It does seem the father has custody. However, that still doesn't mean he gave these women the authority to take the children."

"You can ask him yourself," said Stan. "He's standing right outside." Stan walked to the door and opened it. Alexander Giovanni strode into the room.

"Daddy!" cried Lindsay and Amber and rushed into his arms.

Emma leaned toward Stan. "Who did you get to vacate the West Virginia order and get this order entered?" she whispered.

"I did it," said Stan.

"But you despise family law!" said Emma.

"I figured it was easier than defending you two on kidnapping charges," said Stan.

After a brief discussion between Alex and Agent Jackson, there was a lull in the discourse.

Stan looked at Agent Jackson. "You said there were other charges?"

"Well, yes," he said, closing his notebook and placing it back in his pocket. "Obstruction of Justice, and a few other minor infractions. However, in light of all the new information we have just received, I am going to recommend those charges be dropped. I suppose I have to acknowledge Ms. Parker was just being a zealous advocate for her client. In addition, I regretfully have to admit you two ladies did an unbelievable job of investigating this case. You stayed with my agents, step for step, and sometimes, you were even a step ahead. You ladies have an amazing ability to utilize local contacts and use them to your benefit. Frankly, the Agency could use agents like you. Maybe we could work out some sort of arrangement in the future. You're all free to go."

Having dropped Stan off at the train station, and sending the Giovanni girls on with their father, Emma and Morgan deplaned in Washington, D. C. As they exited the secure area and entered the portion of the airport open to the public, they encountered a crowd of people waiting to greet arriving passengers. Some held flowers, balloons, or stuffed animals. Assorted chauffeurs and limousine drivers held up hand-written signs bearing the name of their passengers. As they passed by, Emma's eye caught a sign bearing her name. She stopped and looked more closely. Darcy stood in the crowd, holding a sign that read, "EMMA PARKER. Please forgive me!"

THE END

ABOUT THE AUTHOR

 While being a life-long writer and fiction enthusiast, Paula Winchester Rank also has more than twenty-five years' experience as a litigator, primarily handling family law matters. Paula's undergraduate degree in Sociology and Social Work has provided her insight into human behavior and interactions. She has traveled extensively, including in the Middle East, Europe, and South America. She has lived in Amman, Jordan, where she worked as a researcher and writer for the U.S. government, as well as in the U.A.E. Paula currently works as an internal auditor for an international non-profit organization. She has two adult sons with her husband, Joseph, and currently divides her time between Riyadh, Saudi Arabia and the Washington, D.C. area.